TALL TALES
from
PITCH END

TALL TALES
from
PITCH END

Nigel McDowell

First published in Great Britain in 2013 by Hot Key Books
Northburgh House, 10 Northburgh Street, London EC1V 0AT

Text copyright © Nigel McDowell 2013

Cover illustration copyright © Manuel Šumberac

A CIP catalogue record for this book is available from the British Library.

ISBN: 978-1-4714-0040-7

1

Typeset by Palimpsest Book Production Limited, Falkirk, Stirlingshire
This book is typeset in 11pt Sabon LT Std

Printed and bound by Clays Ltd, St Ives Plc

FSC

Hot Key Books supports the Forest Stewardship Council (FSC), the leading
international forest certification organisation, and is committed to printing
only on Greenpeace-approved FSC-certified paper.

www.hotkeybooks.com

Hot Key Books is part of the Bonnier Publishing Group
www.bonnierpublishing.com

For my parents

PART ONE
THE FORGETTING

I

Ablaze

Bruno Atlas didn't speak, didn't scream, only thought with eyes shut tight and a mind full of crimson fireworks: *This is it and I'll be gone soon. I'll not be here any more. I'm going to die.*

He heard his mother –

'*Bruno!* I can't see or get to ye! We have to get out before the whole place goes up!'

Bruno dared his eyes open and saw smoke. He felt the dizzy orchestra of noise, the tearing like material being shorn in two, everywhere crackling, splintering, buckling, groaning like a dragon's insides. And just him, alone. On his floor under his bed with knees clutched to his chest, eyes transfixed by flames curling in far-off corners –

'Bruno? Where are ye? Please just shout out to me!'

His mother's voice, each word moving away –

But Bruno Atlas hardly knew where or who he was just then. If asked, he was four-going-on-five turns old (one week

3

from his birthday), and had a lot of nightmares so couldn't sleep much. Sometimes too he wet the bed. But more importantly, he didn't know what to do in this or any fire. Can't blame him then that he just lay where he was, grinding his forehead against the floorboards and wishing. Wishing just to be waking up soon, knowing that it had all been nowhere but in his head, another nightmare.

Something cracked close by him and flames raced like rats up and across his wardrobe, bed, shelves, leapt to his toy chest –

'*Bruno?*'

Her voice, closer.

'I'm—' he started. No more words. He gagged on darkness. But it was enough of a signal –

The door burst open under his mother's fists and in she came, batting away a torrent of smoke that almost defeated her. She staggered on with fingers blackened and twitching, searching for her son. Bruno watched her feet strike about, waver and then turn towards the bed. She didn't see him, didn't know he was there. He opened his mouth but still couldn't manage a word more, had to reach instead for her bare ankle, prodding the knob of bone there, seeing those feet recoil. Her face appeared, bruised with smoke, on the low and almost-safe level he'd discovered. She dragged her hair behind her ears and reached in for him. And he didn't go to her. Because moving would mean it was real. Not just play or another nightmare, but that they had to escape.

4

His bedside table lost balance then and fell forwards, the lantern on top smashing and the pool of oil in its base marrying with flame, chasing Bruno out and up into his mother's arms. Together they ran from the room, he with his eyes closed and hoping for the sudden cold of the outside, both of them quickly lost in the most familiar place in the world, home a prison.

Bruno mumbled into her ear: 'Me da, where is he?'

His mam didn't reply. She'd come to a stop, no notion of where to go to next, smoke too much to see past.

And then –

'This way! *Quick-smart!*'

Some new voice.

He felt his mother turn and bow her head and move with purpose now, past mounting heat ('This way!' went the voice again. 'Almost there!') and then out into sudden, steely night. Bruno opened his eyes and in the same moment his vision blurred with heat and light, the ground zooming upwards, his mother collapsing and him tumbling from her arms like a tender apple onto the lawn, onto his back, flattened lungs feasting on fresher air.

He looked up. Feathers of ash flocked across the night sky: their home migrating. He noticed that their house was the only one on their street streaked with fire.

'Ye okay?'

A face arrived above him, belonging to the voice that had shouted and guided them both to safety. Bruno couldn't make out who it was, eyes too keen on tears. But a man anyway, his coarse thumbs pressing into Bruno's eyes, wiping them clear like two tiny panes.

'Ye okay?' the face said again. 'Ye're grand enough, aren't ye?'

The house burned on behind like a sideshow.

'Da—' Bruno started, but just finished the cough from earlier.

'No,' said the man, 'I'm not yer father.'

Of course he wasn't his father – his father was at his means-to-an-end (or so he called it) in the lighthouse. But in a moment of panic he'd assumed his da had appeared – summoned to save him.

'Ye are,' said this man, deciding. 'Ye're grand enough. Just a bit battered on it.'

Sharp whistles pierced the night. Howling too.

'*Enforcers*,' the man said, his breath reeking of smoke. They sounded distant, the Enforcers, but fast approaching.

And the man was suddenly gone without a sound or bye.

Footsteps and cries filled his absence and Bruno sat up a little, seeing neighbours – in nightclothes, eyes staring and hair harassed, weighed down on each arm with buckets of water – rush forwards and try to douse the flames of the house. A woman's voice gasped in Bruno's ear the same words as the man: 'Ye're alright, aren't ye?' She took him under the armpits. 'Get yerself up now.'

No choice in the matter, Bruno was pulled to his feet. He saw his mother, head lolling, being supported too by neighbours he'd usually only see during the day: discreet in their gardens, tending quiet lives.

Then the whistles and the large dogs arrived proper: Enforcers, all tramping in time, blowing on the slivers of metal between their lips and (only just) keeping a hold on those straining, massive hounds.

Still more of the neighbours clattered forwards with buckets of help. But there was no way to fight the fire now. The water hissed and dissolved in the face of it. Bruno watched his home falter and sink. He was surrounded suddenly by a blanket, tucked tight as a letter in an envelope; bundled away, further removed from the blaze, his mother alongside him soothing, 'Alright, Bruno. Ye're alright.'

Both were settled into the gloom cast by the vast oak in their front garden, its leaves tickled and set alight, the blaze a scorching breeze.

'Get back! Ye'll be dropping those buckets now or else! Be leaving that fire!' ordered one of the arriving Enforcers. His comrades snatched buckets from the neighbours and loosed the contents like quicksilver into the gutter. This Enforcer had a uniform of red and gold, the colour of it clear despite the deep night and the biased illuminations of the house fire; he was the Head Enforcer, the Marshall, and his voice was gravel mixed with gunshots.

'Return to yer homes!' he told them all. 'I needn't bother to be reminding ye it's past Curfew. My men shall deal with the displaced family. This fire is to be left as an example, ntime. An example, terrible as it is, of the continuing presence of the Rebels in Pitch End, and of the Single Season War still ongoing. Back to yer homes, I say!'

People moved slowly, unsure. Too slowly – there were shrieks as the patience of the Enforcers vanished, suddenly drawing pistols or rifles and aiming them at Bruno's neighbours. The dogs bared their teeth, tongues furiously wetting curled-back lips.

'*Now* I say!' cried the Marshall. 'This is no game! And if I find out any of ye are harbouring what shouldn't be harboured, there'll be more bother than ye can think of!'

Everyone retreated immediately. Doors were closed, curtains whipped across. Bruno huddled closer to his mother as she said, 'Quiet now. Don't be speaking out of turn to the Marshall.'

But no matter what he'd told the neighbours about looking after the 'displaced family', the Marshall was taking little-to-no notice of either Bruno or his mother. His eyes were too concerned with scanning their street, ensuring everyone was where they should be. He beckoned to one of his subordinates with a creaking, leather-gloved finger: 'Station an officer outside each home,' he told him. 'No one to leave tonight. Not for any reason.' He paused, glaring at Bruno. 'I always thought this street had something suspicious about it. Something rightly-*indecent*.'

Enforcers scattered.

'Come here, boy,' said the Marshall.

Bruno looked to his mother. She nodded, detaching him.

'Now,' said the Marshall, quietly, with a face half in light, half in dark, but still a solid tower above Bruno. 'How was this fire started? A Rebel hiding hisself in yer wee house?'

Bruno looked to his mother. He saw the rapid swell and fall of her chest.

'*Well?*'

The Marshall's nose was suddenly an inch from Bruno's and his fingers were around Bruno's chin. Bruno examined the Marshall's face: from hairline to eyebrow ran a recent wound, open and livid and deep.

'What's yer name, boy?' he asked.

Bruno could only tell him.

'*Bruno Atlas* – ye know what *war* is, Bruno?'

Bruno nodded.

'Ye do? Good boy. Then ye'll be knowing too that only one thing matters in war: that's the *winning*. Ye don't want the Rebels to win, do ye? No, didn't think so. Now tell me quick-smart – was there someone in yer house that shouldn't have been?'

Bruno didn't know the answer he was supposed to give. He felt cold and warm at the same time, his chest hurt, his eyes wouldn't stop their crying. His finger strayed instinctively to his mouth to be chewed like a bare twig. But he was saved any further discomfort –

Beyond the Marshall, standing in the blinking shadow of the safe, unscathed house next door, Bruno saw the face of the man who had wiped the tears from his eyes, who had called them to safety. And before he knew what he was doing, Bruno stared over the Marshall's broad shoulder, whose head snapped round like it had no bones in it at all. Bruno fell and buried his head in his mother's breast as gunshots snapped into the air and the Head Enforcer charged after the man who made his escape just as swiftly.

'A Rebel!' cried the Marshall as he ran on. 'Get him! Dead or alive unless it's Jonathan Bloom! Remember Temperate Thomas's orders!'

Like grains of sand, the Enforcers and their dogs funnelled as one yapping, yammering flood through the narrow space between Bruno's burning house and the next. They had him without trouble.

'This way ye scum! Ye can drag yer feet all ye like, won't be saving ye.'

Dragged, the man looked like he'd lost the use of his legs. The place where his head should have been was empty, as though it had been lopped off. Bruno shuddered, but kept watching. The Enforcers brought him closer, and Bruno was relieved when he saw that the man's head had only slumped forwards. But his face glistened black like new tar. He was let drop onto the lawn in front of Bruno and his mother.

Again, Bruno's mother told him, 'Quiet. Don't say a word.'

The Marshall approached the man from behind. The other Enforcers fell back.

'Name,' said the Marshall.

The man, this Rebel, didn't reply.

'One more time: *name*,' said the Marshall. He spoke slowly and quietly, but with perfect clarity. The scar on his forehead wept. The man began to stir, fingers clawing at the ground – small movements against large, the flames still rioting in the house behind.

Bruno ruined the stillness by crying out as the Head Enforcer descended suddenly with pistol in hand and jammed it into the Rebel's face once, twice, three times. Nearly a fourth.

Bruno could hardly breathe, his mother's arms tight around his chest.

The Marshall held the gun aloft again, hand steady.

'Don't make me repeat meself,' he said, chest heaving but with a voice so very calm. 'Yer name, yer title, and the location too of Dr Jonathan Bloom. *Now*.'

For the briefest moment, Bruno looked into the eyes of the Rebel – two cauldrons reflecting firelight. He had hoisted himself onto his elbows, looking upwards into the sky – then into the face of the Marshall.

'*Never*,' said the Rebel, his voice just as calm and clear as the Marshall's. 'I will never ever, never ever . . .'

The refrain went on and on – Bruno felt it would never cease.

'*Rebel*,' spat the Head Enforcer, as though he could think of no muddier insult.

He fired.

Bruno shut his eyes and cried, '*Stop!*' and without a

thought freed himself from his mother, scrambled to his feet and threw his body blindly against the solid figure of the Marshall, his small fists striking. But each weak attempt was in vain.

'Stupid child,' said the Marshall. He settled one hand across Bruno's face – the stench of leather like instant suffocation – and pushed him backwards onto the ground.

His mother pulled him close again, but not into an embrace. She pinched his arm and said, 'Never *ever* do that again, ye hear me? Just like yer father. It's not sensible to behave like that.'

'Ye need to watch that one, missus,' said the Marshall. 'He's got too much *fire* in him.' The Marshall grinned, the Enforcers laughed at the joke, and still the flames rose. Like the Rebel, slumped, a heap on the ground, Bruno and his mother's home finally folded, defeated, into the earth.

II
The Sea of Apparitions

Bruno's birthday – no presents or cards or wishes, only a headline delivered to the kitchen table:

PITCH END JOURNAL
April 29th, Year +290

THE SINGLE SEASON WAR COMES TO AN END –
THE REBELS HAVE BEEN DEFEATED!
TEMPERATE THOMAS SAYS, 'ABOUT TIME.'

Bruno glanced down at a smaller headline:

THE REBEL NICHOLAS M. DELBY CHARGED
FOR THE M****R OF MICHAEL ATLAS
(THE LIGHTHOUSE KEEPER)
. . . AND THEN DELBY ESCAPES!
TEMPERATE THOMAS SAYS: 'SHAME ON HIM!'

'*Bruno!*'

His mother whipped the newspaper away before he had time to see more. At five turns old he could read a bit but not much. But enough.

M****R!

'No one says just *dead*,' he said.

'What?' said his mother.

'Dead and that's that. That's what Sabitha said yesterday to me in Hedge School, but not a body else is for saying it! They say things like "at peace" or "moving on" or "passing away" or—'

'Sabitha McCormack should learn to behave herself,' said his mother. 'Marshall for a father or not, she should learn some manners. Too old for her age – five turns going on fifty-five.'

Bruno remained cross-legged on the kitchen floor of their new home – a new cottage, smaller than their old house, cracks rife on the walls and ceiling. 'But we're grateful for it,' his mother had told him after they'd moved in. 'The Elders have provided, and we're rightly-grateful for it.' He'd had to bite back disagreeable words.

Beside Bruno was his Owl-Sentry. He took it everywhere, tarnished, useless thing though it was – his only toy, all else destroyed in the fire. Bruno rapped the Owl-Sentry with his knuckles. Its large eyes glowed, then diminished. He looked to his mother. She was in a different dress: very long, very dark. A neighbour had brought it around the night before at precisely midnight and Bruno had darted into her bedroom just in time to see the dress slither like oil from between layers of greasy paper (when his mother hadn't been looking, Bruno had torn a scrap of this wrapping and wadded it into his pocket) folded inside a large, flattened box. It had the odour of Pitch End ritual about it. A matching hood of material – lighter, less dense than the dress, but just as black – was tucked around her shoulders.

He stood, looking to the kitchen table and seeing more black, more ritual: Forgetting Ornaments, wood carvings of ravens, charred, and damp, black roses with a note attached:

> *I'll be Forgetting him. But I'll rightly miss him.*
> *Mr Pace-the-Witherman*

'Right, old man,' his mother said, dropping in that little endearment, the name she and Bruno's father had given him for no reason he could get out of them. 'It's about time now.'

Bruno felt it had come too quickly. He would remember this, years later: the first sight of his mother taking hold of that long, dark length of material that had been plaguing her shoulders, drawing it up and over, letting it cover her face. Her expression could have been anything then. Bruno shivered some more. He'd seen other women – '*Poor hags*,' Sabitha McCormack called them – drifting around Pitch End wearing these. A lot more since the Single Season War had begun – since the Rebel attacks like the one that had destroyed their house.

15

'*Dead*,' said Bruno. He tugged on one of the Owl-Sentry's wings, tugged it out wide. 'Does it mean never coming back or just never bothering to waken up?'

Bruno's mother didn't speak for a moment. Then words disturbed the veil: 'Yer father's a proper hero now, Bruno. Being – being *taken* from us like that, by those no-good Rebels. But we'll be well looked after because of it. Ye just wait-see. He's a hero. Died for Pitch End.'

Bruno released the Sentry's wing. It sagged, then snapped back into its body.

'But—' he began.

'No more *buts*,' said his mother. 'It's time.'

She kissed his forehead. Felt like cobwebs.

A storm licked the Sea of Apparitions. Waves rose, shattered, regrouped. And when Bruno and his mother arrived at the harbour, they saw the entire population of the town crammed along the tumultuous shore. The one-footed raven population too, teetering on railings and shipping masts, rooftops and chimney pots and men's bowler hats; black spots littering Bruno's vision, ruffling nightmares that croaked: '*Tragedy! Tragedy! Oh the tragedy!*'

Anyone who was anyone was there. Many too who were nobody Bruno could know or name. When the story had emerged that Bruno's father hadn't just disappeared on the same night of the Rebel attack on their house, but had been murdered by one of the Rebels, there wasn't a Pitch Ender who would dare be anywhere else on the morning of Michael Atlas's Forgetting – too much scandal to be leeched, too much indignation to be mined, the lust for tragedy too much to miss.

Temperate Thomas, Head of the Pitch End Elders, led the ceremony.

Bruno and his mother took their place, standing on shingle, the Temperate upraised on the ceremonial casket used for all Forgettings, its edges split and panels cracked. Temperate Thomas clapped his hands for attention, shivered and stamped his feet and clapped his hands some more just to keep them from forgetting warmth.

'Come forward, the Withermen!' he called out.

Four men parted the crowd. Long hair as grey-brown and as lank as dead grass, blank-eyed and heads bowed, between them they carried an oak casket, two on either side. The body of Michael Atlas hadn't been found so tradition dictated that Bruno and his mother would offer just the casket to the sea, filled with Michael Atlas's 'most treasured possessions'. At their approach, Bruno looked for the same thing all Pitch Enders looked for, never tired of seeing, but with a mixture of disgust and intrigue: clock faces embedded in the four men's chests, over their hearts.

Most, like the Temperate, called them 'Withermen'. Some – not many and mostly children – called them 'Wind-Up-Men'. But Bruno preferred Withermen – 'Wind-Up-Men' was too childish for him. Bruno had asked his mother more than once or twice what the clocks in their chests were for, and was it to keep them going all day long, never dying like the people it was their job to deal with? His mother had told him, 'Sshhh, and don't ask so many questions all the time.'

'Hurry now!' the Temperate told them.

One of these Withermen was the Mr Pace who had sent the black roses. He was a friend of Bruno's father. Had been. Bruno remembered trips to North Street to buy spuds and apples and string and candles and wireless batteries (or to South Street – butter, milk, eggs, shoe polish), and his father would stop and speak to Pace and the other Withermen at their parlour on North. Bruno noticed on these occasions how other Pitch Enders scowled, hurried past the parlour. And after, how shop-keepers would flick their notices from COME IN! to GO AWAY! if they saw him and his father approach. He'd tugged his father's hand and asked, 'Why do they not want to speak to the Withermen? Is it coz they're dealing with the dead bodies of people? Do people not like it or what?'

His father had laughed and said, 'Ye're a clever boy, Bruno. Sharp as a tack. Don't bother a bit about what anybody in this place thinks. Speak to whoever ye like.'

Back on the beach for his father's Forgetting, the shingle was a careless racket under the Withermen's boots. They settled the casket at the top of a long, skinny-legged, wooden chute that led to the sea. Temperate Thomas began, though the waves were keen to edit: 'With a veritable ocean

18

of regret . . . tragic loss of such a great character . . . martyr to the cause of decency . . . dedicated father, masterful husband . . .'

And on and on.

'Were it not for these so-calling-themselves *Rebels*,' Temperate Thomas went on, 'that have burned our homes and turned the milk sour in our cattle, blighted our crops and Pitch-knows what else, then poor Widow Atlas and her boy would still be having a brave husband and salt-of-the-sea father to protect and nurture them both. A breadwinner to provide for them.'

Bruno examined the face of Temperate Thomas, the eyes in particular so close together that when Bruno half-closed his own they appeared not as two but as just one big one. He would have tugged on his mother's sleeve, told her of this discovery, maybe made her laugh. His father would've appreciated him for it, told him how canny he was and never to lose that talent for seeing people properly.

'Now, who is to care for these two souls?'

As was custom – no answer nor offer.

Bruno's eyes wandered, looked down. He had a sudden desire to snatch up a piece of shingle, feel the sharpness of it in his hand. He thought for a moment, then licked his thumb and bent down to rub a smudge from his left shoe before bobbing back up again, fragment retrieved, slipping it like lightning into his pocket.

No more words. Temperate Thomas simply nodded to one of the young Trainee Elders. The boy held, at arm's

19

length, a clutch of straw. Into it the Temperate tossed flame from a careful hand, his Talent summoning it despite the gale and the spray and the cold. The flames were white. The Trainee Elder touched the torch to the casket and it took, swift as fire had taken Bruno and his mother's home. The casket remained, obscured by twisting flame and smoke. Only when Temperate Thomas gave a nod did the Trainee Elder yank on a rope and it was launched down the chute and into the Sea of Apparitions.

Too soon, the last reminders of Bruno's father were snatched by the current. Out, beyond the mist, beyond anyone's seeing, the casket would be caught by one of the whirlpools, the Sea of Apparitions hungry for any tragedy to swallow.

Where before Bruno had felt nothing much – bit bored and baffled, not really seeing the point at all in sending out to sea a box that was supposed to contain his father but didn't but which they all needed to pretend was important – he then suddenly moved towards the waves. His mother grabbed and held him back, hands clasped tight across his chest. Water rushed against his ankles but he hardly felt the cold, the pain.

It hadn't been a conscious thought of his, just an instinct – to follow that casket, to watch it leave, watch it end. Bruno started to cry then, cold needling his cheeks, fists clenched. He looked to the Temperate – his expression was perfect pity. Bruno felt a desire to rush at the man, to beat against him as he'd done with the Marshall. Then he looked to his mother, but there was nothing there but black.

'*Forget*, Pitch Enders!' announced Temperate Thomas, his voice rising over everything, touching on everyone's hearing. '*Forget!*'

The ravens encouraged too: '*Forget! Forget!*'

'We do not dwell,' Temperate Thomas continued, 'on the finality of death, but discard past pains like those of the past season – the war we've been fighting against the Rebels. And to rightly put that past behind us, let me offer something to all of ye now.'

Bruno became conscious of another shifting in the crowd. Feet shuffled to position themselves, to allow their owners to see clearly, and only by his position on the beach could Bruno see without needing to strain or move around: two men, *boys*, tripping along, feet hindered by rusted chains, two Enforcers driving them onwards with rifle barrels at their backs.

'Ladies and gentlemen of Pitch End,' Temperate Thomas said, 'we are at the ending of the Single Season War. So now – witness the demise of the Rebels!'

Spitting, insults and profanities, more than Bruno had ever heard or dared to utter himself, were hurled like rocks at these two boys. Two Rebels but with tiny, watering, retreating, blackened eyes, skinny legs and cracked knees. They hobbled as their bare feet met shingle, forced on until they stood only feet from Bruno and his mother. They

21

shivered in the shadow of Temperate Thomas, who gave the smallest nod.

At the wordless command the Enforcers jabbed rifles into the legs of the Rebels. They collapsed on top of one another. They began to cry, squirming, pushing their heads close together, hoping for protection or solace. They didn't speak.

One of the boys reached for Bruno.

'Yer tears are dust!' said the Temperate, suddenly. 'No protest, no repentance will save ye. No hope now. Yer deeds – yer despicable, worthless deeds – are all that will remain of ye, what will endure, what we will scavenge from the carcass of yer lives!'

The crack of metal as Enforcers cocked their rifles, took aim.

Waves clawed the shore.

Unlike outside the burning house a week earlier, this time Bruno wanted to see. But realising what was about to happen an instant before it did, his mother clapped her hands over his eyes. Nothing could stifle the sound though – gunshots echoing far out to sea and up North and South Streets and into the cracks of the Elm Tree Mountains, rocking Bruno to his bones. He almost toppled, all breath slammed from his chest.

Two final crunches of shingle, barely distinguishable one from the other.

And the final words resounded on the morning air:

'It is over,' Bruno heard Temperate Thomas say from

beyond the dawn darkness of his mother's shivering fingers. 'It is over, my friends. Now go forth, and Forget!'

The ravens repeated: *'Forget! Forget!'*

'Long live Pitch End!' the Temperate told them.

The townsfolk chorused their traditional reply: *'And longer live the Elders!'*

III

The End of Time

Before sunlight: 'Up Bruno. Wake now. They're here.'

His mother, veiled face close to his, whispered low but with hands tight on his shoulders, shaking.

'Widow Atlas! Open up! We're here to collect!'

Bruno was soft-headed with sleep but still he recognised the voice of the Marshall. There was a thumping at their front door like the Head of the Enforcers was about to bring it down, collapse further their fragile world – three days since the Forgetting and Bruno had barely left his bed; he and his mother hadn't spoken to each other until this.

'Here,' said his mother, and she slipped her hand beneath his blankets, pressing something into his hands. Her fingers were cold, the thing she passed to him colder.

'We have to hide anything to do with yer father,' she said. 'In case they're finding it. Take it and keep it somewhere safe. I know ye'll think of a good place – ye're a sharp boy. Do it quick-smart.'

She left him, hurrying out and pulling the door of Bruno's bedroom shut.

Bruno lay where he was. He thought to give up whatever his mother had given, push it out from under the blankets, let it fall, drop to the floorboards. Whatever she'd given him, he couldn't care. He just lay, and listened –

'Widow Atlas' (the Marshall) 'we're here to collect.'

'All I had' (his mother's voice, lower than Bruno could've imagined it) 'went in the Forgetting Casket, on out to sea. I have nothing more.'

'Not that nonsense,' said the Marshall. 'We're here for something else. Ye've been reading the Elder Orders we've been giving out these past few days?'

If his mother replied, Bruno didn't hear it. He sat up then, willed by curiosity. His bedroom was at the front of their cottage so he had only to crawl down the bed and listen by the small window –

'He's wanting to collect what?' he heard his mother say, her voice still low.

'Temperate Thomas II,' the Marshall snapped, 'Head of the Elders, has sent us to collect yer *time*.'

Silence then. Or an almost-silence – Bruno was still holding what his mother had given him and only then did he look to it, drawn by sound. A small, circular, brass object. It was *ticking*.

'*Time*,' the Marshall repeated, and Bruno started, covering the object and at the same time noticing that it was bound up tight with a silver chain, as though to hold

25

the thing shut, whatever lay inside having to stay hidden. 'We need all of it,' the Marshall went on. 'Things are changing in Pitch End, Widow Atlas. No more doing what youse all want, whenever ye like. There's to be proper rules, make sure everyone is for staying in line. Now – how many timepieces do ye have?'

Bruno left his bed whilst his mother breathed her soft, placid reply – 'Just a carriage clock in the living room, that's all' – and moved quick on his toes to his bedside table and snatched the defunct Owl-Sentry from its place. Then back and under his bed, the fire doing nothing to deter him hiding in this place. He felt safer, being so alone; felt closer to his own thoughts.

On his belly he opened the back of the Owl-Sentry. This was his hiding place – amongst cogs and gears, rust and verdigris, were plenty of things that he shouldn't have had. Some things taken from his father's oak casket when his mother hadn't been looking that should've been at sea, some he'd kept for no proper reason: a strip of greaseproof paper, a wilted rose, a sepia pictograph of himself and his father and mother, a curl of shingle, a wooden ship that sat in his palm perfectly, small sails as frail as web. To these he added the –

'Ye don't have a pocket watch here, by any chance?' he heard the Marshall ask.

'No,' said Bruno's mother. 'We've never had such a thing.'

A pocket watch. Bruno realised that's what he held, the chain knotted around it with (he noticed only then) a symbol of silver attached: a half-shut eye with a bird in

26

open flight at its centre. A storm-petrel, Bruno decided, noticing the long, thin legs. His father had taught him about such things on their wanderings together – Pitch End birds and plants and seasons and the inevitable tides.

'We're duty-bound,' he heard the Marshall say, 'to come in and be checking. So *no*, a Widow's word isn't good enough for me.'

And in they came – boots and boots, so many footfalls it was as though the Enforcers were on parade, still in readiness for war and not for entering the cottage of a Widow and her five-turns-old son. Bruno shut the back of the Owl-Sentry and listened, watching bland light leak under his bedroom door from carried lanterns. Shadows broke the beams and paused, then passed. He clutched the Owl-Sentry closer to his heart and for a moment its eyes brightened to white, fairly blazed, its head twitching and revolving to gaze at Bruno as though at last it might make a sound.

A hand went against his bedroom door, a new shadow beneath.

'Marshall,' he heard his mother say, just outside the door. 'What exactly is the right-real purpose of taking the clocks?'

'The purpose,' replied the Marshall, 'is none of yer concern. But the fact is this: ye'll do as we say, coz we do what Temperate Thomas and the Elders say. And they say it's about time this town was brought into line. It's about *time*' (he paused, and Bruno heard the Marshall snort) 'that there was a bit *less* time. A bit less doing as ye please. It's too much sitting about thinking and not enough busying that got us into the recent . . . *unpleasantness*.' Bruno knew that the Marshall meant the Single Season War, the Rebels and their attempts (Sabitha McCormack had told him in Hedge School) to get rid of the Elders. But the real words of what happened were being rubbed out, Forgotten as completely as his father would be.

No one will be saying *war*, thought Bruno. They'll be saying *unpleasantness*. Like the way no one just says *dead*.

'Didn't see any other clocks or nothing, Marshall,' said the voice of an Enforcer.

A creak of floorboard, creak of leather.

Bruno watched the shadow of the Marshall shift.

'That'll be doing for now,' he said. 'Have a pleasant Pitch End day, Widow Atlas.'

His shadow retreated, and Bruno saw only a vague darkness at the bottom of his bedroom door: his mother, standing stranded, as the Marshall and the Enforcers left them.

Bruno remained under his bed, and his mother remained outside the door.

He looked down and watched the eyes of his Owl-Sentry dim, die, as the cry went out over the cold and damp of an Ever-Winter morning in Pitch End: 'Surrender all yer timepieces in the name of the Elders! Today in Pitch End is the end of time!'

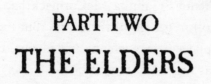

PART TWO
THE ELDERS

IV

Truth

'Ye shouldn't be talking about yer da, Bruno Atlas! He's dead and gone so ye should've *Forgotten*! I'm telling Miss Hope.'

'Do what ye like.'

'I will. Do ye know who my father is, Atlas?'

'How could I not know, Sabitha – ye never shut up about it.'

Sabitha McCormack stalled, then swallowed and said, 'At least my da is still alive. Ye're no better than any of the rest of us, even if yer father was killed by a Rebel. So ye can stop acting like the big man and some bloody hero, Atlas!'

Everyone in the playground laughed.

That's it, thought Bruno. No more. Enough is bloody enough.

He turned, fingers doubling over into a cumbersome but determined fist, sucked in a shallow breath and punched Sabitha McCormack, the Marshall's daughter. Bone on bone, knuckle against cheek – a deep, sickening collision. Sabitha cried out and recoiled and so did Bruno, but he steadied himself quickly and was able to watch Sabitha stumble and fall to the playground.

She didn't move, just lay there, bewildered. Nausea made Bruno's vision run, the world a ruined watercolour. He knew he'd done too much.

The other children in the playground drew in, calling out and announcing their outrage to one another as Sabitha's eyes grew wider and wider again. Bruno knew she was trying to decide whether or not to cry. She was fifteen turns old, same as him, but still she wept near enough daily. Sabitha examined herself, discovered the beginning of some bleeding on her elbows and settled, this time, for screaming.

'Someone get Miss Hope!' she cried, and Sabitha's best friend in the world, Martha Tilly, nodded and ran off towards the Hedge School building. Sabitha continued screaming, weeping too, and the other children drifted close but not too close – she was an injured thing after all, they didn't want to upset her further.

Bruno turned away, finding support on the iron fence that surrounded the Hedge School and its grounds. He was shaking, couldn't control his limbs, breathing incomplete, telling himself: just calm down now. It's fine. All be fine. She deserved it. And there's not a thing I can do now, anyway. No way to be taking it back. Wouldn't even want to take it back!

But no amount of talking to himself, trying to rationalise things, could overcome visiting terrors. He felt deadened and triumphant at the same time. Glad he'd done it, but regretted the fuss it would cause. Bruno felt dominated by the act. As far as anyone else was concerned, he would now be that Bruno Atlas, the boy who punched the Marshall's daughter. Another title to add to the list: *Bruno Atlas, Son of a Hero! Bruno Atlas, Son of the Last Man to Die at the Hands of the Rebels! Bruno Atlas, the Boy Who Tells Lies* . . .

A breeze fussed with his hair. He reached instinctively for the medallion he'd taken to carrying with him, freed from his Owl-Sentry, from around his father's pocket-watch: silver chain, silver half-moon like a narrowed, suspicious eye, small silver storm-petrel in the centre. After ten turns the metal was still without scratch or dent. Beyond the fact it had been his father's, something about its untainted endurability gave him comfort.

Then he heard a shout behind –

'Bruno Atlas! What in the name of Pitch have ye done now, ye nasty little boy?'

Miss Hope, he thought dully, and then folded, opening his mouth to let the gush of his stinging insides splatter the playground.

'Yer father would be rightly-ashamed,' Miss Hope told Bruno. 'If he was seeing how ye are now and what ye've been doing these days with all yer disagreeing contrariness, he'd be right to disown ye! What could Miss McCormack possibly have come out with to warrant being beaten so violently?'

'I didn't *beat* her, I just—'

'No excuses and none of yer usual backchat – just an answer!'

'She said that my da—' began Bruno. He stopped. He glanced at the Cat-Sentry poised on Miss Hope's desk, heard the low purr of clockwork tucked inside its slim body, watched the slow twist of its winding key between sharp ears. Bruno took a breath and continued: 'She said me da wasn't a right-real hero. And that I shouldn't be thinking meself any better than anyone else.'

Miss Hope looked at him, then folded her arms.

'*And?*' she said. 'What is so rightly-awful about that, Master Atlas? If ye're so keen on the truth in our classes (with all those impertinent questions all the time) then I would've thought ye wouldn't mind being told what so many are thinking, oftentimes.'

Bruno didn't reply.

Alone in the classroom together but not alone at all. Miss Hope's words were a lure. She wanted him to lash out and then the Cat-Sentry would sense it, jerk to life, gobble his words, recording them and taking them to the Elders and he would be whisked away, excluded for the good of all from 'rightly-decent' society. It had happened to others.

For a long time, children had been disappearing. Bruno

tried to decide on an exact time, but of course didn't know. How long? Months or turns? He was unsure, but just knew it, felt it, most acutely in more recent times – the classroom was emptying, and not just from children Coming-Of-Age and leaving. Children who'd spoken 'indecently' (too much about the past, talking of things that should've been Forgotten, Temperate Thomas's order to *Forget* expanding to consume all past *things*, not just those who'd died) went and weren't seen in Hedge School again. No one knew where they went. Bruno imagined them kept indoors by mortified parents; locked-in lives, small shames. So Bruno couldn't speak or he'd risk punishment or removal, and he didn't want to give Miss Hope the satisfaction of either.

Miss Hope followed Bruno's gaze to the Sentry. Then a smirk from her.

Bruno thought, to hell with it!

'Ye don't know what me da would think or feel,' said Bruno, 'coz he's dead. I remember him – he died for Pitch End. So don't act like ye can even know anything about his feelings, ye stupid oul bat!'

Shouldn't have said it, he thought straightaway. But, like punching Sabitha, knowing he shouldn't have done it wasn't the same as wishing he hadn't.

One of Miss Hope's hands scrambled to her chest and lay there. Her eyes darted from Bruno to the Cat-Sentry, which hadn't moved, not even a twitch.

'How dare ye!' she managed to say then. 'I really don't

35

have a notion what we're going to do with ye.' And though the usual trace of injured martyrdom was present in her, Bruno saw too the other side of Miss Hope emerging: anger.

'Not a *clue*!' she cried.

This last word was accompanied with a palm slapped on the table and Bruno saw the rest of the tables in the draughty classroom leap from the floor, hang for a blink, and then drop. Bruno's heart began to thrum – Miss Hope had used her Talent. Almost no one in Pitch End was allowed – the Elders of course, and some other generally esteemed members of the community.

He tried not to look at her. He focused on the high, barred windows that held strips of dull sky; on the sounds of subdued play outside – silence, then a low laugh, foot-slaps and then the weight of more weary silence; on the chalkboard behind Miss Hope's head, its black clouded with the ghosts of past lessons, on the Elder Advice stencilled tall and dark on white-washed walls: 'Routine is the Enemy of Rebellion! Too Much Time Makes for Too Much Trouble!'

'All yer daydreaming,' Miss Hope was saying, her breathing shallow. Bruno dragged himself back to her. 'Wouldn't surprise me a bit that ye weren't listening in this morning's Definitive History lesson.'

Bruno glanced at the Cat-Sentry. Still no movement, despite all the things: the volume of Miss Hope's voice, the use of her Talent, the mention of Definitive History – that should have piqued its attention.

'Pardon me, Miss Hope,' said Bruno, 'but I was paying attention rightly.'

And he meant it. The chance to learn some small shred of Pitch End's history – however garbled, ludicrous – was all that Bruno found interesting in Hedge School.

'Is that right?' said Miss Hope. 'Well let's be putting that to the test, Master Atlas.' Once more using her Talent, the long, flat steel ruler that lay on her desk lifted, sliced through the air and slotted into Miss Hope's waiting fingers.

Bruno swallowed.

'Hold out your hands,' said Miss Hope.

Bruno didn't move.

Miss Hope hoisted one eyebrow.

Bruno had to hold out his palms, up and open, too innocent-looking and too pale. He fought a mounting tremble in them.

'First question,' said Miss Hope, and she extricated one sheet from the mass that lay on the table – the catastrophe of Pitch End Definitive History. The sheet was marked with a diagram like a family tree, illustrating the twelve generations of lighthouse in Pitch End. 'Lighthouse number four,' said Miss Hope, 'how was it rightly and so violently destroyed in the year +41?'

Bruno knew the correct and true answer, knew it without thinking. But the answer in his mind was not Miss Hope's desired one.

'*Well?*' said Miss Hope. She gripped the ruler more firmly.

'Lighthouse number four,' began Bruno, 'was destroyed in the year +41 . . .'

Bruno closed his eyes and struggled with himself. The words Miss Hope needed, the ones that would save him from punishment – he knew those well. But they were nonsense to him, illogical. *Lies*. He had a source all his own; one that he believed, knew as more truthful than any Miss Hope had.

He wet his lips, and said, 'It met its end by . . .'

'Go on,' said Miss Hope.

Bruno opened his eyes, decided, and told what he knew to be the truth: 'It met its end because one of the Elders, Elder Dishonest, brought it down with his Talent coz he wanted to murder that farmer who—'

He managed no more – the spill of words, the tide of truth, ceased with Miss Hope bringing the ruler down across his palms. Pain detonated everywhere, not just in the hands but his whole body, set blazing as though he'd dropped into cold water. He wanted to rush his hands to his chest, cradle and protect. But he didn't. Didn't want to give in.

'The correct answer now, Master Atlas,' said Miss Hope.

Bruno watched the tremble – not in his hands but Miss Hope's. Heard it too in her voice. What he'd felt in the playground after striking Sabitha McCormack – what had made him retch – was infecting Miss Hope. But she mastered it quickly, fed off it. She could take comfort,

38

Bruno thought, in the idea that what she did was the 'right thing'. For his own good.

'The right-real answer,' Miss Hope said, raising the ruler for a second time.

Bruno said nothing. The words she wanted crawled up his throat in readiness, but he still couldn't and wouldn't and didn't speak them.

'I can't say a right thing,' he said.

'Pardon me?' said Miss Hope, narrowing one eye.

'I said that I can't be saying anything because nothing I say will be right.'

'How can that be so, Master Atlas? Ye know right-well the correct answer. Two and two equals four, does it not?'

Bruno nodded.

'And this is just the very same. Just give the correct answer. By the mountains – I'm no monster! And as yer teacher I can ask no more than the truth from ye.'

Clever, thought Bruno. Pushing, just like Sabitha had. He knew all Miss Hope's efforts were aimed at making him feel like the stupid one, like his way of looking at things was the wrong way.

'Fine,' he said at last, realising that the lie would cost him nothing so long as he knew it as a lie, never truly believed it. 'The demise of lighthouse number four was as a result of the rightly-nasty and opportunistic attempt on the Mayor's life by one of the Rebels. The bullet from the Rebel rifle ricocheted off one of the pillars of the town hall, hit the back of a jellyfish in the Sea of Apparitions and struck the lighthouse, shattering the glass . . . and that was that.'

Miss Hope's nostrils flared.

'No,' she said. 'That's not entirely correct.'

The ruler fell on his palms again and again and again and Bruno shut his eyes during, wishing himself out of his body, away from pain, far even from Pitch End . . .

'The right-real answer perhaps,' said Miss Hope, stopping, Bruno hearing the exhilaration in her breathing, 'but the very *wrong* attitude. And the *way* we say things is just as important as the *content* of them, is it not?'

Bruno opened his eyes. He didn't look at his hands.

'No,' he said, his voice breaking. 'It's the truth that matters, not how I say some lies.'

'Is that so?' said Miss Hope.

Bruno waited, and then said, 'It is so. And you know it too, not so deep down.'

Neither of them moved. Bruno kept his hands steady, palms throbbing, still expectant of more. Bruno looked into Miss Hope's eyes, blank as frozen puddles, and refused a waver in his gaze. And he knew their thoughts were the same.

'You should never have done it,' said Bruno. 'I know the truth about the lighthouse because of that book, and we'd know more of the right-real truth if you'd never have burned it when—'

'*Silence!*' Miss Hope hissed, and she didn't strike him but instead took her hands to the ears of the Cat-Sentry.

40

Her eyes were shut and her narrow body shook. Bruno thought her almost breakable.

'Why is it, Atlas,' she said between deep breaths, 'that ye always say the things ye should just be keeping in yer head, and then only think what ye should be saying?'

Bruno didn't reply – she hadn't been the first who'd said this to him.

'Go,' said Miss Hope, 'and I don't care what ye say or do with yerself now. I wash me hands of ye. Ye can only go on like this so long. And I for one will not shed a tear on the day the Elders and Enforcers come for ye.'

'I'm not afeared of them,' said Bruno, his voice struggling with a sob.

Miss Hope replied with eyes still closed and hands still clamped over the Cat-Sentry's hearing, in a low whisper: 'Ye right-well should be. And no made-up stories, no *Tall Tales* are gonna be saving ye then.'

V

The Tall Tale of the Dishonest Elder

At ten turns old Bruno saw words he shouldn't have in a book he shouldn't have found: a book of *stories*. And he found it in a place he shouldn't have been. He thought of it ever after, referred to it in the privacy of his own thoughts, as the Day of Discovery.

The only printed words Bruno knew were those in Jack Pitch's *The Wrath*: every Pitch Ender's guide, standard-issue, given at birth. Everything ('And more than anyone should be looking to know or learn!' said the Elders) was detailed within those scarlet covers, all clear and no-nonsense. So to discover a different book – to discover anything other than the usual and the approved in Pitch End – took searching, going places you weren't supposed to. But first, you had to find time.

On the morning of his Day of Discovery Bruno stood

in his back garden, sweating. Swelter Season, wide sky stale and blue-bland, not a cloud, the wider world of the town closed off because all action was dictated by the Work-Dial, a stone disc on a stone stump with an iron needle two-hands high, top and centre. Like *The Wrath*, all Pitch End households had one. After time had been taken from them when Bruno was five turns, the Work-Dial was how the townsfolk were told what to be doing with themselves.

Bruno looked to the needle's imperious shadow – it lay in one of the sections with the chiselled word WORK. EAT & DRINK – the three thinnest divisions on the surface of the stone disc – were separated by WORK and yet again, WORK . . . other than this, only SHUT-EYE.

WORK for Bruno meant Hedge School or, at weekends, house-WORK. For his mother WORK meant Official Mourning in the town hall with the other Widows of Pitch End. Saturday and Sunday she left a list for Bruno – things to be washed, ironed, scrubbed, dusted, emptied, washed up again. But he'd grown good at working fast, accomplishing things like chores quick. By midday on the Day of Discovery he'd finished all his mother's orders. He was alone then, bored and curious.

Bruno went to his room and tugged the curtains closed.

His hiding habit had flourished: from under his bed, under a loose floorboard, he took his old Owl-Sentry. The Sentry had never worked as it should've, but it had been invaluable anyway. It still held safe the brass pocket watch

43

of his father – unable to be opened, though Bruno had tried for long hours. Around it were crammed loose sheets, articles he'd snipped from the *Pitch End Journal*. He shouldn't have had these any more than he should've had a pocket watch. Every night as Curfew drove townsfolk home, the shadow of the Work-Dial's needle settling on SHUT-EYE, that day's copy of the *Pitch End Journal* was left out on every doorstep. There surrendered, the journals were disappeared in the night and taken to the town hall (by Enforcers, Bruno had heard) and there destroyed (he'd also heard). This action was yet another Elder Order, to keep Pitch End firm in its Forgetting.

Bruno knew that if he was discovered not in the throes of WORK as the needle dictated, he'd be done. If he was found not doing as he should be and in possession of newspapers that should've been in the town hall and a pocket watch belonging to his Forgotten father, he'd be disappeared himself in the night, taken to the town hall and destroyed too. It was an oddly thrilling thought. He tried to care, worry a bit about horrific consequence, but couldn't.

He laid out his kept articles, each as stiff and see-through as a torn fingernail, and read their headlines, wondering –

February 31st, Year +292

FARMERS SAY REBELS STILL THE CAUSE OF SOGGY CABBAGES!

44

TEMPERATE THOMAS SAYS:
'IF YER CABBAGE SMELLS OFF, TURN ON THE SPOT
FIFTEEN TIMES WHILST BOILING IT IN A
SAUCEPAN,
AND THAT'LL BANISH THE BLIGHT OF DR BLOOM
AND HIS REBELS FROM IT!'

March 29th, Year +293

FISHERMEN SAY THEY SEE SHADOWS TEN FEET TALL
AT SEA! TEMPERATE THOMAS SAYS:
'DR BLOOM AND REBELS MAY BE RETURNING IN
DARKER FORM!'

April 1st, Year +294

SCREAMS HEARD FROM THE ELM TREE MOUNTAINS
AS PIGS
VANISH OVERNIGHT FROM EASTERN FIELDS!
TEMPERATE THOMAS SAYS:
'DR BLOOM AND OTHER REBELS MAY BE
HIDING
UNDERGROUND IN
MOUNT TOME WITH STOLEN LIVESTOCK!'

Never easing and always at the approach of the Single Season War's anniversary – the terror of the Rebels, gone but never Forgotten, never far. Bruno reread and reread, and longed to sift some truth from these things. All just words to frighten, or was there something beneath it all, truthfully?

He eased back, lay on the floor and gazed at the ceiling. He remained for long, silent, unknowable minutes. Again alone, bored and curious.

On that morning, a journey to the old house was the only thing for him.

The way back to his old home took Bruno towards the shore, then west. He'd see people on route, pass within earshot, hear them talk, but he'd been stopped never. Bruno had a way, he'd realised, of not being noticed. On the journey there were distractions that set the heart going (Elder words spoke from everywhere) – black on white, warning in the form of advice, admonishment in the guise of encouragement, comfort. Wrapped around lampposts or pasted across windows of derelict cottages or just airborne, proliferating and settling on rooftops, doorsteps, on lawns yellowed like old newspaper in the Swelter.

Then Bruno saw Elders themselves. And sure enough they had armfuls more of paper, were rapping on doors and scolding the occupants for not being quick enough to answer or too quick ('Which must mean ye're not occupying yerselves properly with some hard work!'). Bruno watched them press copies of the Eleven Decent Ways into the hands of the too-slow (or too-quick).

He slowed enough to hear . . . The Elders were wanting

donations. And information – 'How many children do ye have? How old? Boy or girl? Oh, here he is now! Nine turns, did ye say? He's big for his age, isn't he? Looks very sprightly and strong, plenty of life in him! Would he be interested, I'm wondering, in spending some time with the Elders? Coz we'd be very interested indeed in having him for a few hours, teach him some of the rightly-decent ways.'

Bruno passed Enforcers, door-knocking too, with harder fists and stamped warrants, demanding to see inside, to catch people out. Bruno knew that a pair – man and wife, both eighty-eight turns old – had been arrested earlier that week for having too much food in their cupboards. 'On suspicion,' said the *Pitch End Journal*, 'of hoarding food to provide to the Rebels! (For more on the latest Elder predictions on the possible return of the Rebels, turn to page two.)'

At the end of his street, Bruno stopped at the base of the large wooden sign on two tall legs that declared:

1,915 DAYS SINCE ANY 'UNPLEASANTNESS' IN PITCH END – ELDERS BE PRAISED!

Bruno couldn't stop himself thinking, 1,915 days since everyone Forgot my da.

Ducking under the sign, his feet sank into Diamond Beach. An outflung arm of sand, colour of faded fool's gold, the beach reached towards the western headland and the lighthouse, its black and white whirl of a tower planted on a sharp shoulder of rock – stone and cement, not built from anything as ill-advised as glass.

This was Bruno's favourite place in Pitch End.

Unblemished by Elder or Enforcer, the scene rippled with silence. He'd come with his father and mother many times, any season. Memories still un-Forgotten returned to him only when he stood on the beach. Nothing much moved. The Pitch End flag hung limp on its pole. He squinted, saw people. Not many and mostly unmoving. Could be flotsam or jetsam, Bruno thought, the Pitch Enders washed up, unwanted, laid out. Could be waiting just for the tide to come in and embrace, take them elsewhere.

A half-dozen gulls passed overhead, wings arched, parting and then alighting, each on one of the wooden bollards carved into the shape of ravens that marked the tide, stalking down to gentle waves, to a sea that shrunk them shorter and shorter, then swallowed. Bruno would've remained there, nestled in memory, were it not for the voice of an Elder nearing –

'Don't worry yer head,' the Elder was saying, in that special voice used by adults who don't like children very much. 'Ye'll be home in time for yer SHUT-EYE. Tell me – would ye like to see what lies under the Clocktower in the town square?'

Bruno moved on and minutes later – five, ten, who knew? – he stood before his old house. The oak in front had been reduced to a stump, its top scorched. Bruno looked left and right and behind him – every tree on Meadow Street had been treated the same. He remembered the Elder Order that came under their front door not long after the end of time:

> Every tree – big or small – on every street in Pitch
>   End is to be cut down to size.
> This is for the precious protection of Pitch Enders.
> For trees are far too easy for people to be hiding in
>   and behind.
> Signed,
> Temperate Thomas II, Head of the Elders

Bruno went in. He stooped, moved deep into ash and darkness, into the ruin of the life he'd had until one week from five turns old. Bruno promised himself every time he went (and returned without detection) that it would be his final time, no more. And each time he broke it – the old house never failed to divulge some curio or other, some scrap, some remainder ripe for taking and poring over and keeping hidden.

On into black, things all around broken and meaningless, and on further into the corner of the former cellar. Bruno stopped, looked up, saw Swelter Season sky fringed with thorns, splintered floorboards and rafters.

He heard the slow trickle of water. He followed that sound, and beneath slabs and scorched soil, not hidden or locked up, just there awaiting discovery – on his Day of Discovery! – he found it.

Immediately different. Vulnerable in his hands and forbidden, but formidable too, its pages singed, the cover rough and vaguely illustrated: a figure on a beach, apparently alone but with hands upraised like surrender. Bruno looked closer, licked his finger and rubbed away grime, revealing more . . . Behind and all around the figure stood tall, dark, faceless creatures. And then the title, a swirl of silver on black –

Tall Tales from Pitch End
By Dr Jonathan Bloom

Bruno heard Miss Hope's voice in his head: '*The villain, Dr Jonathan Bloom, was the leader of the Rebels. He was a cruel, uneducated man. An animal, a monster, rightly-indecent and evil and filthy in his habits, he longed for nothing less than the complete destruction of rightly-decent Pitch End life! He also had shocking bad manners.*'

But in that moment of finding, thoughts of Rebels and the Single Season War and Miss Hope melted from Bruno's mind. In his hands was something undiscovered. And without a thought for obeying Elder Orders – finding the nearest Enforcer and surrendering the book, freeing himself of the thing as a dubious object surely intended to muddy his mind – Bruno folded himself under a pair of scorched beams, opened the book and began to read.

Each tale was devoured. Without break Bruno read – and read on into a true timelessness . . . And when he arrived at the back cover, letting it fall, he looked up and didn't know where he was. Darkness had covered him without notice. He wondered how he'd managed to read with so little light to see by. Slowly he was restored to the world, with head light and limbs numb. He couldn't part with it. *Tall Tales from Pitch End* went home with him.

That night the stories, like sharp pips swallowed, germinated in Bruno's imagination. Within hours, the *Tall Tales* were thriving in every bit of him.

Next morning Bruno sent a message, a whisper, around Hedge School: all had to assemble at first break behind the privy – by the pump that gushed rust-flecked water. And they should not tell Miss Hope. At the advised time, Bruno stood on an upturned bucket, only slightly above the other children.

'What is it, Atlas?' Sabitha McCormack shouted at him as she arrived, standing at the back of the group. She folded her arms. 'It better be good and not all boring like everything ye usually come out with!'

Others agreed.

Bruno took a breath, wet his lips. He held the book open on both hands. The title of the first *Tall Tale* was waiting, wanting to be read. The title alone was enough to get Bruno twenty or so whacks with the ruler, maybe worse. He knew this.

'Come on!' cried Sabitha. 'Are ye simple or what!'

'*Quiet!*' Bruno told them, and then they were. He cleared his throat and began: 'This is called '*The Tall Tale of the Dishonest Elder.*'

Everyone gasped.

He'd expected this reaction. He stood taller.

'*There was once a dishonest Elder (named Elder Dishonest, truly enough) who one dark night murdered the husband of a woman he had fallen in love with. The man was a farmer, and his wife a woman of fine breeding who had fallen in with what the Elders would call "a lower sort of man". Elder Dishonest accomplished his murder like this: first, he sent a letter to the farmer, telling him that he was to be especially rewarded for his work for Pitch End – for his long hours of labour, for his general decency, he was to be given the not insubstantial sum of exactly sixty pitches, ten putts and thirty-three pence. Being a farmer in hard times, the promise of money was enough to lure the man to the meeting place noted in his official, Elder-stamped letter: the western headland, near the fourth lighthouse of Pitch End, at sundown.*

'*But little did he reckon on the scheming of Elder Dishonest. And little did he know that Elder Dishonest was waiting there for him, skulking in a nearby cave. When the Elder saw the farmer approach he skulked deeper, held his silence and waited for the right moment, because Elders are as slippery as serpents, cunning as cats and resourceful as rats when they need to be. And when the farmer turned* his back, was at his most vulnerable, the Elder fired a burst of Talent at him, knocking the man into the sea.

'Now, this wasn't enough to finish the farmer off – the Elder had hoped for a stormy night, high winds and crashing waves, but the water was calm and the farmer simply began to swim back towards the headland. The Elder knew he would have to kill the man, but would also have to make sure it looked like an accident. He looked to the fourth lighthouse of Pitch End, knowing what already people were saying about the new glass lighthouse – that it would surely be knocked down at the first sign of storm. So Elder Dishonest summoned all his considerable Talent and sent cracks scaling the lighthouse, and it broke apart and toppled into the sea, little more than shards that tore the farmer to little more than ribbons.

'So, deed done, Elder Dishonest went home to a snifter of brandy and then sleep, with untroubled dreams.

'Next morning, news spread fast (as it always does in Pitch End) of the farmer's death. No one suspected anything untoward, all claiming they knew such a thing would happen to the lighthouse, even if the night hadn't been particularly squally. And Elder Dishonest was instrumental in promoting the idea that the man had probably been drunk, lost his way, leading to the terrible tragedy. Deeply regretful, sad . . . but still, as the Elders say, "When the drink goes in, the decency goes out!"

'At the same time, Elder Dishonest went to visit the wife of the man he had murdered. He intended to comfort her,

53

console her, offer her a life as an Elder's wife (these were in the days when Elders still did such things as marry). But when he arrived at the farm and made his slow but firm advances, as he had long planned, the farmer's wife rejected him. She was too overcome with grief, she explained, to contemplate a life without her husband. She could not, would not, ever forget him, would never love another, and certainly never consider remarriage. So Elder Dishonest left, broken-hearted.

'*That night, the Elder woke in the dead, dark hours to a terrifying sight: the farmer he had murdered was standing at the end of his bed. He was no more than a shadow, the farmer, but was as tall as the ceiling, imposing as a pillar, and he spoke in a voice like an echo of an echo, saying: "Never forget. Ye will never be Forgetting me. Never, ever forget what ye did!"*

'*Elder Dishonest hid under the covers, recited eleven times the Eleven Decent Ways of the Elders, and when he dared to look out again the vision of the murdered farmer had departed.*

'*The next night, however, the same thing happened again, and still all the words the dead farmer offered were: "Never forget. Ye will never be Forgetting me. Never, ever forget what ye did!"*

'*And so on, for the next night and the next, and the one after that too – always the same vision, always the same words.*

'*Elder Dishonest consulted with his fellow Elders, told*

them he was being haunted by the farmer who had recently (and tragically) died. They advised him to take a penny and engrave on it the name of the farmer, then fill a bowl of milk, drop the penny in it, then boil the milk. When the surface was bubbling, the Elder was to drink the milk in one go, penny and all. This, he was told, would rid him of all traces of the dead farmer.

'Elder Dishonest did just this.

'But still the farmer appeared to him: "Never forget. Ye will never be Forgetting me. Never, ever forget what ye did!"

'Elders advised Elder Dishonest to shoot a hare, sever one of its paws and use it to dust the floor of his bedroom where the shadowy form of the farmer usually appeared. But this did not work either. Finally, they told him that he had one final option – to go to the spot where the farmer had perished, and hope there to encounter the man's unsettled soul, and direct it out to the Sea of Apparitions, where all who die in Pitch End must go.

'Elder Dishonest stood that night on the western headland, amidst the wreckage of Pitch End's fourth lighthouse. The world was not calm as it had been on the night he had murdered the farmer: waves soaked him, cold wind chewed at his bones, and guilt gnawed at his soul. And there, on the shore of Pitch End, the farmer he had murdered appeared to him once more.

'Elder Dishonest fell to his knees and demanded of the farmer, "Why do ye haunt me like this? Ye're dead and gone, Forgotten, so why do ye not leave me be?"

'And the farmer replied, "Because I am not truly Forgotten. No one is so easily gone, even the dead, if they have people left behind to remember them, miss them. We linger on still. A Shadow, a presence that is everywhere and nowhere as long as we remain in the minds of the ones who loved us, stays. And at times we can rise, face any great evil, put a stop to things done in the name of darkness – like the killing of a man in cold blood."

'From the churning waters rose other figures, other Shadows, others who Elder Dishonest had wronged, cheated, even murdered – tall, thin, with faces dark and voices sharp, their lament added to the farmer's as they chorused to the night: "Never forget. Never forget. We are the Undying Voices, never Forgotten!"

'Elder Dishonest knew then what he must do to be rid of the farmer forever – he shut his eyes, whispered a final prayer to the sea, begging its mercy, and then let himself fall into the waves, into the clutches of Shadows who bore him downwards into the dark.

'His body was never seen again by human eyes, his voice never heard to tell others what they should be doing or thinking or feeling, and there was not a person left behind who remembered him fondly, who mourned him even. No one left at all in Pitch End who wished to be remembering that most dishonest of the Elders, Elder Dishonest.'

Bruno looked up. Like before, he was surprised to find himself in the world.

His audience were wordless.

Eventually, one of the younger ones went: 'That was brilliant!' At the same time another, older, started to wail: 'I don't wanna see one of them Shadows!'

'Shut up youse two!' said Sabitha. 'Quit yer whingeing, it's only all made up!'

But Bruno saw Sabitha look askance at her own shadow, its mid-morning length enough to blot some of the playground.

'That Shadow wasn't for hurting the Elder,' Bruno explained, looking at the boy who still cried on. 'He just wanted the Elder to know that he wasn't just going away. He'd still stay because he'd murdered him. Things don't just go.'

As he said it, he wondered: his own father had gone, not been Forgotten by Bruno, yet he'd never seen a Shadow of him. He'd never returned, despite how lonely Bruno felt, how much in need and how lost.

He spoke again to the one weeping – 'Don't worry. It's not that scary a story.'

'It *was* scary!' Sabitha shouted, before any other words could be voiced by any other mouth. 'The story was meant to be like in *The Wrath* when Jack Pitch talks about what'll happen at the end of the world – *scary*. Missing the point as usual, Master Atlas!'

A few sniggers – the same words Miss Hope used when Bruno was disagreeable.

'It can be what ye want it to be,' said Bruno. 'Not just one decided thing. It's not like *The Wrath*.'

57

'So the things in that there book,' said Gahern, a boy younger than Bruno, 'they're written down like in *The Wrath,* but they aren't the right-real truth?'

Bruno thought, and then nodded. Then shook his head.

'How is it written down if it didn't happen?' asked Martha Tilly, looking not at Bruno but at Sabitha. 'Where'd it all come from?'

Bruno began, 'Someone . . .' But could barely understand it himself. 'Someone must've just . . . *made it up* . . .'

Some children scoffed, others looked thoughtful, or doubtful. But none bored.

'Rubbish!' Sabitha decided. 'Ye're nothing but a liar, Bruno Atlas! I'm gonna tell my father!'

'There's other things in here,' said Bruno, feeling like an Elder on his small but significantly raised height. 'They're stories too, but they've things in them about what happened turns ago – about why the slogg-barges are stranded in Mickleward Marsh, the way the Elders got into power so quick and why the ravens only have one foot and are able to talk and—'

'*Atlas!*'

Miss Hope's voice across the playground.

'What is that book ye're reading from? It had better be *The Wrath*!'

Knowing that it wasn't and knowing that there was no way to hide or deny it, Bruno shut the book, finger turning down the corner to mark the page, and waited on Miss Hope's approach.

58

The book snatched from Bruno's hand and less than a minute later – her face a squirm of shock and fear and disgust – Miss Hope delivered her verdict, a small tear leaking from her left eye: '*Lies*. Pure lies and nonsense and hearsay and . . .' She could find no more words to articulate the crime that this book had committed by its very existence, and by Bruno's reading it.

'I'll be putting an end to this!' she announced.

Miss Hope carried the book at arm's length to the squat, rusted brazier that was a permanent fixture of the playground at Hedge School. Permanent, because every Tuesday afternoon the children spent one hour creating their 'Weekly Confessions' – scraps of paper bearing confessions of things done or thought or said that week which the children knew as 'indecent' (using the Elders' Eleven Decent Ways as a guide), then submitted to the flames.

'Stop!' cried Bruno. 'Don't burn it! Ye can keep it or lock it up or something but just don't bloody burn it!'

He ran forwards but Miss Hope held him at bay on the strength of her Talent.

Bruno could only breathe then, move his eyeballs, want to weep – no other movement was possible, and no intervention. He watched.

Miss Hope opened the book (eyes averted), and laid it amongst the charred remains of confessed indecencies. And with her Talent – indignation so intense, so incendiary – drew flames from nowhere and tossed into them into the brazier.

Bruno wanted to cry out but his jaw was held shut by Miss Hope's consuming Talent. He decided instead, the Shadows in the story as his guide: I won't forget this. I won't forget what was written there. Because Bruno had the sense – contrary as it felt – that what he'd read in *Tall Tales from Pitch End* was of greater importance than anything he'd been taught. Anything he'd read in *The Wrath*, anything from the lips of Miss Hope or any Elder. Then the strangest thought, electrifying: that more than any other thing in Pitch End, those *Tall Tales* were true.

VI

The Wintering

'Come collect yer daily dose of Decency-Draught, guaranteed to fortify!'

'Donate to the Elders, folks – dig deep! Their comfort is our joy!'

'Potatoes! Carrots! Parsnips! Ten pence a bag, twenty pence a pair!'

'Fresh fish! No fish fresher than fish just outta the sea and into yer hand!'

Noon in Pitch End. Bruno was sitting on a mooring post not far from where his father's Forgetting had taken place ten turns before. His hands lay open, palms up, beseeching the sea, seeking the cool caress of mist, something to soothe where the ruler had struck. But the more minutes that passed the more traces of Miss Hope's punishment showed – rising and livid and undeniable. Bruno tried to close his hands, winced, but promised himself he wouldn't cry. He looked out, around –

Market-sellers were trying to out-holler one another, hunched under awnings with wares on the road, or leading donkeys as dull as damp brushes, saddle-baskets stacked up with nothing much. Outside The Fish in the Pan pub Enforcers were seated on barrels, throwing a game of BOX and downing pints of black beer, smoking and comparing the size of their rifles. Cat-Sentries were padding across the spine of the rooftops, awaiting an errant word or action, always the everywhere-eyes-and-ears of the Elders. Fishing boats were returning from their mornings, seagulls whirling above like furious halos, heckling and swooping and trying to unpick fish from bulging nets.

This was the sum of everything, all sight and sound of Pitch End.

'Alright – two bags for twenty pence! Bargain!'

All was so familiar, nothing in Pitch End new. Like waking each morning and being presented with the same set of dull and threadbare clothes to wear, not a thing ever changed. Bruno shut his eyes, weary, and tried to consider the future.

Fifteen turns old. He would Come-Of-Age in June when he took his Leaving exam and finished at Hedge School, and then he'd be handed his decided life. Regardless of exam results, this was how it would happen for all those Coming-Of-Age: an envelope slipped under the door at night, a white card inside with a single dark word that would be his calling for the rest of his life; one of the following:

ENFORCER
FARMER
SHOPKEEPER
FISHERMAN
STREET-SWEEPER
MARKET-SELLER

Or, rare though it was –

TRAINEE ELDER

Others in Hedge School whispered their desire for this last. Hoped for it, then dared not to. Bruno had decided too: if he was made a Trainee Elder, he would run away. But he knew what his card would tell him; generations of fathers gifted their lot to sons. Everyone stayed as they were. The word contained in his envelope would be:

LIGHTHOUSE-KEEPER

The job itself wasn't his worry. He liked time spent alone, and isolated in the lighthouse on the brink of the western headland would bring plenty of that. Even Coming-Of-Age didn't bother (for as long as he remembered, Bruno had always wished himself many turns older than he was) – it was the fact he had no choice. He thought the cards likely had already been written, since birth or before! His role in life noted, ticked off. Something else to think about was

63

what he'd do in the lighthouse. Last time the place had given out light was at least two turns before, the Temperate's explanation being: 'Why would we need a light to be guiding boats into our harbour? Doesn't anyone we'd ever want coming into Pitch End know the way already? Might be seen as an open and rightly-warm invitation to any foreigner passing by! No – best darken it, and we'll all sleep safer in our beds.' So what other work would they have for him?

He tried to clench his fists and managed it, though the pain cost him unfortunate tears, a slow roll of syrupy blood and a great deal of inward swearing.

'How's Bruno? Ye daydreaming as usual?'

Bruno opened his eyes.

From one of the rusted fishing boats dragging itself towards the jetty, Mr Pace had called. Bruno managed to wave, contemplating as he'd done many times the prospect of stowing away aboard one of these vessels. He could slide too easily into daydreams of distant and glittering shores, brighter places, happier people.

Before Bruno himself could reply –

'Less chat, more graft!' the Harbour Master shouted back at Pace, repeating another favourite bit of Elder Advice.

Ten turns since his father's Forgetting and Bruno noticed the unkindness of time on Mr Pace; watched him leap from the boat and stumble, hurry along the jetty like a half-lame hound and work to fasten the tow rope to a mooring post, panting.

'Make sure ye tie that up good and tight this time, Wither!' shouted the red-eyed Captain. 'Don't want it drifting off loose again! Got it?'

The Captain and Harbour Master exchanged a grin, a chuckle.

Pace didn't reply, just tipped his hat to the Captain.

'Ye shouldn't let him call ye that,' said Bruno. 'Ye're a fisherman now and not a Witherman.'

'Bruno,' said Pace with a sigh, setting his foot against the post and tugging on the rope, 'old Pace here will *always* be a Witherman.'

'Even not dealing with the dead any more?' said Bruno. 'Not sending them out to sea?'

They shared a small look. And in the small silence Bruno heard the low, slow *tick, tick, tick* of the clock in Pace's chest.

'I've towl ye a dozen times before,' said Pace, lowering his voice. 'Some things shouldn't be talked about. How are ye anyway? How's Definitive History these days?'

Bruno didn't reply.

'That good, eh?' said Pace. 'Here, take this for yerself. Get some sherbets or whatever ye buy these days for fun.' He added a black penny to Bruno's hand.

'Thanks,' said Bruno, and he pushed it into his trouser pocket.

'What happened to yer hands there?' asked Pace. 'That blood on them?'

'Nothing,' Bruno said, clasping them together. 'Just got into a bit of a fight.'

'Ye need to watch yerself,' said Pace. 'Did I ever tell ye about the time I got into a scrap with Scabby McCormack?'

'*Scabby?*'

'Oh aye,' said Pace. 'Called him that coz he had all these scabs on his knees, always falling over, big clumsy lummock he was, always bullying too. But one day, I decided I'd stand up to oul Scabby, so I took me fist and I—'

Pace stopped.

'Scabby McCormack,' said Bruno, thinking aloud. 'Was that Marshall McCormack? Because it was his daughter that I was—'

'Anyway,' Pace shouted suddenly, 'shouldn't Master Bruno Atlas be in school? Lunchtime must be near enough over by now, I'd be thinking.'

Bruno looked around – a Cat-Sentry had arrived close on one of the mooring posts with ears stiff and sharp.

'I should be going now too, Atlas,' said Pace. His head was dipped.

Bruno checked the Work-Dial near the jetty – the needle's shadow was vague, but was inching back into the realm of WORK sure enough.

'Aye,' said Bruno. 'Better be off.'

Pace leaned close to Bruno and muttered, 'Sorry about that, but ye're as clear as a rock pool for thinking, Bruno. Ye need to learn to hide yer worries away from them that would want to be knowing them. Take care of yerself.' Pace chanced a hand on Bruno's shoulder, a shaky squeeze, then hobbled off towards The Fish in the Pan.

Bruno remained, wondering about how easily he could be read, and worrying. He watched one of the fishermen clamp a hand around the fat purse of a black bream's body, the other sliding a blade in and up – tail to eyes in one swipe – and then plucking the tangle of guts from inside, flinging them into the sea. The fisherman looked at him, then laughed at the disgusted expression on Bruno's face.

Yes, thought Bruno, I'm much too easy to read.

He stood and turned, dread crawling across his body like a fever, symptoms being: Hedge School, Sabitha McCormack, Miss Hope, Definitive History . . .

But on his feet and only a moment later, came a sound. Loud enough and clear enough to stop everyone and thing dead: men on the markets, the Enforcers, fishermen, the fold of waves, the breath in Bruno's chest . . .

The sound of *laughter*.

Sudden light in the sea mist, a shred of blue-white, wavering, moving towards the jetty.

Another burst of laughter, the urgent blast of a foghorn –

'Bruno, come away from there, quick-smart! Come away!'

Pace had returned. Stooped a few feet behind Bruno, he held out a shivering hand. But Bruno didn't shift, eyes too besotted with approaching light.

'Load yer weapons, prepare to fire,' a voice behind him ordered.

'What is it?' another voice demanded.

'Nothing,' said the first voice. 'It's – it's just *nothing*.

Now get back all of ye! Wither – tell that boy to get back!'

Finally Bruno turned – a half-dozen Enforcers were behind, all kneeling with rifles aimed towards the mist. Towards the 'nothing'.

'*Bruno!*' shouted Pace, his throat nearly tearing with the effort.

Then Bruno saw: the prow of a boat rushed clear of the mist, a lantern with a blue-white flame swinging high on the mast, speeding towards the jetty as Pace cried out yet again, straining to snatch Bruno away. But he'd already turned, running as the first boards of the jetty snapped in two under the charging boat. Bruno barely leaped clear of it before the Enforcers thought to fire, bullets finding echoes in the rust-stained hull as the boat came on and on, unstoppable –

A moment of exquisite terror: Bruno imagined the boat charging on and not stopping until it met the Elm Tree Mountains, cleaving Pitch End in two –

A scream –

Another pounding moment –

The Cat-Sentry on the mooring post, too keen to bear witness and record, was crunched beneath the fishing-boat –

It came to a slow stop; shuddering, reluctant, and only inches from where Bruno and Pace were sprawled on the ground. On a hull rough with barnacles, fragmented letters tried to declare: *The Wintering*.

Echoes of the boat's arrival bounded through Pitch End – Enforcer gunshots, the snapping of wood and grind of metal, and the masts of fishing boats moored along the (now ruined) jetty clashing like frantic limbs.

Slowly, Bruno and Pace got to their feet. Slower still, market-sellers and fishermen began an approach. And further away again, the noise of the boat, the following press of silence, was drawing others: more Enforcers, more Cat-Sentries . . .

'Everyone just be staying where they are!'

And Marshall McCormack.

'Be leaving that boat!'

The Marshall passed close and Bruno examined his face: a scar descending from hairline to brow like a seam of bright silver was the only flaw, a thin chink in otherwise immaculate armour. And though he knew he should have Forgotten, Bruno remembered that night from which all things could be traced – scar a fresh wound, inflicted on a face that had interrogated, ordered, insulted, executed . . .

'*Wither!* Be staying back! And get that child away too.'

Child? thought Bruno.

An Enforcer swooped on Bruno and Pace and took them by the scruffs. Bruno twisted, half-turned, and succeeded in shrugging him off.

'This is an official Enforcer matter,' the Marshall went on, voice not loud but as clear as struck glass. 'No one is to be taking even a *step* closer.' He brushed past Bruno, whispering to an Enforcer, 'It's like we were warned. This is the missing boat. Get Temperate Thomas.'

'Why not just send a Sentry, sir?' asked the Enforcer.

The Marshall gave him a look.

The Enforcer obeyed without more reply, running up South Street towards the town hall.

The Marshall turned on the watchers.

'Did ye not hear me?' he said. 'Away now. The Dial says WORK, if ye know what that means and ye know what's good for ye!'

'Ye heard the Marshall,' said another Enforcer, laying a hand on Pace.

'A'right! A'right!' said Pace, shrugging him off. 'We're going, rightly-obedient.'

Pace began to steer Bruno away through the crowd who were all retreating under order, but all slowly, curiosity like a glue on their soles. Bruno dragged his feet too, trying to snatch a better look at the boat, his breath swift, excitement and some fear fluttering in his chest – the boat, that laughter, the rush of its arrival, all as fierce as an accusation. Maybe, and just perhaps, Bruno thought, things can change in Pitch End.

Just as he was about to lose sight of *The Wintering* there was another scream from the crowd.

Bruno broke free of Pace, turned and was pushed to the ground once again, this time by a rush of Enforcers – a soaring of shrieks, human and gull, and through the stampeding legs of the townsfolk, Bruno saw a man aboard

70

The Wintering, standing tall and screaming. A screaming which shifted into laughter – manic eyes wide and red-rimmed, mouth wider still and black.

The Enforcer's bullets had no effect at first. The man shrugged them off like pellets of paper, but increasingly he cowered, body forming a shield around something. Bruno looked and looked and noticed a large crate tucked under the man's arm, something he was keen to protect, splintered and bound with knotted lengths of seaweed. Then, brief and in no more than a glimpse, there was something else seen by Bruno: the cracked face of a clock, without hands, protruding from the man's chest . . .

'*Gumbly-the-Witherman*,' Bruno heard Pace breathe.

Only the Marshall managed a true shot.

It struck the Witherman's cheek and he stopped, looking directly at Bruno. Then Gumbly collapsed, the crate tumbling from his hands and pitching into the water.

Every Enforcer stormed *The Wintering* in a heartbeat. Marshall McCormack too, medals gleaming, pistol releasing a ribbon of smoke following its fatal shot. He crouched over the fallen Witherman.

Bruno got up, most senses asunder but still wanting to watch, to know, to capture every exchange, every moment, remember it.

Enforcers searched the fishing boat, kicking doors open and upending more crates – 'Come out with yer hands in the air in the name of Pitch End!' – and then returned to the Marshall to report. 'No one else aboard, sir.'

'Of course there isn't,' said the Marshall, and he slapped the Enforcer around the neck. '*Fool*. Now retrieve that crate from the water.'

Rubbing his neck, the Enforcer grabbed one of his fellows and the pair of them returned to the jetty.

'*School*,' said Pace, his fingers grinding into Bruno's shoulder.

Bruno watched the Enforcers wade into the water like tentative children, rifles held aloft, submerged to the waist before they could reach the crate that Gumbly-the-Witherman had been carrying.

A nudge at Bruno's leg – he looked down and saw a Cat-Sentry flow past and up South Street. Like the proudest feline returning with a bird between the teeth, Bruno knew it would hasten to the Elders then to present what it had just witnessed. Then it would be for Temperate Thomas to decide what these events meant for the people of Pitch End.

'I said be *going*,' said Pace. Bruno heard – almost felt in the chambers of his own chest – the fraught *tick, tick, tick* of Pace's clock-heart.

'Ye what?' asked Bruno. 'And miss more of this? What's in the crate? Where do ye think he's come from? Do you think he—'

'*Quiet*, Bruno,' Pace told him again, teeth gritted. 'In the name of Pitch, none of yer arguing. Not now. And tell not a one about this. Not a single soul, do ye hear me?'

'But why is Gumbly—'

Then Bruno noticed – the Marshall was watching. His eyes met Bruno's, then shifted downwards. Bruno looked too – his father's medallion, silver chain, silver eye with silver storm-petrel enclosed, was lying on the ground, its chain snapped. Must've fallen off when I got pushed, Bruno thought, and he kneeled and gathered it up in one hand. And when he looked up again, he saw the Marshall flinch as though he'd been stung, or shot.

'Why is he looking at it?' Bruno thought aloud.

'I towl ye,' whispered Pace, 'ye give too much away, Bruno. Now away with ye before it's too late.' So Bruno said nothing more, only turned away. But in turning he saw a final thing. On the side of the crate being brought from the water was a symbol splashed in silver paint: a half-shut eye, a storm-petrel inside, and words stencilled below:

DO NOT BE OPENING THIS CRATE UNLESS YE WISH TO BE BRINGING A RIGHTLY-EARLY END TO EVERYTHING!

VII
Old Town

When Hedge School wound up that evening Bruno fled swifter than usual. Freed, he sprinted up the steep slope that ended in the meeting of North and South Streets, and there stopped in the quiet of the town square. The heart of the town, Bruno supposed, but a heart arrested. Dominated by the town hall and the tall, lopsided Clocktower – its hands unmoving, frozen at midnight (or midday, depending on who you talked to) – all of Pitch End rose slowly then steeply towards this alarming pinnacle, marking the town's highest point, from which everything could be observed.

Bruno could've (should've) gone home. Without delay and like everyone else in town – to tea and toast, then bed and sleep filled with unmemorable, rightly-decent dreams. But Bruno didn't want to go home. Couldn't. He needed to know that what he'd witnessed on the jetty was a real thing, not a daydream he'd sunken into. That he'd seen the Witherman shot, the crate fall, the symbol on its side. The warning not to open. Because soon, he knew, the event would be as fully Forgotten as his father, same as all the dead and bygones and past things of Pitch End. Wiped away by the Elders.

So he crouched amongst shadows at the base of the Clocktower, under the blank watch of statues: the seven sons of George Pitch, founder of Pitch End. He waited and watched, only a little worried. '*Loitering and snooping, staying out of sight – can't be good and can't be right!*' the Elder words reminded his head.

He hoped for something to happen. Pitch End Curfew (dictated by the arrival of dusk) would soon be in effect, and he tried to keep his thoughts from what would happen if he was discovered. The noticeboard by the town hall's double doors advised:

NO ENTRY WITHOUT ELDER APPROVAL
&
ONLY ON RIGHTLY-DECENT BUSINESS

(REMINDER: ANYTHING DESCRIBED AS

'RIGHTLY-DECENT BUSINESS'

MUST FIRST BE APPROVED BY THE ELDERS.)

Bruno swallowed.

Somewhere above a one-footed raven cried out, took off.

Cold dashed his finger. Then his wrist, nose – the ground began to darken in spots of rain.

But his waiting was rewarded in the next moment. There was a fresh arrival of noise and, at the bottom of the cobbled slope that burrowed into still-lingering sea mist on the shore, Bruno saw a consolidation of darkness. A horde of Enforcers, all on horseback and all oncoming like a wave. He ducked lower, wishing himself smaller, but still watching – the Marshall was at the head of the tide.

They slowed and just about stopped in front of the town hall and Bruno expected them to move inside where they had their barracks. Instead, the double doors opened and, wordlessly, four Enforcers emerged, struggling to carry between them something long and wrapped in black. Bruno watched more: he saw a limp hand, a clutch of fingers, a bulge of swollen flesh, seaweed trailing. *Gumbly*. His body, but no crate.

The voice of the Marshall went: 'Hurry it up.'

Something in his tone made Bruno's scalp prickle.

Gumbly's body was lifted and flung over the Marshall's stallion where his leather-gloved fingers held it fast. A dig of his heel, the low command of, 'Into Old Town,' and the Marshall galloped off, Enforcers all following.

Bruno shifted. Old Town was the last place he'd expected the Marshall to head and he felt certain he'd be seen, his shock sending out signals. He pressed himself to the Clocktower, eyes shut. He listened.

The hollow rap of hooves faded, a sodden silence left in their wake.

He opened his eyes, looked to the entrance to Old Town, to the pair of crumbling pillars topped with ram's heads. Thought for a moment longer . . . To hell with it! He followed the Marshall and his horde.

As steeply as the slope from Hedge School to the Clocktower ran upwards, all ways into Old Town delved just as steeply down. It was part of Pitch End no one wanted to be found in. Shops opened at odd hours, if they did at all – under a full moon maybe, or on the first day after the Breaking of the World celebration, or when the weather was fairer, or fouler. Few called anywhere in Old Town home, and any that did had to put up with being ignored or called gypsy or no-hoper or vagrant, or seen as simply 'indecent'.

Vegetation was allowed to flourish, slated rooftops and windows sprouting vast, crooked limbs of vast and crooked trees. And huddled amongst dark foliage – a gleam, a keen eye, but raven or Cat-Sentry? Every doorway or window as dark and deep-set as a sunken eyeball or broken mouth, there were plenty of places to remain concealed, to watch but remain unseen. But Bruno wondered, as he entered a narrow laneway – a 'darkway', as most Pitch Enders called them – why the Enforcers would come into Old Town at all? The security and respectability of their barracks was only an echo away.

The sky groaned, lamenting unspeakable storms, releasing more rain.

A sudden flare of light by Bruno's face – he ducked, and the window beside and above him blushed with light.

'Put him – *it* – on the table. Carefully.'

The gravel-and-gunshots voice of the Marshall. Heavy footsteps beyond the window, then a loud thud.

'I said be *careful* on it!' the Marshall shouted.

A few apologetic mumbles.

'The chest,' said the Marshall, 'it's that – that *thing* fixed in the chest. Temperate Thomas wants it removed. For looking at more closely.'

The clock, thought Bruno.

A new voice now, high-pitched: 'I see. Well then, let's have a wee gander.'

Silence, into which Bruno poured himself, straining, trying to hear. But no good. So he picked himself up onto tiptoe. He found only a tiny, frayed sliver of seeing where the curtains should've met but didn't quite. An Enforcer stood in front of the window inside, a thick-set barrier of scarlet.

Bruno looked around and noticed a wizened trunk, branches like keen fingers clinging to the side of the building the Enforcers were in. Bruno had never climbed a tree before, but the fire of his curiosity made him bolder – he grasped a branch, settled his foot on another, and began to scale the side of the building.

Any creak or complaint from the tree was lost in rainfall.

But when he reached the roof he was without any cover, felt too exposed. A breeze rushed over, the rooftop fluttering like many worried eyes – a canopy of leaves where the roof had once been, a little slate and a wide opening, lantern light from the room below illuminating the underside of foliage. Bruno crawled towards this opening, moving along branches. He slipped, snatched at a handful of leaves, and for long moments heard nothing but his own blood thudding. He remained where he was, trying to breathe and just be without shivering.

Then he moved on.

At the opening he gathered fragments he had to slot together of the picture below – a hand with a tremble, the shine of a bald head, a dark fireplace. Bruno could only see pieces, but felt at the same time that he was seeing more clearly than he'd ever done in Pitch End before; he was seeing what he wasn't meant to. Then he saw the doctor he knew was called Pinchbeck, the top of his bald head bent close to the table. The Marshall was at his elbow, and around them both Enforcers were planted, some close, some at a distance. And on the table itself –

'By the mountains!' squealed Dr Pinchbeck.

A clatter of metal, a shiver that shook the room, all Enforcers uprooted, gasps and a momentary snatch of the table – Gumbly spread, blood, pale flesh, blank eyes and a clock face embedded in his ribs where his heart should've been, and yet more blood leaking. Everyone below had recoiled but one: the Marshall. And it wasn't the sight of the clock or gore that had shook them all, Bruno realised. The Marshall stepped forwards, hand outstretched, and from Gumbly's neck he snapped a chain. He let it hang, touched by lamplight. And there was no mistaking, no keeping the fear from Bruno as once again he saw the same symbol. A medallion spun on the end of the chain, an eye with the storm-petrel inside.

'*Rebel symbol*,' the Marshall breathed.

Before Bruno could think to move, to leave Old Town, he had that sudden, unmistakeable sense of being watched. He looked up. A Cat-Sentry was less than a foot away, coiled. Its eyes whirred, its legs lowered and it leapt away as Bruno snatched for its tail and had it in his grip for a moment before it opened its mouth and screamed a recorded human scream, fierce enough to carry over all Pitch End and shocking him into release. It tumbled into the below and struck the lantern – a smash, gasps, light snatched away.

Bruno didn't move.

So much silence, only rainfall, and then the order, the voice of the unseen Marshall:

'Get him.'

VIII

Cinder-Folk

If Bruno moved he was sure he'd be caught. If he didn't move – same end. His fingers enclosed the medallion around his neck, the chain knotted in repair after the earlier break by the harbour.

Rebel symbol. Rebel medallion?

My father a Rebel? Bruno thought. A blunt thought, one that left him unable to move, to think further, clearer; to feel anything close to safe or innocent any more. Like knowing he was destined from birth for a lighthouse-keeper because he was born who he was, for having the father he did – he felt in the same way suddenly predestined then, the same way condemned.

Then came the grumble of Enforcers and their foot-scrapes to distract him, boot against stone and the groan of the tree as bodies heavier than Bruno's began to climb. Realising he had no choice at all he pushed on through leaves, the tree bearing him up but unwillingly. He needed to reach the other side of the roof, slip down, hope no one was there to meet him and then follow one of the darkways deeper into Old Town, hide until he was sure it was safer. Then run home?

'Hand me my rifle! I see someone in the tree there!'

Bruno scrambled. But not much further on and his support deserted him: a snap and he slipped. He didn't bother to grapple or grab for anything more, though, but decided to let himself drop, just fall, holding his breath and hoping for a landing not too severe . . . his spine slammed stone, in a puddle as large as a pond, soaking him. He blinked. The world tilted, spun and refused sense.

'The other side! *Go!*'

Bruno shut his eyes for three long seconds, then opened them. He stood. Dead ends everywhere, blankness upon blankness. And which way would the Enforcers come from?

'Down here! He fell into this darkway!'

Finally he sank backwards, lost, awaiting capture. But there was nothing behind him but hands – they closed across his chest, dragged him off his feet and through a tall, narrow door that was bolted, rain shut out. A voice said to him, '*Hush*. Not a word or breath.'

Bruno obeyed.

He heard the splash and stop of the Enforcers outside.

'Where'd he go to?' said one. 'We have to find him, else the Marshall will bloody have our guts for supper.'

'Some of ye should've stayed on this side,' said another.

82

'Not just stood about below doing nothing and not watching!'

'It's alright saying that now,' said the first. 'Saying all afterwards is easy enough.'

'Why don't ye just—'

'Oh, just shut yer trap ye—'

The bickering went on, and Bruno let relief remove him from it. He'd not been captured, not by Enforcers anyway. He realised then that he'd been released from the arms that had brought him inside, but to safety or not?

Bruno turned, wanted to know, but his senses were like dull lights against the dark. He heard rain puttering softly onto a stone floor. Then he saw something move, the motion reminding him of a weak stirring of ash in an empty grate. He wanted to step back and step forwards at the same time; retreat and investigate both. In the end he didn't move at all, just watched the dark making shapes, things shifting, waking. He saw a mouth yawn – pink and black and scarce of teeth – then shut. Then a pair of eyes, yellowed, teeth below the same colour with gums dark. He thought of tallow and spent matches. And finally came a voice, a male voice that matched the dark in its foreboding: 'Ye say *thanks* in our tradition when someone creeps up and saves yer life.'

The eyes blinked, staying suspended in the black.

Bruno wanted to speak but couldn't even think, and before any speech came a figure rushed towards him, a rustling thing that pressed him to the wall and took his face in its hands.

'*Name*,' said the voice, the eyes, the man.

'Bruno.'

'Not first name,' said the man. 'No good to me. Tell me yer family name.'

'Atlas,' Bruno supplied.

The hand that held him loosened and dropped away. The eyes closed and for a moment their owner might not have been there at all. And then he reappeared, eyes wide.

'*Atlas*,' the man repeated. He raised his voice and called back, 'What ye think on it, Da? Name of Atlas safe or no?'

The reply was a long time coming. But then, in a slow, deep voice: 'Atlas family were good to us Cinder-Folk, times long-gone. Helped out our Silas once, got him outta trouble with the Enforcers maybe thirty-and-two turns back. I'll be pleased to meet this Bruno of the family of Atlas. Make him welcome enough.'

'He says ye're alright,' said the man close to Bruno. 'So ye must be.' And the man moved closer and gave Bruno something curious, utterly unfamiliar – a kiss to the forehead.

'Bruno Atlas,' he said. 'See us. Meet the final Cinder-Folk family.'

Behind the man more eyes popped into life – three pairs, two wide and unblinking, another slower to open.

'Connor's my name,' said the eyes nearest Bruno. 'Or ye can call me just Conn, if ye like to.' He half-turned and called, 'Come here and be introducing yerselves, boys.'

84

The two livelier sets of eyes – not so yellowed, but bloodshot – jogged forwards.

Bruno blinked, things becoming clearer: the bodies of two small boys formed around the pairs of eyes. He blinked again, looking back to the man called Connor, and saw his face: hair black and long and matted, meeting a beard. All three, father and sons, wore long dark coats that dragged.

'These here,' said Conn, 'are me two boys. Twins, good luck and precious gifts them both: Dominic and Donal. Don't be fooled by their friendly ways though – they'll have yer arm broke in a tick if ye try anything stupid.'

Bruno decided not to move much at all.

'Dom is all ye need to be saying,' said one of the boys. 'Not *Dominic*.'

'And just D for me!' said the other.

'Ye can't be just "D"!' said Dom.

'Now, boys,' said the father, 'none of yer squabbling. Go there and give Granddad a hand getting his introduction.'

Only then did Bruno look again to the fourth pair of eyes. The twins moved off and began to lead the final eyes towards Bruno. An older man – back hunched, all of him shaking and the same long dark coat – approached. This had been the man who'd spoken earlier, confirmed the goodness of the name Atlas. His voice was low, but strong. 'Bruno Atlas,' he said. 'Son of Michael Atlas, the lighthouse-keeper.'

'Yes,' said Bruno.

'Wasn't a question!' said the old man. 'I know what I know, remember what I rightly-remember, no matter what them Elders say or want!'

He coughed, harsh and hacking, deep gasps between.

'Ye should sit yerself down, Da,' said Conn. 'Help him, boys. Bruno Atlas, come sit.'

But Bruno didn't move as the twins led their grandfather back. He'd heard, same as all in Pitch End, of the breed of people who lived in Old Town: darkness in their lives and morals, ways and means below everyone else. He couldn't shake off so many turns of being told so.

'Ye're afeared of us,' said Conn. He sighed. 'Don't blame ye much. Spending all day and all night listening to those Elders, no wonder ye can't think for yerself.'

'I can,' said Bruno, taking Conn's words as a challenge. 'I do think for meself.'

'Then decide,' said Conn, his eyes coming close. 'Go on back out into the rain and run on and hopefully the Enforcers won't get ye, or stay and listen and learn some things.'

Bruno said nothing. Then, 'What did ye call yerselves earlier?'

'Cinder-Folk,' the man said. 'The last Cinder-Folk family left.'

The name 'Cinder-Folk' shook small bells in Bruno's memory, but the sounds they gave out were only Elder words: 'Stay outta Old Town – gypsies, no-goods, thieves

86

and vagrants giving themselves fancy names like Cinder-Folk, Free-Seers, Fire-Brands . . . but all still no good and rightly-indecent!' But he was sure somewhere else in his past 'Cinder-Folk' had been mentioned, not in an Elder's tones.

Bruno felt a tug on his sleeve, looked down and saw the twins. Their eyes were still wide, but smiles wider.

'Stay,' said one of them, the boy Bruno thought was called Donal.

'We'll look after ye,' said Dom, who was a little taller.

So Bruno allowed himself to think other than what he'd been told. He followed the twins and Conn towards the old man.

'Make yerself comfortable,' Conn told him, and Bruno sank to the floor. He felt some soft but fraying carpet beneath his fingers.

No one spoke, the rain still in fervent conversation with the rooftop. But after a time, Bruno saw a small, thin flame rising on the floor in front of him; Conn, his sons and his old father became clearer. Like their clothes and hair and eyes, their skin had been darkened, and Bruno thought maybe they might have rubbed it with ash or charcoal. Or perhaps they'd simply been living too long out of the light. At their waists, Bruno noticed many small packages bound in string. They knew Bruno's wondering and answered without being asked –

'To hide ourselves,' said Dom, showing Bruno his blackened hands.

87

'We make things,' said Donal, showing his belt laden with small bindings.

'Old Cinder-Folk traditions,' said Dom.

'We keep things going, not Forgetting,' said Donal.

Bruno focused on Conn, whose hands worked the air as though trying to free an invisible skein. And continued to watch, waiting, half-knowing what he was about to see . . . flame leapt from Conn's fingertips, joining those already gathered in front of them.

'My teacher,' said Bruno, the memory of the morning in the playground five turns before scorched into his mind, the burning of *Tall Tales from Pitch End* always close with him. 'My teacher,' he said again, 'she can do that too, with her Talent.'

'We have a Talent for fire,' said Conn. 'Cinder-Folk always have.'

'Our mam,' said Dominic, 'she was the best ye ever saw with Talent.'

'Ye shoulda seen her,' said Donal. 'On Cinder's Eve, she'd make the biggest bonfires ever!'

'Where is she?' asked Bruno, and regretted the question instantly.

'She died,' said Conn, 'near ten turns ago. When things went bad for us all.'

'And for me too,' Bruno found himself saying.

A kettle was produced by Dominic, enamel cups by Donal. Bruno heard the thick slosh of water inside the kettle as it was settled over the flames. Conn took a bundle of leaf and string from his waist and opened it. His fingers pinched up a little of what was inside and added it to each cup. Not too long and with water boiled, Dominic filled the cups and Donal offered one to Bruno.

'Ye'll not want to drink it,' said the old man on the edge of the dark, before Bruno could say anything. 'Ye'll want to refuse.'

Bruno looked to every eye. He hesitated. Then he took the cup and drank, determined – it tasted sweet, then sharp, and he felt suddenly more awake, more alert.

'It'll strengthen ye,' said Conn.

'How can ye hide here?' said Bruno, his mind clearing, ripening with questions. 'Why do the Elders not come for ye?'

'Why would they?' said the old man, his agitation returned. 'If ye think a thing is less than human, has no voice to speak with nor any brains to be thinking with, then why bother yer head by chasing after it, trying to stamp it out?'

'They don't care,' said Conn, 'coz we're hardly even here.'

'That's what I said!' said the old man.

The twins sniggered.

'How come ye're the only ones left?' asked Bruno.

The silence this question brought was absolute. Every head fell. Minutes passed, and then a deep, long sigh, and firm words: 'I'll tell ye,' said the old man. 'I'll tell ye the truth, how we came to be the last. I'll tell ye the *Tall Tale of the Cinder-Folk*.'

That's where I knew it from, thought Bruno. That's where I've heard the name 'Cinder-Folk' before. But he said nothing. Nerves jangling, memory racing, he listened as the old man spoke in a voice still low, still strong –

'Once upon a time, in the part of Pitch End we know nowadays as Old Town, there lived a peaceful people known as the Cinder-Folk. Peaceful, but wondrously powerful too – not just in Talent, but in their ability to brew concoctions, to bind leaves and weeds and powders to cure any ill.

'Now, there was one such member of the Cinder-Folk respected above all others: a woman known as Clara, and she was the most potent and revered of all Cinder-Folk. One night she was in her caravan, speaking softly to the raven she kept as her own special pet, and same time brewing a heady concoction that she hoped would soon cure her neighbour of her heartache at losing her beloved, when there was a knock on her door. She opened it to an old man, who was blue and bent with cold and coughing something terrible into a rag. She noticed he was wearing nothing on his feet. "May I come in," asked the man, "and rest the night here? For I've nowhere else to go, my home having been destroyed by a recent storm." Clara had no reason to doubt the sincerity of the stranger, and she was in any case a kind, compassionate woman. So she opened the door and admitted the man. She boiled water, added a snatch of leaves to a cup and served him a hot tonic.

'The old man pronounced the drink "Most wondrous!"

and asked then: "Tell me, what leaf did you add to make it so rightly-effective?" Clara wondered for a moment, but saw no harm in confessing her secret to this harmless old man. She told him the type of leaf (which I shall not repeat, for fear of giving away Cinder-Folk secrets myself), and he smiled, saying, "Thank you, my dear. I shall know what to look out for now."

'But Clara had a warning for the old man: "Do not," she said, "be using too much of the leaf. Nor must you take it without first allowing it to mature for thirty-six nights and a day. For too much, and at the wrong time, can poison a being, and there is no known cure, even to the Cinder-Folk."

'The old man nodded, and after only half an hour's rest he was on his way, as sprightly as a youngster.

'The very next night though, the old man returned once again: "Help me," he said, "for I have been robbed this very night in the shadow of the Clocktower, and have not a penny on me to buy food!" Clara happily, easily, asked the old man in. And once again, she provided for him – bread baked with moccle seeds, and another cup of her brew from the previous night. And once again, the old man pronounced it all, "Most wondrous!" and asked after the seeds in the bread – their kind, where he could find them. Seeing no harm in the old man – only a fierce curiosity, which is no sin at all – she told him where they were to be found (again – a secret I shall not divulge!), and what their qualities were. But again, she offered a warning:

"Too many of the seeds," she said, "and they will make you jabber incessantly, speaking only the most sacred – and darkest – thoughts in yer head."

'The old man thanked Clara again, and said he had best be on his way, for he had a meeting that he simply must get to.

'On the third night – and with Clara expecting just such a thing to happen – the old man returned. His story this time? "I am all alone in the world, my dear. I have seen you create great wonders these past two nights, and you have been most generous to me. But I wonder, can you gift me one more thing?"

'Clara thought, then asked, "What? What is it you ask of me?"

'The old man licked his wrinkled lips. "To know the secret of eternal youth."

'Clara stood on the threshold of her home, lantern in hand, and this time she decided not to offer her hospitality, but not to resort to rudeness either, for there is no greater sin for the Cinder-Folk. "I cannot help you on that account," she explained. "Such things are the preserve of nature, and I have no control over them. No good can come of meddling with the nature of Time." And she made to close the door of her caravan.

'No sooner had she reached for the door, however, than the old man grabbed it and wrenched it clean off the hinges. Before she could cry out or snatch up one of the many small bindings of leaf or twig that she kept as defences *he forced her to the ground, hand on her mouth, and told her, "You will tell me all your secrets, Cinder-Woman, and I shall have all the power you have and more too!" He reached for the jar containing Clara's supply of moccle seeds, pulled her mouth open and poured them in. Her raven, caged tonight, raged: wings clashed against the bars as it watched helplessly. And then, the effect of the moccle seeds sinking in, Clara began to babble her secrets to the air: how to divine water, how to predict the whims of the weather, how to raise a child who would not be unruly, how to soothe a broken heart, how to reason with Shadows . . . all this, and how to attain eternal youth: "The secret to youth must be in taking the youth of another – to steal this gift, this period of bliss and danger and wonder and fear, from a child. That is the only way to return something aged to something young."*

'"Perfect," said the man. "And how can I do this?"

'Clara glanced towards her raven.

'The effect of the moccle seeds was fading, and Clara regained enough of herself to throw off the aged man, get to her feet and cry out for help. But the old man had stolen her knowledge and recalled her warning from the first night . . . he snatched up the tin containing the leaves needed to concoct her empowering draught and willed her to the wall, forcing the leaves past her lips, into her mouth, down her throat. Too many of these leaves. True to her own warning, Clara collapsed, and was dead within an instant.

'The man turned to face the raven. "So," he said, "is it you, a dark creature, who can give me youth, make me young again? Take the youth from a child?"

'The raven didn't move.

'The old man flung the door of the cage open, and as he did the raven took flight, a flurry of claw and feather and beak, tearing the old man's eyes from his skull. The old man snatched out and took hold of one of the raven's feet and pulled, breaking it free of the bird's body (this, they say, is how the first one-footed raven was created).

'Wailing, blood streaming from his sockets, the man then fled the caravan, on his way upending Clara's lantern. The one-footed raven escaped too, on its way picking up a stray moccle seed and swallowing it down (this, they say, is how the first one-footed raven of Pitch End learned to speak).

'Meanwhile, the fire quickly consumed Clara's caravan. Flame leapt to the next caravan, and then the next, the air rent that night by screams from the Cinder-Folk as many, most, perished in their beds, some still enveloped in sleep, ignorant of their end.

'But the old man was not without his torment – try as he might to leave Old Town, he could not: just as he veered close to a street that might take him safely from the flames, Clara's raven descended, crying, "Fiend! Liar!" and coaxed him back towards the fire. In the end, the blaze everywhere, there was no place to hide, nowhere to shelter. A figure appeared and approached the man, stepping through

94

the flames, unscathed, holding them at bay with his Talent. An Elder, who kneeled and took the blinded man by the hair and demanded of him: "Did ye find out the secret I asked of ye? Did she tell ye?" For they had made an agreement the previous night: the old man asking for a great fortune, and the Elder promising it to him, if only he could force the Cinder-Folk woman to divulge the secret of eternal youth and power.

'"She wouldn't tell me," said the man. "She said not to meddle in matters of Time. Please – help me, Elder. Save me from these flames!"

'But the Elder did not, for he was selfish and uncaring. "You did not do as I asked, therefore our agreement is forfeit. I shall leave you to the flames."

'The man in his fear cried, "Wait! She didn't say anything, but she did look to her raven as she died! A clue, surely!"

'The Elder thought, wondered, and then said, "Very well. I am grateful for your information. And to express my gratitude, your death shall be quicker, less painful than if I simply left you." The Elder flicked his hands and flame consumed the old man, leaving him to a fate no different to that of the Cinder-Folk, his cries no more distinct than theirs as they perished in the rising fire.'

Bruno looked to his empty cup. His thoughts were flying, circling then settling on when he'd first learned that *Tall Tale*, five turns before.

'Ye've heard it,' said Conn.

Bruno looked at him.

'Ye don't seem rightly shocked, so ye must've already read it or heard it told.'

'Read it once,' said Bruno. 'In a book I found.'

'Then ye've already started,' said Conn. 'Already begun yer learning, knowing the things them Elders don't want ye to know.'

'They're true, then?' asked Bruno, heart bursting with hope. 'The *Tall Tales*?'

'I said it was the truth before I started, didn't I!' said Conn's father.

'Nothing's that simple,' said Conn.

'More truthful than what them Elders put about,' said the old man.

'Some bits are true enough,' said Conn. 'What Da just told – that's how the tale was written down and how it was told to us when we all heard it, round the fire as children.'

Bruno was confused – *some bits?* Surely a thing was either true or not?

'We weren't called the Cinder-Folk till after the fire,' said Conn. 'That's one thing. Another is the Elder – some say there was none that night. Or that the old man who tried to steal the Cinder-Folk secrets, who killed Clara, was an Elder himself.'

Conn sighed.

The twins copied him.

'I believe in it,' said Bruno.

'So do I!' said Dominic.

'Me too!' said Donal.

Conn's laugh was small, not quite bitter.

Then came a sound that made everyone in the room start – the tolling of a bell.

'Town hall bell,' said Conn's father, his voice lower, as though drifting, close to dreaming.

'Never rings,' said Conn. He looked to Bruno. 'Ye're being summoned. Ye have to go. *Now*.'

'I don't want to,' said Bruno, though he got to his feet as Conn did, as the twins did, and followed across the room as they rushed to listen with ears pressed tight to the door. 'Tell me more about the Cinder-Folk,' said Bruno. 'I need to be knowing.'

'There's need and there's want,' said Conn. 'And for now, ye have all ye need. But here, take this. This is what ye'll be needing more.'

He took Bruno's hand, opened it – inside he laid a small, dark coal.

'What is it?' asked Bruno.

'If ye ever want to know more,' said Conn.

'Ever want to be calling us,' followed Dominic.

'Ever want to find us,' said Donal.

'Ever want a hand!' called the grandfather.

'Ever need *help*,' said Conn in a whisper, 'then just add a spot of blood to it and it'll fairly glow, will send signals. And we'll be there, Bruno Atlas.'

A final kiss was passed like a father to a parting son.

Conn opened the door to the rain, to a Pitch End Bruno

97

had almost forgotten, so completely had he sunk into the *Tall Tale*. The town hall bell called, almost unbearable in its insistence. And then, not knowing why, Bruno reached for his father's medallion. He held it in both hands and let Conn see. He didn't speak.

Then Conn sighed, again.

'Bruno Atlas,' he said, with a small shake to his head. 'Ye're a dark horse, aren't ye? Following in yer father's footsteps? There's a task and a half.'

'What do I do?' asked Bruno.

Conn told him, 'All anyone can ever do in Pitch End: just stay as ye are. And then hope that when the time comes ye'll not be alone, and that ye'll know what to do for the best. Be Bruno Atlas, and all that comes with it. Coz this is only the start. Things are changing, and all I can say is good luck to ye. Ye'll be needing it.'

IX

The Tall Tale of the Faerie Fort

Leaving Old Town, Bruno had no choice but to join other Pitch Enders. In a throng close to frantic in their efforts to cross the square, they pushed and elbowed and bickered towards the town hall. And for once he felt a kinship with them. All soaked, all worried, all intrigued as the bell sounded its thunderous summons. But as Bruno passed between the tall, wooden double doors of the town hall's entrance, he alone was stopped. A hand shot out of the darkness and clamped itself around his upper arm.

'Straight into the Discussion Chamber,' said a voice on the end of the arm. 'None of this troubling to stand about or gawking.'

Bruno blinked raindrops from his lashes. His fear took shape – the Marshall, standing stern as the rifle at his side. The medallion beneath Bruno's shirt, resting over his heart, needled his chest like something alive, aware of its own rising importance.

Bruno swallowed, and could only jerk his head as a response to the Marshall.

He was released, but slowly, and even when the Marshall had let go, the place he'd gripped still throbbed.

Bruno sidestepped into the town hall, quick as was respectable.

The next thing he knew was astounding light. Blood-red like an ill-omened sky and blazing, throbbing in the enormity of the entrance hall, stood a tree with long emaciated boughs bearing countless numbers of delicate tapered leaves, all a wild scarlet, each like an avid but noiseless flame, all aglow.

The Tall Tale of the Faerie Fort.

Fished from the dark waters of memory, the *Tall Tale*, the words that composed it, rushed to the surface as Bruno remembered. He heard the last section of the story as though a voice was reciting it to him alone in a low, conspiratorial whisper . . .

'. . . *and George Pitch, founder of Pitch End, took the scarlet bulb he'd been blessed with by the faerie woman and planted it that very night in the gaze of a full moon (as she'd instructed). He formed a small mound of earth and inserted the bulb just below the surface. Then he wept with thoughts of his wife, murdered in the night by the forces attempting to take control of Pitch End, and his worry for his seven half-orphaned sons. And the tears fell on the small mound, nourishing the bulb below the surface. As the faerie woman had told him, George Pitch*

100

lay beside the small mound and slept as an anxious father would beside an ill child – restless, always turning, dreaming terrible dreams of the fall of truth in Pitch End and the rise of evil, of Forgetting and ignorance. And of the coming of a group of men who would seek to control all life in the town. When George Pitch awoke in a blazing dawn, he looked up and beheld a vast tree that had sprouted overnight from the scarlet bulb – each leaf was scarlet, the mass of foliage trembling in the breeze like an inferno. And George Pitch recollected what the faerie woman had told him before she had returned to her natural form and slipped back into the Sea of Apparitions: that any nightmares George Pitch might have had whilst sleeping next to the growing tree would never come to pass, so long as the tree, this Faerie Fort, remained. For the tree was to be a beacon of hope, not only to the Pitch Enders, but to all creatures – visible and unseeable, meek or mighty. And should the tree ever falter or fail, be felled or forsaken, then it would mean the end of Pitch End and all within it.'

Bruno had paused on the threshold to gape but was being pushed on by those anxious townsfolk keen to claim good seats in the Discussion Chamber. None were concerned by or interested in the Faerie Fort. None of them had read the *Tall Tale*, Bruno decided, and he thought of Conn's words: in reading *Tall Tales from Pitch End*, he'd started something. Started to learn what the Elders didn't want knowing.

101

He moved and looked closer. Not all the leaves of the Faerie Fort were imparting light. Some were no more than delicate slivers of weak ash and, at the coaxing of a stronger breath of wind, detached suddenly, dissolving in a flicker.

'A penny for the Elders is a penny for Pitch End!'

Bruno's attention shifted to a Trainee Elder by the door to the Discussion Chamber. He was shaking a wooden box with a dark slot, shouting, 'Be generous now!'

As townsfolk passed, their fingers sought whatever coin they couldn't afford, and with longing and Ever-Winter in their eyes, they deposited it.

Bruno slipped his hands into his pockets and found the penny Pace had given him. His hand shut on it.

More arrivals: Cat-Sentries, wending between legs, the collective hum of their clockwork sending a shiver through Bruno and, following behind like human familiars, the procession of Pitch End Widows. Bruno tried (but knew it impossible) to discern which Widow was his mother. An identical half-dozen, scalp to toe all in black, veiled, their lace-plaited hands held together to enforce the decisive gesture of Official Mourning, dark umbrellas wedged awkwardly between. He thought of calling out, clearing his throat even. He had so much to tell her. So much had happened. Perhaps his mother would acknowledge him, stop, speak?

But Widows didn't speak. Just mourned, shuffled. They dropped their umbrellas at the feet of the Trainee Elder and shuffled on into the Discussion Chamber like dry leaves coaxed by a breeze. The Trainee wrinkled his nose.

Bruno looked back to the double doors.

Now's the time, he thought. Stay now or retreat? He considered, as he'd done at the base of the Clocktower, and then decided: better to know than not know. And he knew, somehow, that there were words that would be said within the Discussion Chamber that he wanted to hear. Not wanted – *needed*.

A tremor ran through his bones: the sound of wood on stone, the rub of metal as the doors to the town hall were shut and sealed by Enforcers under watch of the Marshall.

No way out. And no way in for those too slow to present themselves.

Bruno stepped over the umbrellas, passing the Trainee Elder, and there was another rattle of the collection box as the boy told him, 'Give money for the Elders!'

'Sorry, no change,' said Bruno, the penny Pace had given him safe in his fist.

X

Temperate Thomas

Bruno stepped into the Discussion Chamber and saw a town divided. The Pitch Enders were all on long narrow benches enclosed in long narrow cages of cast iron, doors at either end. Trainee Elders were directing each arrival to their row, their place. On the stone walls of the Chamber, lightbulbs the colour of dark earwax snarled on curled brass brackets. Bruno stopped, and again thought about retreating, but before he could do anything, one of the Trainee Elders rushed forwards, had him –

'What are ye?' the boy demanded. The Trainee's robes were too big, his sleeves folded back so his hands could be free. He looked at Bruno, dabbing the sharp point of a black pencil on his tongue and holding it, poised, over the page of a thick ledger.

Bruno didn't know what to say.

'Do ye have a tongue in yer head?' the Trainee Elder shouted. 'I said – *what are ye?*'

Bruno saw some in the cages nearest look over.

'I don't know,' said Bruno, at last.

'What does yer father do?' asked the Trainee Elder. 'And no lies, for I can be quickly checking.'

'He's dead,' said Bruno.

The Trainee Elder rolled his eyes, and then shook his head as though Bruno were being deliberately difficult.

'What did he do before he was Forgotten?' asked the Trainee Elder.

'He was a . . .'

(*Rebel* blazed in Bruno's mind, sizzled on his tongue, but he bit it back.)

'Lighthouse-keeper,' said Bruno.

'Oh,' said the Trainee Elder. He scratched his forehead, chewed on his pencil and looked around (Bruno guessed) for assistance. Other Trainee Elders, only a few turns older than Bruno, were busy around the edges of the Chamber, noting names and counting heads. Bruno pictured them later that night sitting down together to deduce who'd been decent enough to present themselves, and who hadn't bothered.

'We need to keep 'em moving or he'll not be pleased.' Another Trainee Elder had joined the first – same pencil, same ledger, same too-big robes.

'I'm trying to put this one in his rightly-proper place,' said the first. 'But I dunno where he goes.'

They spoke about Bruno as though he wasn't there. Or that he was, but had no voice of his own.

'Well,' said the second Trainee Elder, 'let's see.' He turned to face Bruno with narrowed eyes. 'Have ye Come-Of-Age yet?' he asked.

Bruno shook his head.

'Well, that's easy then!' said the second Trainee Elder. 'He's with the other children and the teacher, first row on the right, remember? Temperate Thomas told us to put them there. Ye need to be asking the right questions.'

A *tut-tut* and the second Trainee Elder moved off, leaving the first with thunder in his eyes. 'Ye could've just said ye hadn't Come-Of-Age,' he spat at Bruno. 'Showing me up like that. Follow me, boy.'

Bruno followed.

Flesh pressed tight to iron, Pitch End was sorted from the lowliest (any from Old Town, farmers, fishermen, lamplighters) at the back of the Discussion Chamber, to the more respectable and rightly-decent (shopkeepers, Enforcer's spouses) at the front. Bruno marvelled at how the Pitch Enders could retain smart appearances even behind bars: ladies coiled in damp furs and wide, wind-battered hats, men squeezed into best Sunday suits. He looked closer though and saw some flaws – wellingtons under too-short trousers, cheeks smudged with flour or muck, an absent button, a split seam . . .

'In here with ye,' said the Trainee Elder. From amongst a clatter of keys at his belt he found one that unlocked the cage door leading to Bruno's place: first row on the right, beside the other Hedge School children.

Bruno hesitated. Front row was too close, too conspicuous.

'In ye get and stop waiting about!' said the Trainee Elder, and with sudden strength he shoved Bruno in beside Dennis Wire, a boy the same age as him but broader, bolder.

Dennis acknowledged Bruno's arrival by rising and hissing, '*Stupid* Atlas. Why do ye have to stand next to me? Ye better not start talking rubbish, right?'

Bruno tried to ignore him.

The door of the cage was slammed, locked.

Both boys sank to their seats, Bruno clasping damp hands together. He wanted to reach for his father's medallion – so much a habit now, a comfort – and had to stop himself. He sat on his hands. He shut his eyes for a moment, saw a chaos of colour, and then opened them again and looked around, hoping for sight of a friendly face – Pace, maybe? He saw no Mr Pace but noticed Sabitha McCormack in another cage, front row left. He saw the bruise on her cheek, and the memory of that morning was like someone else's: from a different life, a different place altogether, so much had happened since that dwarfed it. Sabitha's mother sat next to her, head boasting a vast, purple hat with a long pheasant feather. As the Marshall's daughter and wife they were as privileged as you could be in Pitch End without being an Elder. There was less cram in their cage.

Sabitha saw Bruno, narrowed her eyes and for a long moment offered him the tip of her pointed tongue, then withdrew it, smiled and turned away to face the front.

Bruno looked ahead too.

Barring the way to a raised platform at the front of the Discussion Chamber was another high cast-iron gate, small spikes ornamenting its top. No danger of it being scaled, Bruno thought. Onstage and behind the gate – not imprisoned, more protected – were seated nine of the ten Elders of Pitch End.

Seeing them, Bruno thought how long it had been since they'd last appeared in the town. Their place was within the town hall, its sanctity and theirs inextricable. No doorknocking, no donation-seeking. Hedge School in lost years had been interrupted almost daily with Elders coming. No forewarning or word, just stalking silently into the back of the classroom; they used to send Miss Hope as much as any of the children into distress: listening and correcting where needed, suggesting answers when doubt formed a silence. Punishing when they felt it was warranted. Their dress was the same though – plum robes and tall, lopsided mitres. But all looked so much older, aged beyond known turns; all bearded and with hair so white and sparse Bruno thought a stiff breeze could've banished it like a row of dandelion clocks.

Every Elder eye was shut.

Bruno tried to guess which were deep into some 'Rightly-Superior Thinking', as they called it, or which might be concealing a sharp attention to what was being said (or unsaid) in the Discussion Chamber. Or which of them might've just dozed off.

One last empty seat – central in their row – awaited the arrival of the Head Elder, Temperate Thomas.

Below was overtaken by fevered Pitch Ender talk. Within the cages, no entire sentence was distinguishable; just bits, but still running together:

'What if it's those Rebels coming back? I just knew it—'

'—would happen again. Told ye last week, dint I? I said—'

'—something like this was going to happen, felt it coming for weeks! Mountains protect us!'

And Bruno thought there was neither sight nor shock that could've quietened the Pitch Enders just then, their fear so decided, speculation so intense. But when a concealed door with the appearance of stone opened up behind the Elders, silence flooded the Discussion Chamber.

Bruno strained in his seat to see.

All Pitch End waited.

And then he came.

Temperate Thomas was an Elder of different cloth. His robes might've been plum, same as the other Elders, but they were clean and vivid, not grubby nor worn. His mitre was straight, a proper extension of the high curve of his forehead, an extra foot of authority. As he stepped from the doorway slowly, moving in solitary procession towards his seat, careful and precise in his movement, a whisper passed along Bruno's row, ending in Dennis Wire telling him: 'Head down, Atlas, or he'll have it lopped off ye.'

The children bowed, Bruno included. He knew that everywhere, all Pitch Enders were doing the same. But Bruno angled his head not so low that he couldn't continue to watch the progress of the Temperate –

The Head of the Elders was accompanied by his own constant Sentry, a unique kind – a cat, not brass but silver, with its surface polished to a mirror. This Cat-Sentry was perched on the tip of a tall staff, also of brightened silver, carried by the Temperate in his right hand. And as gaslight allowed a clear view of the man, Bruno noticed, amazed, how little change had come over the Temperate in ten turns. Like a rock worked upon by the sea but remaining unchanged, it was as though he had evaded the seasons, escaping the ageing that had crept in upon his fellow Elders. As this ageless man came to a stop before his empty chair, Bruno had an uneasy thought: that Temperate Thomas would survive them all, merely step across generations, enduring, always in control, ruling and dictating, defying death itself.

The Temperate didn't speak right away.

Pitch End squirmed.

'My fellow Pitch Enders,' he began, finally, and the room (Bruno included) exhaled, their heads all lifting as though relieved of a communal weight. 'What can I say, 'cept that it does my heart so much good to see ye all here tonight. I wish to extend many, many thanks for yer rightly-prompt attendance. It is, in such prosperous times as these, greatly appreciated. Especially too as we're only days from the three-hundredth anniversary of Pitch End. It tells me much of the solidity of our fair town, of the unshakable foundations of decency and common sense that've become the cornerstone of our great community, that ye've answered the Elder's call so quick-smart, and with such perfect diligence. For this, I am rightly-humbled. *Long live our Pitch End values!*'

'*But longer live the Elders!*' replied the townsfolk.

Bruno forgot himself, saying only the last word in a whisper.

Dennis glanced at him.

The Temperate's face twitched. 'Indeed it gives me much faith' (he went on) 'and a greater courage to pursue what intentions I have here tonight.' He paused, words trembling on his lips, and Bruno wondered, are those tears in his eyes?

'Please be forgiving me,' Temperate Thomas muttered at last, not troubling to dismiss the tears wriggling down his face. 'But I'm so moved here, I cannot say – I just . . . words cannot . . . *But*,' and he stood tall, stamped his staff on the stage, so that his Cat-Sentry had to leap to his shoulder, and shouted, 'I *must* be strong, as all of Pitch End has been these past ten turns!'

Bruno wanted to run or to look away or cover his ears, but he knew that despite want or will, the Temperate had him and all of the Pitch Enders captured. They could only remain and watch and obey.

'Since I've taken up the post of Temperate,' the Head Elder went on, beginning a slow crossing of the length of

111

the stage, 'it has been my aim always to preserve the spiritual and moral welfare of this town. Watching, but not meddling. Never telling, only advising. But now is the time, I'm most afeared, for something more than watchfulness and advice.' Temperate Thomas paused for a tick, and then continued, his tone no less welcoming, but hardened: 'Once again, my friends, we have malice and menace stalking our streets.'

At this, a muffled explosion of discussion and movement, like small fires –

'I knew there was trouble, I just knew it!'

'Soon as I woke up this morning I felt it! Dint I tell ye?'

'And on the three-hundredth anniversary too! Mountains protect us!'

Bruno shrunk, too vulnerable where he was, suddenly afraid that he would be plucked from the crowd and called to testify about what he'd witnessed on the jetty that day. For what else was there? What else had transpired to warrant the meeting?

Temperate Thomas remained impassive, though Bruno noticed the head of his Cat-Sentry twitch. Its eyes focused, ears flickering in the slow, painstaking act of minute recording. Bruno knew that every word, every face, every expression of every Pitch Ender was being remembered.

The Temperate resumed his speech, and obedient silence followed.

'Now,' he said. 'I know how much all of ye have been obeying the Elder Order of Forgetting. I know

112

how diligently all of ye have banished those bothersome memories that can keep a man from sleep, worry a person, plague and destroy them: death, loss, the whole mess and mangle of bygones. But it will be, for the smallest amount of time, only necessary now to refer to that treacherous and distant land we call . . . *The Past*.'

Gasps, nods and many Pitch Ender's hands working to bless themselves.

Bruno's hand crawled to his chest, to rest over his father's medallion. He thought of Pace's words and told himself, don't give anything away. Don't be so rightly-easy to see through and into. He lowered his hand.

'Now fortunately,' said the Temperate, perching on the very brink of the stage, 'I have remembered all things. And there is nothing, my dear Pitch Enders, which endures in the mind like pain. And the remembrance of the past in our fair town is most painful, and a burden I bear for all of ye. It is for this reason that I have asked that you all Forget! Forget, letting me shoulder the pain, as any rightly-proper leader must. And I have remembered all in perfect detail, so let me tell ye what rightly-happened, without any gossip or hearsay, just the right-real *truth* of it.

'Ten turns ago, during the Ever-Winter of +290, Pitch End was under siege. For a period of no more than a week, things got . . . *nasty*. Our town was going to be overcome by what we may describe best as *Indecent Forces*.' Bruno turned and saw the words echoed mutely on lips throughout the Chamber. 'This is the period known as the Single Season

113

War where a group of individuals who had christened themselves the "Rebels"' (here, the Temperate gave a short and mirthless breath of laughter) 'so-called because they believed they were rebelling against some imaginary power in Pitch End which they saw as their duty to defeat – launched an attack on nothing less than our very way of life. A way of life that had hitherto been so very peaceful, so rightly-respectful. A group of criminals and miscreants lead by a man called Dr Jonathan Bloom.'

And suddenly, like well-practised children, one-footed ravens in the rafters began to crow:

'Jonathan Bloom,
Jonathan Bloom,
If he came in the room,
Would go to his doom!'

Bruno began to shiver, wanted to shut his eyes, shut it out – the Chamber bounced the name back and forth – *Jonathan Bloom! Jonathan Bloom! Jonathan Bloom!* – and the cover of *Tall Tales from Pitch End* was sharp before his eyes.

The ravens continued, though in a lower key, as the Temperate resumed:

'After the Rebels were defeated, our Enforcers (led by our redoubtable Marshall) rounded up all but a handful of the remainder. Most were keen to turn themselves in without fuss – notice how they lacked the true loyalty and resolve we have built since! But others managed to evade us. Now, there is no criminal in Pitch End who our great

Enforcers couldn't catch, I'm rightly-convinced of this. And so it gives us no choice, my fellow Pitch Enders, than to surmise that the likes of Dr Jonathan Bloom, Nicholas M. Delby, and their followers who managed to escape retribution did so only by utilising . . .' Here a suitable pause, a search for a weighty (but unfamiliar enough, Bruno thought) word to baffle and awe the Pitch Enders. '*Nefarious* means. Means that have only today come fully to our light.'

The Temperate wet his lips, shut his eyes, and said, 'I ask now . . . No – I *demand* now – that one amongst us present themselves, so that they might rightly-enlighten us all on these subjects.'

A final pause, and Bruno knew what was next. Knew, and could do not a thing.

'I call to the Elder platform,' said Temperate Thomas, 'Master Bruno Atlas.'

XI

The Book of Black & White

Bruno didn't move. If he moved or spoke, then it would all be real, so if he didn't then –

'Bruno Atlas to the platform!' cried Temperate Thomas.

'He's there in that cage with them other children! The one on the end with the shifty look about him!' Sabitha McCormack had stood and pointed with a smart hand at Bruno. 'I knew he was bad news all along,' she added. Her mother took her outstretched hand and pulled her back to sitting.

Bruno looked to his feet and wondered how fast they could run.

The snap of the lock, the groan of the cage door and he looked up to face the Marshall. '*Out*,' said he. Without waiting, the Marshall took Bruno in the same iron grip as outside the town hall and brought him towards the platform. Bruno knew then why the Temperate had ordered that the children be put in the front row. Knew he should've

116

realised earlier. The door of his cage was shut, and then the whispering –

'He's the son of that man who was murdered by the Rebels, int he?'

'I've seen him always hanging about the place, gawping and dallying.'

'A bad eye he has in his head, just look at him!'

'Mountains protect us!'

Bruno was deposited by the iron gate separating the Elders from Pitch Enders.

'Bruno Atlas.'

Bruno looked up and into the eyes of the Temperate, who held a small cast-iron key in his hand, threaded through with a chain that hung from his neck. He unlocked the gate, the jangle and clash of its opening echoing in the Discussion Chamber.

'I permit ye,' said Temperate Thomas, 'as the Head of the Elders, to enter and walk amongst us.'

There was no choosing for Bruno, no classroom disagreement, not where the Elders were concerned. He could only take in some air and try to still the shiver in his spine as he stepped through the gate. The Temperate slammed it quick behind him as if more Pitch Enders, uninvited, might try to rush through. He applied key to lock to reinstate the Elder's safety and sanctity, and then gestured to a short, steep flight of three steps that led to the platform. Temperate Thomas's manner was as courteous as a shopkeeper to a customer in strained times, and stiff with ritual rightness. Three steps . . . but three more draining ones Bruno couldn't imagine taking. Three steps that brought him into the focus of all the townsfolk.

How could it be so difficult to stop your own body shivering? Bruno wondered. Why so difficult to swallow deep, slow breaths, not have a chest filling and emptying so quick? Why so difficult to hide emotion? And what about the medallion against his chest, beneath only flimsy cloth, hidden, but surely not for long – what would happen when it was discovered?

He faced Pitch End.

Miss Hope was on the end of the first row beside the children, her arms folded, head high, and such a look of triumph on her face that Bruno expected her to rise up and declare, 'I knew all along! I told ye just this morning this would happen!'

In the row just behind were the Widows, ranged like morbid Forgetting Ornaments, unmoving. He looked to each, but no indication came that any was his mother. But wherever Bruno rested his gaze the reception was unsettled: townsfolk turned away, shielding their eyes and whimpering as though he could smite them by a mere look. Those whispers swelled into hissing syllables, the din too much to carry a single, unbroken sentence –

'—Atlas!'

'—indecent!'

'—nasty!'

'—Rebels!'

Temperate Thomas raised one hand; silence his command and silence the response.

'Please sit,' he said, voice low, the hand that didn't hold his staff willing Bruno backwards into the vacant chair that was the Head of the Elders' own. He found it soft beneath him, velvet-covered, not hard like the benches of the Hedge School or even the chairs he and his mother suffered at home. And then a behaviour that Bruno didn't know how to process: Temperate Thomas smiled at him.

'Good boy,' he said. 'I think we'll get along rightly-well. We'll get this nasty matter dealt with quick-smart.'

These words had been only for Bruno, but then the Temperate turned back to the Discussion Chamber and cried, 'Bring out the crate!'

Bruno didn't need to turn to see or know.

Rotten, cracked, heaved by two Trainee Elders from the wings, on came the crate he'd seen that morning under Gumbly's arm on *The Wintering*. Tentacles of brittle seaweed crackled like wire, trailing across the platform, almost tripping the boys up on their journey. Bruno still didn't look, but imagined a symbol the same as his medallion, and the warning splashed on the crate not to open it.

Then, too overcome with curiosity, Bruno turned to watch.

The Trainee Elders abandoned the crate at the feet of the Temperate, then hurried off.

'Here,' said the Temperate, facing his people, voice

beginning to throb, one hand around his staff, the other a fist, 'is the very crystallisation of all things rightly-evil. Everything we must now oppose. What we must seek to eradicate in the coming days. *United* – we must all stand *united*!'

The Temperate's fist loosened, lifted, and the crate itself rose from the stage, guided by his Talent. The crate hovered at his chest, revolving slowly. The Discussion Chamber filled with the tough groan of wood – crooked nails wrenching themselves from the lid of the crate at Temperate's Thomas's command. A sharp clatter as they dropped to the stage. The lid opened. From its depths emerged a book. Large as a flagstone, as ancient and careworn in appearance as its container, scarred with rough stitching, both blackened (singed, like something only just saved from fire) and whitened (dashed as though with paint, or fouled by gulls). Bruno found himself inching forwards on the velvet seat, wanting and needing to know more closely.

The Temperate let the crate sink but left the book to hover. It was held shut, Bruno noticed, with a rusted lock and clasp.

'*The Book of Black & White*,' announced the Temperate.

Some shallow ripples of recognition spread through the crowd.

'Oh yes, my friends,' said Temperate Thomas. 'That very book indeed.'

Temperate Thomas distanced himself then from *The*

Book of Black & White and resumed his stride across the stage.

'Jack Pitch,' he said, 'was the first son of our great and rightly-noble founder George Pitch. Our spiritual leader, the man who penned *The Wrath* from whose pages we've been all taking our core values these many turns, worshipping the three elements that nurture our town – sea, mountains and sky – just as he dictated. But let me tell ye of Jack Pitch's brother, the seventh son called Arthur, who was a very different type. One who didn't always hold the most . . . *decent* of ideas. Arthur Pitch, who fought with his brother, fell out with him, became estranged from him, and who began to form his own ideas on morality. Arthur Pitch produced the book we see here. Evil, monstrous, rightly-diabolical – just a few words I could use to describe this . . . *piece of work*. It was from this book that Dr Jonathan Bloom took his most dearly held ideas.'

More than ripples rushed through the Chamber at the mention again of Dr Jonathan Bloom – a swell of horror in the faces of the crowd.

'Gumbly, one of a pair of remaining Withermen – Withermen, I should say, were men who had an unhealthy obsession with the dead ten turns back –' (Liar, thought Bruno,) '– who had decided on a more decent vocation as a fisherman, had been missing, along with his crew, for six weeks to this day. Ye may not have known this. We do try, as Elders, to keep these small worries from ye,

121

shoulder any heartache alone. But this morning – after much worry and prayer on my part – Gumbly and his crew did at last return to us. I had my suspicions, my fears. And though it gives me no satisfaction to say it – I was rightly-correct. Gumbly was true to his own past as a Witherman. Showed his true colours, as we say. And all of them were black. The crew on the fishing boat were nowhere to be found. He was alone. I think it safe, my fellow Pitch Enders, to assume that the other members of the crew have *passed on*.'

A single shriek from the crowd – perhaps the wife or mother or sister of one of the dead crew?

'*Murdered!*' decided the Temperate, shifting speculation into fact. 'And we've only one suspect for these cold-blooded and needless murders: Gumbly-the-Witherman. Now, why did Gumbly murder his fellow crew members? Why was he in possession of *The Book of Black & White*? How did he get his hands on this – what we believed to be long-long-lost – volume of wickedness? Who was he intending to deliver it to in Pitch End?'

The Temperate passed a moment in silence. Bruno thought, has he even read it? Is he going to say what it actually is, what's in it or what it's about? Then Bruno realised: the Temperate didn't need to give the Pitch Enders more, something definite. He just had to command fear, and the townsfolk would obey.

'The question,' said Temperate Thomas, turning to face Bruno, 'of why all this is happening to us is what we'll be

122

getting an answer to now. Wouldn't that be true, Master Atlas?'

Bruno said nothing. Or no words left his mouth, but a voice – sounding like his voice, truly – spoke out, declaring with certainty: 'Oh yes. I know rightly what's been going on and what's being done to Pitch End.'

He tried to trace the voice but couldn't see any mouth that had moved. Not the Temperate, though he thought the man's Talent so potent it might've summoned the words from the air like Miss Hope had summoned the flames that had destroyed *Tall Tales from Pitch End*.

The Temperate nodded, allowing another smile.

Bruno knew he had to speak for himself then or be lost –

'I didn't—'

This was all he could muster before Temperate Thomas's Cat-Sentry leapt from the Temperate's shoulder and into Bruno's lap, and again this voice (not from Bruno but still Bruno's) finished for him: 'I didn't know who to tell first, but I want to tell all now and make my own confession. They sought me out because I'm the son of the last man who was killed by a Rebel.'

The Cat-Sentry. Must've recorded my voice, Bruno thought. How long had he been followed, listened to, so that a strong enough store of spoken words could be strung together and used now against him?

His voice came again, calm, matter of fact: 'Gumbly brought *The Book of Black & White* back to Pitch End

123

so he could be giving it to Dr Jonathan Bloom. He brought it back because the Rebels are coming back to Pitch End.'

Enough, decided Bruno.

He moved to rise, cry out and protest, but in trying he realised he couldn't move at all. His jaw was stuck shut. All he could shift were his eyes. He looked to the Temperate – the man's fingers were dabbling, and Bruno understood that he was being pinned to the chair, held immobile and silent and guilty by Temperate Thomas's Talent.

Bruno struggled but only in his heart. It was an impossibility to escape.

'Ye've been keeping this secret to yerself?' asked the Temperate.

The Cat-Sentry, in Bruno's voice, replied, 'I have.'

'And ye've been glad of it, haven't ye? Glad the Rebels are returning?'

'I have.'

'So glad ye'd be willing to fight against all of us? Everyone in this room? Would ye ever be as bold as that?'

'I would,' said the voice that Pitch End now knew as Bruno Atlas.

'And what is this here?' said the Temperate, his Talent teasing the chain from Bruno's throat, the medallion slipping free and left to hover in the air. Bruno's eyes watered in frustration – he looked to the crowd for some support, some face to offer help, an expression other than fright.

But still no Pace, no mother. He realised that he had no one.

'It's nothing less,' said Temperate Thomas, 'than the Rebel symbol itself! Same as on the crate that contained the rightly-infernal book!'

And within all cages there was an uproar that was absolute and unfettered – the Discussion Chamber swept with outrage, townsfolk plucked from their seats, standing and shaking their bars, raging . . .

'We must band together now!' declared Temperate Thomas, turning anew to face his people, voice rising with the rabble. 'We must seek out the traitors, ones like this boy! We must destroy whoever would seek to undermine our way of life and aid the return of the Rebels to Pitch End! If it's the last thing I do, I'll purge this town of doubt, dissent and lies! And if there's anyone who stands in the way of this, in the destruction of the returning Rebels, then they'll be tossed into the Sea of Apparitions with stones around their ankles!'

Bruno shut his eyes, wishing himself away, away from noise, accusation, a madness that couldn't be ignored or blocked out . . .

'Listen to me real close now – I'm gonna get ye outta here.'

Bruno opened his eyes. He saw no one close, not even the Cat-Sentry, which had left him to shadow Temperate Thomas. And yet a voice had whispered in his ear.

'Don't bother to be looking for me,' said the voice. A

125

girl's voice? *'I don't want ye to see me yet. Just be listening, right?'*

Bruno couldn't nod or agree by any means. He had to continue listening.

'Count to ten,' the voice told him, *'and be ready. I'll tell ye when.'*

Then he sensed (but didn't see) that someone had left him. Bruno remembered he was supposed to be counting: *One, two . . .*

The Temperate turned to face him.

Five, six . . .

'Now, Atlas,' he said. 'What else do ye have to be telling us?'

Seven or eight now? Or –

'And how will I be for getting the truth out of ye?'

He stepped towards Bruno, who felt a force like a hundred hands take him. Skin and muscle and bone all pulled back against the chair and he released a scream, his truest sound since mounting the stage –

'I'll get it out of ye, so help me, by any means I need!'

Then a gunshot –

A single shriek –

Bruno saw a light bulb pop, then darken. Then another bulb at the end of another cage. Gunshots from someone unseen, taking out each, darkness seeping into the Discussion Chamber and engulfing it.

Bruno saw nothing but felt the Temperate's Talent slide from his body, his father's medallion dropping to his chest.

126

And as his limbs were freed, his mouth slackening, cheeks damp with tears, a fierce and unseen mouth blasted the word into his ear – *'Run.'*

XII

The Dark

Bruno crouched. He saw nothing, but heard too much. Many screams, and the slow rise of a weeping-wailing –

'They're here already, those Rebels!'

'They've got Talent to take the very light from the place, they'll be rightly stealing the stars next!'

'Mountains protect us!'

He didn't hesitate.

Bruno felt with his fingers towards the short staircase, his way out. On his belly he went down the steps and then his hands met iron, fingers clutching and feeling for some release in the gate, but he knew already there was only one way: over and on into the mass of bodies in the Discussion Chamber whose cries and worries were too much to be soothed, even by the Temperate –

'Calm yerselves, my friends! Don't be afeared! All is well when yer Elders are present, no harm shall be coming to any of ye!'

Then another voice, closer, and which could only be the Marshall –

'What'll we do, Temperate? They're losing their bloody minds here and my men aren't much better!'

'Lock the doors,' replied Temperate Thomas. 'We have to keep them in. I'll keep an eye on the Atlas boy. And try and get them bloody lights back on.'

Now, thought Bruno, or I'll never.

He stood, stuck his feet amongst iron coils and climbed the gate, trying not to remember Old Town and the tree and how poorly it showed him as a climber. But caution wasn't an allowed luxury.

'The boy,' he heard the Temperate breathe, perhaps to his fellow Elders, perhaps to himself. Then again – '*The boy.*'

Bruno's hand struck something sharp – spikes that he wedged one foot between, then his second.

'Stop the Atlas boy!' cried Temperate Thomas, for all who could hear.

Bruno had to leap before he wanted to, his left foot still held tight between spikes as he went forwards. All around was yawning black, the howling –

'Watch for the Atlas boy!'

'Don't let him escape!'

'He knows what the Rebels plans rightly are!'

He fell onto his front, one shoe left behind, impaled. His chin collided with the ground and he tasted blood, the sharp tang of it curling across his tongue like a slow 's' drawn with a rusted coin. He didn't move. He settled only for breathing.

'Pitch Enders!' Temperate Thomas called. 'The Atlas boy is amongst ye, trying to make his rightly-indecent escape! If we are to find out where the Rebels are hiding, what they're planning, we need to be finding Atlas and making him tell us! Do not let him escape!'

And then Bruno was up and plunging forwards, one-shoed and staggering, hands outstretched, other fingers touching his, eliciting cries of: 'I felt something! He went close by me!'

Bruno took two more steps, had to stop or risk more notice, and as he stalled a burst of flame scorched the spot where he'd just stood, where he'd been detected by a Pitch Ender's hands moments before. Blue-white, its heat tightened Bruno's face, showing eyes and more eyes within the cages, the same eager glitter in all. The flame rose as tall as a man and then dissipated. Bruno heard the panic in his own breathing and clapped a hand to mouth to hide it.

'If ye detect him,' Temperate Thomas's voice went out, the darkness stealing back in, 'then cry out and I shall be revealing him!'

The Temperate's Talent, Bruno thought, that's what that sudden flame was.

Bruno moved faster, bent-backed, knowing that if he didn't escape quick then he wouldn't escape at all. And in their need to please, to be the one to capture the traitor

130

Bruno Atlas, the Pitch Enders screamed from all over the Discussion Chamber, claiming –

'Here!'

'No, over here he is!'

'No, I've got him, Temperate! I've got him by the hair!'

'That's *my* hair ye bloody fool! Be letting go!'

Temperate Thomas's Talent flashed close and far, throwing light into cages, Bruno still slipping away from its reveal. The townsfolk were a single thing to him then, one animal, all claws snatching. One body caterwauling with one mouth, and one thought on its mind: capture Bruno Atlas and earn the Temperate's praise.

'He's definitely here, I have him, my Temperate!'

This time right. Bruno was caught – pushed and torn at, he slammed against one cage and another and then went no further. Hands held him.

'Let my son go.'

'Ow! That Widow bloody bit me!'

Bruno was released and he moved out of range less than a moment before Talent in the form of fire rose behind him, higher and wider than before, showing the cage at his back: one man, six Widows.

'Marshall!' the Temperate announced. 'Arrest the Widows of Pitch End! The Atlas boy's mother is amongst them!'

The fire faded. Bruno lost sight of the Widows. He could go no further. How could he leave his mother to the whim of the Elders?

'*What are ye waiting about for?*' It was the same voice,

same whisper that had ordered him earlier and had, Bruno guessed, taken out the light bulbs. *'Ye can't help yer mam now. She'll be grand, she can look after herself.'*

Bruno waited, fresh insults thrown around him by Pitch Enders –

'Those Widows are always lurking about, saying nothing! Not natural!'

'What have they to hide behind those veils!'

'Who even asked them to wear them? Who gave them permission!'

'Bruno,' said the whisper close to him, *'ye have to go. I'll open the door, then ye have to go through, right?'*

Bruno didn't answer. But sure enough the doors to the Discussion Chamber were opened within a minute and new light reached in to dispel the dark – the brilliance of the Faerie Fort.

'Stop him!'

Temperate or Marshall? Maybe both. Bruno ran – out of the Discussion Chamber, beyond the Faerie Fort to the double doors that held the town hall shut in usual times. Bruno couldn't stop. Running too quick he flung himself against the doors. They refused to move. Bolts, bars, a large lock.

He heard naked footsteps hurrying across stone but with no visible owner. He knew what he'd hear next –

'Stand back from the door, quick-smart!'

Bruno moved away a little, eyes on the entrance to the Discussion Chamber and cowering as the bars and bolts were rushed back and three gunshots chased one another into the lock. It sprung off, shattering to scatter itself across the floor. The doors eased open and wind rushed past to filch more dead leaves from the Faerie Fort.

A sudden impact on his shoulder made Bruno cry out, feeling something sharp bite down. He turned, saw a flash of silver and heard his own voice issue from the mouth of Temperate Thomas's Cat-Sentry as it clung onto him, claws moving deeper – '*Come back, Da! Come back! Please come back to me!*'

A blast – another gunshot that exploded the Cat-Sentry on his shoulder as spectacularly as the lock, reduced to bits barely as big as crumbs. Bruno stood stiff with shock, hands feeling his face, hoping all of him was still there. 'Ye could've killed me,' he murmured, though still not knowing who he spoke to.

Bruno felt hands push him on, firm as the Temperate's Talent, towards the open double doors. '*Head for the lighthouse, and ye'll be safe there. I'll be after ye, not far. Run on and don't be stopping for anyone, ye hear me? Don't let anyone see ye.*'

'But how can I stop people seeing me if—'

'*Just think it,*' interrupted the voice, '*and that'll be enough. No one can see ye if ye don't want them too. Go!*'

And Bruno fled into welcome dark, the sanctuary of night.

XIII

The Emerald Ghost

'Anybody about in here?'

Bruno had decided to be brave and speak, but maybe he spoke too soon. (Speaking when I should be silent, he thought, silent when I should be speaking – just like Miss Hope always said.) He'd done as he was told, run without stopping – shedding his second shoe along they way – and was standing on the threshold of the twelfth lighthouse of Pitch End. He bit his lip and waited for anything that might be lurking. The injury on his shoulder itched, wanting attention, but he didn't touch where the Cat-Sentry's claws had gone in – he was afraid of what deep damage he'd find.

Bruno just breathed but couldn't think right, waiting with Pitch End at his back, the rainfall a shroud to soften its lights and rages. Then he heard something behind, a sound like a stumbling on the rocky rough track that led across the outcrop to the lighthouse. Bruno stepped forwards to pull shut the lighthouse's small, heavy door and with its sudden slam sending echoes into the high, hollow reaches of the lighthouse, he felt more alone than he'd done before. A feeling short-lived –

'*Did ye have to slam it so loud? And ye nearly took me arm off with it!*'

Bruno heard footsteps, a deep breathing through nostrils. He stepped back against the door and said, 'Who are ye?'

'*The Emerald Ghost,*' said the voice (same as he'd heard in the town hall, that had told him to flee to the lighthouse). There was laughter, and the voice said again, '*I think I spooked those fools in the town hall good and proper, eh?*'

Bruno couldn't decide whether it was a boy or girl. He didn't reply, just stood repeating the word, 'Ghost,' to himself. His hand touched the cold door for support.

'*Any food in here, do ye think?*' asked the voice. '*Must be something for eating, I'm bloody starving!*'

There was movement in the dark and the longer Bruno stood the more was revealed: three windows, crescent-shaped, their sills showing the thickness of the lighthouse's walls, moonlight outlining the steps of a dark staircase in the centre, corkscrewing upwards. A tall cabinet like the dresser they had at home, but with shelves empty. And around the edges, stacks of paper. For what? Bruno thought. He stepped forwards and his knee struck a large wooden table. Something rattled across its surface, fell. Bruno reached down for it and came back with a pencil. It was one of dozens on the tabletop, some loose, some bound together.

'*Maybe in here there's something.*'

The low doors of the dresser sprang open.

'*Some Rebel meeting place this was!*' said the voice, as more paper dislodged from inside the dresser by unseen hands. '*No provisions, not even an apple for eating!*'

'Why can't I see ye?' Bruno asked.

'*Too dark,*' said the voice.

'Didn't mean that,' said Bruno, quietly, then louder: 'I meant how come I couldn't see ye in the town hall?'

'*Didn't want ye to,*' said the voice. '*Best not to let ye see me properly, I thought. Ye're too easy to work out, Bruno. Ye'd have just looked right at me or something, given the game away!*'

Bruno stepped forwards again and asked, 'Well, how did ye get here as quick as me?'

'*I know rightly-quicker ways,*' was the reply, and Bruno heard a smile in the voice. '*Oh yes, rightly-better than anyone else in Pitch End! But I can't tell in case ye get caught and tell that Temperate all the secrets.*'

'I wouldn't,' said Bruno, frustration obliterating any other feeling. 'Maybe the truth is ye're just too scared to show yerself!'

Any searching through the dresser ceased. The voice said, '*Did ye say scared?*'

And then Bruno did see. Allowed was how it felt: a slow divulging, vague then resolving into a pair of narrowed eyes, a deepening frown, moving fast towards him like a defiant returning ghost refusing mortality . . . a girl cast in an emerald cloak with matching hood, a mass of blond hair like coils of wire standing out from her scalp, and as Bruno wondered at her reality he felt pain in his belly as she arrived at him, poking him hard with one finger.

'Don't *ever* call me scared, right?' she told him. The same finger she'd poked him with came close to his face, folding into a fist. 'Got it?'

She took a shotgun with a foreshortened barrel in hand and aimed it at Bruno.

'*Louise*,' said another voice, making both Bruno and the Emerald Ghost start, and turn for the source. 'I'd appreciate it if ye weren't blowing Bruno's head off, seeing as we need all the allies we can be getting, things developing as they are.'

There was a rasping noise, light that flared then diminished and then a person that Bruno could immediately see. The voice belonged to Pace-the-Witherman.

'Bruno,' said Pace, 'this is Louise Green. One of the last remaining Rebels.'

'Pleased to meet ye,' said Louise, and like another person entirely she smiled and offered Bruno her hand. He took it, shook it, and she skipped away to continue the hunt for food.

Pace moved forwards, avoiding the central spiral stair. He had the appearance of an unwilling guest with poor news. Loosely, his mouth held a pipe shaped like a buxom mermaid.

'Ye alright?' Pace asked, smoke escaping with each syllable.

Bruno nodded, but wasn't sure whether the Witherman had seen. He returned the pencil to the table and his shoulder shot with pain. Pace moved quickly towards him, quicker than Bruno had ever witnessed. His hands – more delicate than Bruno had ever witnessed – touched the wound from the Cat-Sentry.

'Well that'll need seeing to,' said Pace. He chewed on his pipe, and then called, 'Louise! Get me a needle and thread. At the back of the dresser there's a compartment, ye'll find things in there.'

Pace dragged a chair out of the dark and pushed it under Bruno.

'Sit,' said the Witherman. 'Ye've had a lot of shocks tonight, I'm thinking.'

And only then, at the sight of Pace's sympathy, his care, did the fullness of the night's events come to Bruno. He wished for something like sleep, a blank relief.

'At last!' he heard Louise exclaim. A crunch: teeth sinking into apple.

'Louise,' said Pace, 'the box, quick-smart.'

Quick across the room came Louise, apple in one hand and a small wooden box in the other. She gave the box to Pace. A symbol stained its lid, one that Bruno didn't need to fully see to recognise.

'*This*,' said Bruno, bringing out his father's medallion. 'This is the symbol of the Rebels. Gumbly had one of these medallions. It was the symbol on the crate he brought back, the one with that book in it.'

Pace sighed. One of his gnarled, weather-bitten hands shifted into his shirt, bringing back yet another medallion.

'We were all with Dr Jonathan Bloom,' said Pace. 'Yer father, the Withermen, all Rebels, all fighting agin the Elders. It was Dr Bloom that was giving the four Withermen – Waghorn, Grave, Gumbly and meself – these.' Pace hooked another shivering finger around half of his buttonless shirt and pulled it wide, revealing the cracked clock face, handless like Gumbly's, implanted lopsidedly over his heart. Bruno heard: *tick, tick, tick –*

Pace let his shirt fall closed. He settled the box with the Rebel symbol on the table and from inside took a long, sharp needle, already threaded, and a match.

'Why did he put the clocks in yer chests?' asked Bruno.

'Official version told to the Elders,' said Pace, as the match was struck, the needle dipped into the flame, 'was so it would keep us Withermen just working on, never tiring, never dying, always there to look after the dead. That was near twelve turns ago, before Rebels and all the fighting. And Temperate Thomas liked that idea alright. No objection, like he had no objection to those clockwork Cat-Sentries Dr Bloom came up with. Be looking away now, Bruno.'

Pace held the needle ready but not steady, a slight quiver in the silver thread. Bruno watched it, wouldn't look away.

'Good,' said Pace. 'Look if ye can, if ye have to. Not a bad way of being.'

Pace pressed the needle to Bruno's shoulder. Pain like

139

none he knew made Bruno shut his eyes, no decision then, and his hands gripped the sides of the chair, bare feet arching. He struggled to hold onto waking, trying not to topple or cry out.

'My da,' he said, hoping for a distraction, but no past pain could replace the present one.

'Aye,' said Pace, his fingers working on the wound, gently tugging. 'Yer da was a Rebel too. One of the fiercest.'

'But he was killed,' said Bruno. 'Murdered.'

Pace made a noise between a snort and sniff.

'Not a bit of it,' he said. 'Nic Delby was yer da's best friend, had been since they were younger than you. It was the Elders that made out Delby killed yer father. No more killed him than I did.'

'Delby ran away though,' said Bruno. 'All the Rebels, they just went.'

Louise returned, 'Damn wrong! We never went away!'

'Louise and the other Rebels are in hiding,' Pace told Bruno, 'up in the Elm Tree Mountains.' He raised his voice a little. 'How's the army coming along, Louise?'

'Coming along grand,' said Louise, 'just need a few last things.'

'Or a lot of little ones, eh?'

Louise said nothing for a moment, then, 'I'm trying me best! It's not easy to be getting into the town hall for a good snoop around!'

'Well, Bruno,' said Pace, 'I think ye're just about' (the Witherman leaned close and Bruno heard a small snap) 'done.'

Pace picked the bitten-off thread from between his teeth and returned the needle to its box.

Bruno dared adjust his shoulder, a small shrug – the pain was almost none. He reached, touched it, feeling the small, neat line of stitches.

'Ye'll live,' said Pace. 'Now, we have to decide what's next. Coz one thing we know – ye're no longer safe in Pitch End. Nor me neither, not if they've got Gumbly.'

'I saw them,' said Bruno. 'In Old Town, they were going to take the clock out of his chest.'

'Thought they might,' said Pace. 'He should never have come back to Pitch End. He was unstable enough at the best of times, but this morning at the harbour . . .' Pace didn't finish.

'He was missing,' said Bruno. 'Maybe he was trying to escape?'

Pace made the same sound as earlier – amusement in a sniff-snort.

'No,' he said, 'Gumbly didn't go out to sea for escape. Him and all on *The Wintering* went on Elder orders. See, last time I ever spoke to Gumbly, he told me something secret. He said that Temperate Thomas had offered the crew of their boat a load of money and praise and all kinds if they succeeded on a special job he had for them. He ordered them to go to a certain place out at sea, and they were to drop their nets and be dragging them along the seabed. Any fish they caught had to be thrown back. What they were looking for was something else. Anything with

141

a certain symbol on it. Doesn't take a lamplighter to see which symbol they were told to be looking for, does it?'

'Looking for things that belonged to the Rebels,' said Bruno.

'Too right,' said Pace, taking the pipe from his mouth, jabbing it in the air as he spoke. 'See, Temperate knew that when the Single Season War was ending, Dr Bloom wanted to make sure no one ever found *The Book of Black & White*. So the Rebels left by night, took to the sea, taking the book with them.'

'Why?' asked Bruno. 'What's in the book that's so bad?'

Pace didn't look at him. Louise, little more than a shadow, was close, but when Bruno looked to her she turned to face one of the half-moon windows, checking the sea, its black thoughts.

'Like I was saying about Gumbly,' whispered Pace. 'He was nervy enough as it was, but this morning it was worse. Like he'd gone mad. Like he'd seen things he shouldn't. Memory and imagining can drive a being mad, that's what Dr Bloom used to say.'

Bruno watched him.

Pace smoked his pipe in earnest. 'Ye'll see soon enough, Bruno,' he said. 'But we need to concentrate on getting ye to safety now.'

'My mother,' said Bruno.

'Ye can't be helping her,' said Pace. 'Not yet anyway. But she's strong enough. She can fight, look after herself as well as any Widow.'

Bruno wanted to disagree, couldn't think of anyone less able to 'fight' than his mother and the other Widows.

Pace turned to Louise and asked, 'Did ye get what I towl ye to?'

'Course!' she replied, turning back to them, moving in. 'Nothing the Emerald Ghost can't be getting if she needs to!'

And from under her emerald cloak, Louise revealed –

'My Owl-Sentry!' said Bruno.

'Good girl,' said Pace, taking the Sentry from Louise. 'Now' (he handed Louise the box with the Rebel symbol) 'there's matches in there. Ye know what to do. Something that'll distract.'

Louise nodded, then said, 'A diversion!' She mounted the staircase and climbed, ran, the whole thing shaking and creaking under her rush.

'Ye were rightly-smart ye know,' Pace told Bruno, cradling the Owl-Sentry. 'Keeping things safe inside this old thing. No Enforcer nor Elder would've thought to examine something so meagre.'

'How did ye know about it?' asked Bruno.

'Yer mam told me,' said Pace.

Bruno wondered how much his mother knew, how much she'd hidden herself. How much he didn't know her.

'Take what ye need from inside,' said Pace, handing the Sentry to Bruno. 'But most of all – yer father's pocket watch. Ye're gonna need it.'

'But where am I gonna go to? The Enforcers and everyone are after me, Temperate Thomas. If he finds me I'll—'

'Be in no worse trouble than ye are now,' said Pace.

Bruno half-turned away, but could find no solace in the dark, walls too close, everything overtaking him. He held the Owl-Sentry to his chest.

'I haven't asked for any of this,' he found himself saying. 'It's just happening. Just because of things other people did.'

'And what's wrong with that?' asked Pace.

'There's no choice,' said Bruno.

'Always a choice,' said Pace. 'Let me show ye.'

Bruno turned back to face the Witherman.

'Ye can choose,' said Pace, 'to try and escape, get to safety. To fight back agin the Elders. Or ye can choose to stay in Pitch End. Now do ye want to see what ye'll be doing for the rest of yer life if ye choose the second thing?'

Light blazed from above, rushed like water down the walls, washed over their feet, the room around. And Bruno was shown: the stacks of paper he'd seen in the half-dark were bound like books, lengths of red leather in readiness beside. Pace picked one and handed it to Bruno. 'Read,' the Witherman told him. Bruno saw:

The Wrath
By Jack Pitch
2nd Edition
(With Rightly-Decent Additional Advice By
Temperate Thomas II)

'Making new copies of *The Wrath*,' said Pace. 'Writing them out by hand to be given to all Pitch Enders, with some extra little pearls added by the Temperate.'

Bruno said nothing. He felt shamed. Shamed at his surprise. What had he expected? What life did he think he'd have in the lighthouse? Think he'd be apart from Pitch End, isolated, alone but independent on the western headland, no longer answerable to the Elders? He realised that he'd never had a choice. Not until that moment.

'Day after day,' Pace was saying. 'Turn upon turn just scribbling and—'

'*Enough*,' said Bruno. He waited, aware of Louise descending the steps then stopping, watching. Then he decided. Bruno let the book drop from his hand and said, 'What do I need to do?'

'Good on ye!' shouted Louise. 'Here,' she said, and a satchel was flung to Bruno. 'Ye can put the pocket watch and things in that. I'll find ye some new shoes too, bound to be some of yer da's here.'

'We need to hit that Temperate where it hurts,' said Pace, smiling. Bruno heard *tick-tick, tick-tick, tick-tick* . . . the Witherman's heart as swift as a rabbit's foot. 'That Temperate might be acting like *The Book of Black & White* is the most indecent thing in Pitch End, but he needs it more than anyone. So we're going to steal it.'

'How?' said Bruno. 'It's Curfew, there'll be Sentries about everywhere.'

'I'll see to 'em!' said Louise, searching again through

the dresser. 'I'll do something rightly-stealthy to sort them out.'

Bruno didn't feel much consoled.

'But what if I'm seen by someone else?' he asked.

'Ye won't be,' Pace whispered, still smiling.

'Like I towl ye earlier on,' said Louise, 'if ye don't want someone to see ye, they won't. Ye see ye need to just—'

Pace said, '*No*. Don't be telling him. There's some things ye can't be just told. Some things ye need to be learning for yerself.'

XIV

Unseeable

The moon a wound, a nick on the night sky; an absence of stars; lizard-tongue clouds licking up the little moonlight – the scene as Curfew seized Pitch End, townsfolk all home but Bruno Atlas not where he was supposed to be. On a darkway just off South Street, in an old pair of his father's shoes they'd found in the lighthouse – which were two sizes too big – he was waiting with Pace-the-Witherman.

'Alright and ready?' asked Pace in a whisper.

Bruno didn't respond. He adjusted the satchel on his back, contents of the Owl-Sentry inside, listening to the slow clop of hoof on cobble. Then he saw the head of an Enforcer's horse appear at the end of the alley, moving uphill towards the Clocktower.

'Now or ye'll never,' said Pace. 'Hurry or he'll just pass . . . *now.*'

And Bruno shut his eyes, trying to believe Pace, remembering what he'd told him to do and feel and think, and stepped out almost into the Enforcer's path. He hoped some more –

Bruno opened his eyes.

The Enforcer moved on.

Bruno watched the slow flick of the horse's tail, its head half-turning for a moment as though it sensed. He stepped back into the darkway beside Pace.

'Well done,' said Pace in a fierce whisper.

'I have *Talent*?' muttered Bruno.

'That's the politest and most Elder-like word for it, but yeh,' said Pace. 'All Pitch Enders have it, if they would just learn to use it, learn to feel something. See, it's all that energy – all that feeling – that comes to the surface when ye're Coming-Of-Age. Emotion. Rage and pain, bitter stuff and happier stuff too. It all comes bursting out in a hundred different ways, and that's what fuels a Talent. Learning then to master it is the difficult bit.'

'The Temperate,' said Bruno, 'in the town hall, he was able make fire, like my teacher did once. He was able to move things and hold me back and . . .' Bruno stopped, horrified not excited by the possibilities. 'Can ye do anything with Talent?' he asked Pace.

'Well for some it's different,' replied Pace. 'Some can just do silly tricks, others can make things move or jump about. Others can destroy things. Some people, rightly-special, can do all that and more besides. Some can even create. And yes, some can do whatever they can imagine if they're controlling their feelings properly.'

148

'How are we gonna stop Temperate Thomas if he can do anything he can think of?' asked Bruno.

Pace sighed. 'Ye always ask the difficult questions, don't ye?'

Bruno felt he should shy, look away, but he didn't.

'Never mind that now,' said Pace. 'Just come back.'

'What?' asked Bruno.

'I mean let me see ye again. Can't keep talking to the wall, can I?'

'How can I let ye see me?' asked Bruno.

'That's up to yerself,' said Pace. 'Ye're the one who chooses who ye want to see ye and who ye don't. Ye have to choose how, and how much. But my advice – just imagine a person seeing ye, knowing ye, and they will.'

Bruno let his thoughts unlatch, relent – strange, but it had been easier to make himself unseeable than to want to be seen again. Then he thought of not being seen by Pace, perhaps ever again. Of being alone, left behind, haunting Pitch End, unable to do anything –

'There now,' said Pace, suddenly. 'Ye're back with me. See, ye've got the hang of it rightly. A natural, just like yer dear da.' A small, grim smile passed over the Witherman's face, and then he said, 'Right, let's see what we can be seeing.'

He leaned past Bruno and both looked out onto South Street; high on the slope, Enforcers surrounded the Clocktower and town hall, all on horseback, pale chill bursting from the animal's nostrils. Every few moments, light reached across the sky from the west, passing above their heads like a roaming gaze. But the reappearance of this sudden signal from the lighthouse, the first in two turns, hadn't drawn away many. Either that, or the number of Enforcers was more than Bruno had known. He counted ten, then another ten at least . . . then more. But probably even more again, hidden in darkways.

Bruno's own gaze wandered, landing on the town hall: unlit, pillars as close to one another as townsfolk passing gossip, a closed fist of a place with secrets clutched safe inside.

'What'll the Temperate be doing now?' asked Bruno.

'Planning and plotting,' said Pace.

'Worrying?' asked Bruno, then thought it wrong.

'Maybe,' said Pace. 'But not doing nothing, ye can bet on that.'

'Why worry over one person?' said Bruno, remembering the words of the Cinder-Folk. 'Why bother so much about me? One person isn't enough to bring back the Rebels.'

'Well,' said Pace, still peering around the corner of the alley, 'that's where ye're wrong. Even a small whisper, a whimper of rebellion – that's enough to make that Temperate as nervous as anything, and he'll want to be silencing it quick-smart. He knows it only takes one and then it'll start all over again, just like ten turn ago.'

And then, as though in reply –

'I saw the beam from the lighthouse indeed, Marshall – I thought I gave an Elder Order two turns ago for the thing to be darkened, permanently.'

150

Bruno didn't hear the Marshall's reply to the Temperate.

'What are ye at just loitering about here?' Temperate Thomas shouted then, surely to the Enforcers. 'The eastern fields need to be concentrated on, and the Marsh! Whatever's going on in the lighthouse could be a rightly-devious ruse to lead us off like wild barnacle geese!'

Bruno forced himself to lean out to look, though he clung close still to the shadows.

'Temperate,' said the Marshall, 'I've decided to keep a strong presence of men here, and send some to the light-house to have a look. It was for protection as much as anything.'

'*Protection?*' said Temperate Thomas. 'Thank you, Marshall, but neither myself nor the other Elders need protection. And specially not from some boy, Rebel or not. So, it's decided,' said the Temperate. 'Be searching the windmills and the farmer's cottages, checking for trapdoors. I'd say be especially and rightly-suspicious of bookcases and the like (why would someone need such a thing!). Be as fly as a fox, Marshall. Imagine yerself as a serpent almost, or even worse: a *cat*. Because be certain of it – that's how those Rebels will be thinking. I send the Temperate's most blessed blessing with ye all. *Long live Pitch End!*'

'*And longer live the Elders!*' came the automatic reply.

The Marshall cried, 'This way, men!'

Bruno and Pace retreated as Enforcers charged on to the shoreline and east, towards the fields. The tumult of their hoof beats still audible, Bruno returned to the edge of the darkway.

'There,' Pace told him, pointing. 'He's still there.'

Temperate Thomas stood at the base of the Clocktower.

Freed of cloud then, moonlight let them see clear: the Temperate, his focus on the face of the Clocktower, on its motionless hands. Bruno looked closer. In Temperate Thomas's arms was something large, something black and white.

'How are we ever gonna be getting that book?' asked Bruno.

Before an answer from Pace, the doors of the town hall opened and such dark figures were released that Bruno's first guess was of Widows, his own mother. But no Widow would be treated with such cordiality by Temperate Thomas – Bruno watched him bow to each as they joined him. Bruno counted nine, then realised: the other Elders.

Bruno took another step forwards, leaning out into South Street, but Pace grabbed his arm, hissing, '*Stop!*'

Cloud returned to gorge, moonlight lost as Bruno saw the Elders come together, for a moment all drawing close to the base of the Clocktower. Words returned to him that he struggled, for a moment, to place; then he remembered Diamond Beach, the Day of Discovery, bright, hot, and an Elder's awkward words to a collected child, '*Tell me – would ye like to see what lies under the Clocktower in the town square?*'

Bruno heard a rough grind of stone, saw a darker

opening in the stonework of the Clocktower, and the Temperate leading the Elders inside.

'Where are they going?' asked Bruno.

The sound of closing stone as moonlight returned, but too late – the Elders had vanished.

'Let's go,' said Bruno, so keen to follow. But Pace still had his arm.

'No,' said the Witherman. 'We wait for the signal, the plan.'

Bruno looked all over South Street.

'But it's safe,' he said. 'I can't see any Cat-Sentries.'

'And they don't see us,' said Pace. 'But it don't mean we aren't here, does it?'

Bruno didn't move.

'Listen now,' said Pace suddenly, 'do ye hear it?'

Bruno did listen: first nothing, then something . . . a high-pitched cry. And then he saw her – only a smear of emerald, an apparition, but without any doubt Louise as she rushed across the town square squealing for all the weary world to hear.

'That's the "rightly-stealthy" signal she was on about?' said Bruno.

Pace was laughing, in his own ragged way. 'Keep watching,' he managed to say.

Cat-Sentries snapped into sight. Leaping from rooftops and out of chimney pots, squirming from drainpipes and uncoiling from gutters, from behind lampposts. They all moved swift towards Old Town, all in pursuit of Louise.

'Well,' said Pace. 'She gets the job done. Come on.'

The Witherman marched past Bruno, back hunched, legs struggling to take him up the slope of South Street. Bruno followed, still thinking himself unseeable, his own eyes watchful of the dark, of upstairs windows, doorways, darkways.

'Must've used Gumbly's one to get inside,' muttered Pace as they reached the Clocktower. Then words to Bruno, holding his hand open and out – 'Yer pocket watch.'

Bruno didn't tell Pace, but he'd taken with him not just his father's pocket watch but all his secrets, all prized things: the scrap of greaseproof paper, tooth of shingle, shreds of *Pitch End Journal*, the muddy sepia pictograph of himself, his mother and his father, and the coal Conn had given him. All were saved in the satchel. He removed it to search.

'Quick-smart now,' said Pace.

Bruno's hand brought out the small, brass pocket watch. Pace took it in both hands with as much delicacy as he'd adopted for stitching Bruno's wound. He turned it over and held it to his ear between few fingers, like something too hot or too cold to the touch, and listened. He grinned. His middle finger slid underneath the base. There was a click that carried too far in the quietness of the night, Bruno thought; a sharp twist, and the lid of the pocket watch split, flowered into four triangular sections, all folding back to reveal the face. Bruno moved in to see, finally: three pin-narrow hands allowed him to know the time – something he hadn't for too many turns. And incredibly, at that moment both hands mirrored the stopped Clocktower: midnight.

Bruno heard *tick, tick, tick* . . . and felt strengthened by it.

Pace exhaled, the beat of his own clock-heart quickening.

'Thank the mountains,' he said. 'She's still working well.'

Bruno felt a desire to snatch it back, examine it further, know it for himself, but Pace had shifted his feet and his intense, careful attention to the Clocktower. His fingertips pattered the surface like he was trying to detect some weak spot and he settled them in the end into a small gouge, a nip in the stone. Bruno looked closer, saw a circular gouge, something more deliberate than a nip – and with four extending, petal-shaped spaces.

Pace laid the pocket watch, open, into this carefully carved absence in the stone. It fitted without flaw. He turned it. There was the same, slow grind of stone Bruno had heard minutes before and the same doorway opened, a tall slab of stone eased out by the darkest darkness behind. A breeze like a held breath, cold as iron, enwrapped him.

'Go on now,' said Pace. 'Ye don't have much time. They'll be down there with that book.'

'*Me?*' said Bruno.

'Ye think I'd be better?' said Pace, the rapid tick of his clock-heart unnerving: *tick-tick, tick-tick, tick-tick* . . .

So Bruno returned his satchel to his back, turned and

155

treated the doorway like an opponent, squaring himself before it, one he didn't know how to conquer.

'This is the most important thing now,' said Pace. 'Everything depends on it. We need that book, or the Temperate, he'll—'

'He'll what?' asked Bruno.

Pace didn't answer, at first. 'I want ye to see it for yerself,' said Pace. He sighed. 'Like I said before: some things ye have to see with yer own eyes, no use being told. Now go. I'll be waiting for ye right here. I'm going nowhere.'

Bruno knew to ask no more.

Only one thought made him move forwards, carried him on inside: now's the time to prove myself. Prove I'm not just all thoughts or all wrong words. Now for action, for doing something.

Once more he heard the grind of stone as Pace edged the door shut on him, Bruno hoping himself unseeable, and hoping his newfound Talent wouldn't fail him.

XV
Old Before Time

Enough of an insecure structure from outside, inside the Clocktower Bruno looked to four walls bothered with cracks and felt he could've pressed fingers into them, pulled the place apart with little enough effort. Cracks that branched, spread upwards, reaching high into the gaze of the four faces of the clock – four hazy discs of moonlight. At the highest point of the tower, Bruno saw shadows like discarded morsels, shifting and turning and approaching one another at a hop, snapping and complaining and then retreating – the one-footed ravens, apparently as enthral to Curfew as any Pitch Ender.

Bruno stepped forwards.

Two staircases were in sight – first being a way up, clinging to the inside of the Clocktower, steps crumbling like soaked bread; second staircase the way down, a spiral thing with a smudge of light somewhere far beneath. Bruno kneeled by the second, fingers poised on the ground. He peered down, listened, but heard nothing.

He took a breath, then began a slow descent, keeping his hand on the central spine, light brightening at the bottom like the opening of a lantern valve. And at each turn of the stair Bruno heaped his thoughts on his Talent, intoning: I am nothing. I am no one that anyone wants to see. Unseeable, nothing at all . . .

And then the end. A long, long passageway.

The light ahead was bright but inconstant, tucked around a final, distant turn.

Bruno took a step, then stopped once more – the walls had eyes and ears. Cat-Sentries, from uneven floor to sloped ceiling, were settled in their own small niches, each one in a different state of repose and disrepair. Some looked like they could be made to work, Bruno thought, with some attention. He decided some might just be in hibernation, a faint throb of light in their eyes. But others were hopeless, had shed eyes, limbs, one ear or both, and had plenty of dust to adorn them. He counted quickly and calculated, adding rows and columns . . . the number seemed improbable, until he looked closer –

Below each Sentry was a name, inked on paper and pinned – *Horatio Crywolf, Morris Leadbeater, Elsa Hope, Pace-the-Witherman* . . . this was where the words of the Pitch Enders had been stored. Turn upon turn of things spoken, private and public, held for the kind of event he'd been at the centre of earlier. Words that could be used to incriminate. Bruno's hands became fists and he would've begun to take each Sentry and smash it, crush it underfoot, tear out its clockwork insides, if it weren't for remembering why he was there, what his mission was. And for Temperate Thomas's voice –

'That's it, my dear Elders,' he was saying. 'Let us see what we've been gifted by those so rightly-generous, rightly-pestilential Pitch Enders this week.'

He laughed.

And Bruno – ignoring the Cat-Sentries, hoping they were more dead than dormant – couldn't go anywhere but onwards. His hearing strained to catch any word. But there were less words and more laughter, and the passageway echoed with the fall of coins . . .

'My, my,' he heard the Temperate say, more delight in his voice than Bruno would've conceived of, 'Elder Brackett, that's a rightly-valuable haul ye have there! And what about Elder Horrfrost, how's the rheumatism these days? Well, ye've been a busy bee, there's plenty of black pennies there. May the mountains protect ye. Elder Pester, how have the farmers been doing? Keeping to their agreement of quarter for them, three-quarters for the good of the town?'

Finally, Bruno reached the turn and – teeth clenched, every breath and every blink desperately reduced – he ventured one last, sliding step and saw:

Temperate Thomas and his Elders were gathered in a circular chamber, a low ceiling demanding a stoop from them all. There was a stone table with many squat, greasy, shrinking candles, dribbling, shedding small light on objects

Bruno couldn't discern. Ten stone chairs surrounded a larger, heavier, wooden chair with the appearance of a throne that was placed at the centre of the chamber. It was blessed with bulging velvet cushions and armrests sculpted to resemble raven talons. And on the cushion, like a long-lost now restored king: *The Book of Black & White*.

Bruno thought to snatch it but knew he couldn't have: the Temperate stood before this central chair, a wooden casket in his arms with its lid open, a smile on his face for each Elder as they offered a small, drawstring bag ('Elder Writtle! Well this is a rightly-generous haul ye've managed to get out of them this week, I tell ye!'), shaking out the contents – whether meagre or 'rightly-generous' – and letting them cascade into the casket.

'Very good,' said Temperate Thomas. 'A very profitable week indeed.'

The lid of the casket was shut, locked by a key that hung with many others from a chain around the Temperate's neck, and left on the stone table.

Monies surrendered, all Elders but their Temperate sank into stone chairs around the edge of the chamber, each knowing their place. The candlelight shivered under the assault of so many long sighs. Some of the men began to loll within moments, as though weighted with such a longing for sleep they couldn't resist.

'Well now!' said Temperate Thomas loudly, a few Elders starting, clutching heart or knee or hip with wince and groan. 'How rightly-glad I am to be seeing ye all tonight, my brave, brave Elders. I often think of the great burden on ye all. The great worry we all carry for the welfare of our town. We may not be young men, but we are young and pure in our hearts!'

The Elders mostly nodded.

Temperate Thomas smiled.

Bruno was bewildered (and perhaps a small amount awed) at how the Temperate was addressing the Elders. At how much he had them in his command, and with words so close to the words he'd thrown to the Pitch Enders in the Discussion Chamber; the very same way too of sliding, without a stumble, from flattery and gratitude to firm resolve.

'And we are allowed one moment of pure contentedness, I'm thinking,' said Temperate Thomas. He turned, stooping, letting his fingers slide over the surface of *The Book of Black & White*. He lifted the vast book – a 'volume of wickedness' thought Bruno, remembering the Temperate's earlier description – and brought it as close to his chest as an infant needing soothing. 'Indeed, we can be content, for it has returned to us at last. Returned, as I always said it would, did I not, Elders?'

Again there was nodding, a few grumbles of agreement, and then one solitary shout – 'We've a bit of it anyway!'

Bruno tried to source the voice, but saw no face likely to have just spoken.

But Temperate Thomas seized on it.

'Right ye are, Elder Shoemark!'

He moved fast then, bowing low to a man with one eye open and the other shut, and a nose the colour of burnt bacon. 'We do indeed have one wee bit, but we've only been able to do the littlest of what is possible, isn't that right?'

Elder Shoemark's mouth replied in a long glistening thread of saliva.

'One page is all we've had these ten turns,' said Temperate Thomas, moving away from Elder Shoemark. 'One ripped, half-ruined but rightly-useful page from this book. We've become desperate in our ageing. But no more. Soon we'll have more than just a respite from the ravages of ageing. Remember what Jack Pitch tells us in *The Wrath*: *Power can be now and forever, but be knowing that the body and the mind are rightly-not.*'

Bruno's legs began to ache with so much standing and not moving, mind vibrating with concentration. And questions, always more questions, answers just as out of reach as *The Book of Black & White* . . .

'We'll not be about forever!' cried another Elder without warning. Temperate Thomas rushed to console him, coming so close and so quickly to where Bruno stood, unseeable, that he recoiled.

'Aye, Elder Pester,' said the Temperate, covering the Elder's hand with one of his own. Bruno noted the difference: Elder Pester's hand was riven with burst blood vessels, tangles of swollen vein, fingers purpled where the Temperate's hand was merely smooth. Not utterly untouched by age – mottled with mauve spots, like the first warnings of damp on a wall – but not as distressed.

'Ye're right enough,' Temperate Thomas went on. 'We won't be about forever. And we've to do something quick if we're to stop the rot of mind and body. For what would they do without us, these people in this town? What would become of Pitch End without our rightly-decent guidance? Sure, they wouldn't even know what to do with themselves at all! Would probably not even get out of bed, so afeared they'd be, if we weren't around. Did ye see how they feared the book, just because I was *telling* them to? Not even a question about it!

'The Elders have been here longest of all – since before the Single Season War, before the Renaming of the Streets and the burning of the gypsies in Old Town . . . before and before that, and we shall stay on. We must be without time. Our continuing on, our staying where we are, always in their minds and daily ways – that's what we must ensure. That's what this book will give us. And not just the book has been returned to us. Our friend the Witherman has gifted something else too.'

From beneath his robes the Temperate took a pocket watch – cracked, without hands, clockwork twisted and mangled – and Bruno knew it as the clock that had been fixed in Gumbly. The state of the clockwork led his imagination to places he didn't like, images of what it had taken to remove the thing from Gumbly's chest.

'Ye see, Elders,' said Temperate Thomas, 'didn't I say if

163

we merely planned, waited, then these Withermen would see to themselves. No need to go hunting them down or be taking these things out by force. Just advise, for example, that a Witherman needs to attend a rightly-secret meeting in a rightly-insecure building in Old Town, and then what should happen? The building collapses. Unfortunate. Then advise another that they should be for always checking their daily meat for maggots, can't ever be too careful! Shame they didn't listen. Found dead in their bed, foaming at the mouth.' The Temperate smiled. 'Now, we'll be adding this one to the others we've collected.'

The Temperate turned and Bruno leaned forwards, noticing again the small objects on the stone table, then knowing what they were by their similarity to what Temperate Thomas placed amongst them – two other mangled pocket watches, joined by Gumbly's. The clocks belonged to the two other dead Withermen.

'*But*,' said the Temperate, his voice low, like thoughts being wondered aloud. 'I'm thinking we may have to reconsider such rightly-patient action, given the return of the book. Time is truly in short supply. We will have to deploy all our considerable power now to locate the other pocket watches. Starting first, of course, with the one in the heart of the last Witherman. Once all are collected, and with *The Book of Black & White*—'

Then the most unexpected thing of all. An impatient knocking behind Bruno, behind a patch of wall free of Cat-Sentries.

'And sure it couldn't have been better timed!' said Temperate Thomas. Bruno had the space of a heartbeat to move as the Head Elder rushed by him. Bruno held a breath as the Temperate again dragged the chain from the collar of his tunic, the end weighted with keys.

'Best behaviour now!' he called to the Elders. They groaned like ancient elms.

Temperate Thomas found somewhere to insert the key; the wall became a door, sweeping forwards, and out stepped a child, a girl – *Sabitha McCormack*. Bruno had to struggle to keep that breath in as the Temperate offered Sabitha his hand, saying, 'Ye're most welcome, my child. Were ye finding yer way here alright?'

'Course I did,' said Sabitha. 'Like ye told me, I went to that shop in Old Town where the Withermen used to keep the dead, opened the trapdoor, climbed down and then went left, then right, then kept going till I got here. Easy.'

'And yer father?' said the Temperate. 'Told him nothing, did ye? Kept this our secret, as I Elder-Ordered it?'

'Course,' said Sabitha, and Bruno saw her roll her eyes.

Bruno felt as though he was witnessing something only imagined. Dreamed up by someone else. The feelings, his fear, his shock, took him. He had to fight to bring his emotion under control, to focus on remaining unseeable.

'I don't need my daddy with me to go places,' Sabitha was saying. 'I'm rightly-good at finding my own way. Miss Hope says I'll go far and—'

'Sshhh now,' said Temperate Thomas, and he lowered

165

his voice. 'Ye're entering a rightly-special place, young one, so we must be especially respecting of it. Ye're very lucky, ye know. Very lucky to be invited here.'

'What kinda place?' asked Sabitha, and though she tried to roll her eyes again, give all appearance of not being bothered, Bruno knew she was flattered; nothing she liked more than feeling she was seeing something special, being allowed in someplace that others weren't. Her curiosity overtook anything else.

Maybe, Bruno thought, I'm not that different from her.

'What kinda place?' asked Sabitha again, but she got no reply.

She moved into the chamber where the Elders sat and Bruno shut his eyes, not trusting himself to remain unseen, feeling his Talent might falter under such stress. He held his eyes shut until he felt them pass; opening them again he watched Temperate Thomas lead Sabitha to the wooden throne in the centre of the chamber.

'Sit,' said the Temperate.

'It's that book!' said Sabitha, still standing and now pointing at *The Book of Black & White* held in the Temperate's arms. 'The one ye were making all the big fuss about. Can I have a look at it?' And she made to snatch it from him but was stopped – her hands outstretched, fingers spread, weight tipped forwards onto tiptoe, the Temperate with his Talent holding her back.

'Now,' said Temperate Thomas, 'I said to ye that this is a rightly-decent place and ye need to have respect for it.

Ye need to be doing as I say exactly when I say it, and no contrariness or being awkward. If there's one thing I don't like it's a child that doesn't know right-well what's best for them. Understand?'

Sabitha didn't move; couldn't, even in agreement.

'I think ye do,' said the Temperate. 'I see in yer eyes that ye're a good girl. And ye will go far indeed, if ye learn to do as ye're told.'

Sabitha was released, easing back, arms slowly falling to her sides. Bruno looked closer – a tear was sliding down her cheek.

'No need for tears,' said Temperate Thomas, and he lifted it from her with one long finger. 'Ye couldn't be in a safer place, truth-told, with those Rebels back. Sit yerself down, child.'

Sabitha turned and eyed the chair. But there could be no debate. She sat.

'Good girl,' said the Temperate.

As much of an urge as he had to snatch *The Book of Black & White*, Bruno felt an urge rising just as strong to snatch away Sabitha. He couldn't know what was about to happen, but the fear he saw seep into her, a girl transformed from the Sabitha he knew – with hands tucked under her legs, head lowered – this was enough to make him wish he could take her from the Elders.

The Temperate had returned to the stone table.

'Sabitha,' he said, 'do ye know what Jack Pitch says in *The Wrath* about a child's obedience to a person's Elders?'

167

'I'm not a child!' flashed Sabitha, and Bruno saw her reclaim some of her old self. 'I'm Coming-of-Age soon!'

Temperate Thomas half-turned. She demurred.

'It says,' he went on, turning back to the table, 'that a child's greatest duty is obedience. That their greatest interest should be in pleasing, satisfying and furthering the well-being, livelihood and love of their Elders.'

'I thought Jack Pitch was meaning parents and stuff,' said Sabitha. 'When he was saying "elders" he meant older people, not *Elders* like you.'

To his own surprise, Bruno felt a rush of pride for her.

The Temperate turned. In his hands he held a long, flat, narrow box.

'I am going to show ye something,' said Temperate Thomas, moving towards Sabitha. Bruno noticed that *The Book of Black & White* had been left on the stone table. 'Something no one else knows,' the Temperate went on. 'A piece of paper no one else in Pitch End has seen, except us Elders. Would ye like that?'

Sabitha turned in the chair, said nothing, but had fire in her eyes like Bruno had seen in class when she'd been praised by Miss Hope for reciting some dull, nonsensical fact of Pitch End Definitive History.

The Temperate smiled. He opened the narrow box, and Bruno saw something pale, curled. Temperate Thomas eased it free – a slow, reverent delicacy working his fingers – and Bruno remembered what had been mentioned only minutes before about a 'ripped, half-ruined but rightly-useful page'.

The container set aside, the Temperate approached Sabitha, unfurling the page. Bruno saw how ruined it was – black, no discernible words, scarred and pitted.

'What is it?' said Sabitha, and Bruno could see her interest dwindling, expression saying that nothing (in her opinion) like a charred page could ever be interesting.

'This,' said the Temperate, 'is what keeps myself and the other Elders as we are.'

'I don't like it,' said Sabitha, deciding.

'Now, now,' said Temperate Thomas. 'Ye know what happens to bad little girls and boys who disobey their Elders, don't ye?'

'They get taken away by the Rebels,' said Sabitha. 'But I wouldn't let that happen – I'd bite and scratch and fight, my father taught me how. And if I couldn't get away he'd come to save me!'

'But yer father wouldn't know,' said the Temperate. 'Because the Rebels, those clever divils, would put a Changeling in yer bed and it would look like yerself and talk like yerself and kiss and cuddle Mammy and Daddy. They'd be none the wiser, and in the meantime ye'd be with the Rebels. And all because ye were rightly-disobedient to yer Elders.'

And then, with a passion Bruno knew too well, Sabitha screamed: 'That isn't true!'

Temperate Thomas's response knocked Bruno off balance.

He fell against the wall as the Temperate lifted a stiff hand, a rush of Talent consuming Sabitha, holding her fast, forcing her to sit bolt upright in the chair.

He laid two fingers on her forehead.

'Be still now,' he said. 'Just remember what Jack Pitch said: *A child's greatest duty is obedience.*'

He withdrew his fingers. Sabitha's eyeballs twitched. None of the other Elders reacted.

Bruno's fear splintered him, tore his attention, and he thought his Talent must've faded for a moment as Sabitha's eyes turned, widened, seemingly spying him there. He forced his thoughts back to his Talent, screwed and stuck them . . .

'If ye're so keen to know about *The Book of Black & White,*' said Temperate Thomas, 'then I'll tell ye. I'm all for learning, for the right-real truth of things. Ye see, Arthur Pitch was fascinated by Talent. He went further into exploring it than anyone else ever in Pitch End's noble history. He was obsessed too, as I shared earlier in the town hall, with immortality. In living forever. Or, eventually, staying young forever. So he got all his thoughts down in this book. He believed that if ye could only get control of all that feeling, all that fire that makes Talent come through when ye Come-Of-Age – if ye could keep it, make it powerful, then ye would never grow a day older. Ye could stay on the verge of Coming-Of-Age, always. The key to it all is in the pages of *The Book of Black & White*. Secrets, if ye know how to be reading it.'

Temperate Thomas laid one finger on the dark, ruined page, and dragged. He let one digit descend in straight lines, top to bottom as though he could discern words there that Bruno couldn't. The movement drew a scratching, like a needle working against stone, which in turn drew more sound from the chamber: from Sabitha, a low moan as though fending off nightmares; from the Elders, groaning too and shifting in their stone chairs, an uncomfortable, indecent excitement agitating their bones. It made Bruno want to look away, be away. But he couldn't. He had to know.

The place on Sabitha's forehead where Temperate Thomas had touched began to sag, squirm, wrinkles appearing and deepening, multiplying like streams threading across land, carving small, dark paths. And at the same time the opposite was happening in Temperate Thomas – his few wrinkles softened, bright relief blushing his cheeks, the dark spots of age that peppered his hands fading.

Bruno had wanted to know, and now he wanted to forget; wished, for the first time in all the enforced Forgetting of Pitch End, to unknow something. But he knew he would never forget this.

'Ye see!' said the Temperate, holding his hands up like a triumphant criminal, one happily caught in the act. 'Ye see, my Elders! This is with only our one ruined page, just as we've been doing for ten turns. But with *The Book of Black & White* it can be not just one child at a time, but

171

many. And not just one Elder but all of us together! We must find all the remaining pocket watches, use them to restart the Clocktower and, as it says in Arthur Pitch's own words, use it to—'

From somewhere then, Sabitha found strength; one of her hands fixed around the pointed ball of Temperate Thomas's throat, the torn page from *The Book of Black & White* falling from his hand. He spluttered, hoping for help but the other Elders were too old, too unable to move.

And Bruno saw his only chance – he crept forwards fast, fingers reaching for *The Book of Black & White* long before he touched it . . . but the deeper he went into the chamber the more exposed he felt, not wholly unseeable but just a discreet presence hoping to remain unnoticed. He felt as though the book itself knew that it was about to be taken and was eroding his Talent, determined to reveal him.

His foot caught on uneven stone and he stumbled. He looked up – the Temperate was looking at him.

No more hesitation – Bruno scooped *The Book of Black & White* from the stone table, turned and ran as Temperate Thomas snatched out for him, hoping that Sabitha's strength would hold longer –

A wail from the Elders, hollowed chorus as Bruno tried to refocus – *I'm nothing, no one can see me, I'm not here, I'm gone* – as he passed into the long passageway, but again, in his too-big shoes, Bruno stumbled, and he knew before it happened what he was going to do.

He fell.

The slam of his body, the slam of the book, woke the slumbering Cat-Sentries, and their screams – all recorded, human agony – shattered his Talent completely.

'The *book*! Get the *book*!' The cry of the Temperate –

Cat-Sentries pounced and tore at Bruno, same as Temperate Thomas's own in the town hall, but with no Louise to save him he fought one-handed, the other scooping up *The Book of Black & White*. Pain ripped his cheek, but not as deeply as in the town hall – these Sentries were slow, sluggish enough that he could fling them off, kick and send them cracking off the wall.

On he charged, up spiral stairs almost on all fours, turn after turn, satchel thudding on his back, climb feeling like forever then rising into the body of the Clocktower, shouting, 'Pace! Pace, let me out!'

The door didn't open.

'Stop! In the name of the Elders of Pitch End!' came Temperate Thomas's cry against the caterwauling of the Sentries.

Then the door moved and Bruno was out and through before it had opened even half.

It was raining again, a world in agony.

Pace retrieved the pocket watch from its niche and handed it to Bruno.

The door rolled shut.

Silently, Pace laid his stooped weight against one of the statues. Bruno noticed 'Arthur Pitch, the Seventh Son' chipped across its chest. The statue leaned –

Footsteps rose fast in the Clocktower –

And Arthur Pitch toppled, falling across the doorway.

A thud inside – the uncanny urge, Bruno felt sure, of Temperate Thomas's Talent. How long before he forced his way out?

Bruno looked to Pace and followed the Witherman's gaze – at *The Book of Black & White* that Bruno held in his hands. The weight of the thing dragged on him. But Bruno's worry, heavier still, was threatening to anchor him where he stood. He thought: what have I begun?

XVI

The Passing Gate

'Pace,' said Bruno, breathless but feeling he needed to tell, let someone else know. 'I saw the Temperate. *Children.* He's been—'

'I know,' said Pace. 'And now ye know too, and know how rightly-important all this is.'

Another impact of Talent shook the statue of Arthur Pitch.

'Where do we go?' asked Bruno.

'Only one place safe now,' Pace breathed. His body shivered, back stiffening like a coil of wire trying to straighten itself. 'Outta Pitch End altogether.'

Then the Witherman moved off, faster than Bruno could've thought. Bruno followed, *The Book of Black & White* growing heavier the longer he bore it.

Across the town square and then at the entrance to Old Town they stopped –

Enforcers. Cigarettes poked from their mouths, a

smouldering constellation. They were collected on the very same darkway Bruno had ventured down hours before, in what he considered a different, more innocent life. And, so swiftly they could've been dragged from ten-turn hibernation, posters bearing the face of Dr Jonathan Bloom gawped from every window and door. Bruno doubted whether the man was as demonstrably and diabolically evil as the posters made out – eyes just slits, brow heavy and primitive, hair tangled like madness and in his right hand a dagger that looked like it had been dipped in something dark. A gruesome legend had been rendered above his face in drops of the same stuff that coated the knife:

HAVE YOU SEEN THIS SWINE?

Bruno adjusted *The Book of Black & White*; the weight of a stone in his arms, it felt too obvious, even rendered unseeable, to carry. He opened his satchel and stuffed it in, its bulk pushing everything else aside, then shouldered it again.

They waited. Bruno looked to Pace for guidance, but he said and indicated nothing.

A palpitation of thunder, short flickers of lightning and Bruno was shown shuddering Enforcers. He thought: they're barely older than I am, and they're afeared of everything.

Knowing this made his own fear fade a little. Just enough. He took the decision. '*Now*,' he whispered. He tugged on

Pace's sleeve, both sinking deep into the protection of their Talent, hurrying forwards, clinging to buildings, dodging Enforcers, leaping puddles like pewter that held disturbed reflections.

They reached the end of the darkway, and between them and the high stone wall that surrounded Pitch End was a narrow strip of swampy ground – Mickleward Marsh. It encircled the town, shore to shore, between buildings and the wall. Narrow-looking but deep, Bruno had heard. But, he wondered, where's the Passing Gate?

An Enforcer close by provided it – a lantern was hooked on the crook of his arm and, as he paused in his patrol on the edge of the Marsh, the Passing Gate bloomed: high and wide, magnificently rusted and corroded, a mass of every kind of metal Bruno could recognise, welded and nailed and woven together. Stretching (and to Bruno, it really *did* look stretched) from the ground – a series of spikes leaving not a hand of space to worm under – to a stone arch humped like a raised eyebrow over more spikes. A plaque, tarnished, declared in all Elder verbosity:

THIS PASSING GATE WAS SEALED ON THE ORDERS
OF TEMPERATE THOMAS II
WITH THE EXPRESS HOPE OF PRESERVING
THE RIGHTLY-DECENT PITCH END WAY OF LIFE
(AND TO KEEP OUT FOREIGNERS)
ON 30TH APRIL, YEAR +290.

HE – OR SHE – WHO OPENS IT, AND LEAVES BY IT,
MAY CONSIDER THEMSELVES FOREVER BANISHED . . .
AS THEY'LL NOT BE LET BACK IN.
HAVE A PLEASANT PITCH END DAY.

'What do we do when we get out even?' Bruno whispered to Pace. 'Where to?'

'Mount Tome,' said Pace. 'Central peak of the Elm Tree Mountains, that's where ye're heading. Other Rebels who've been hiding out, same as Louise, they'll be waiting for ye.'

Yet another pull of thunder, fiercer rain, all silver and black.

Bruno was overwhelmed with sudden worry then: if he left Pitch End, violated the Gate – was 'banished' and not let back in – would he never see his mother again? Never come home again? He may have spent so many turns imagining leaving the town, but on the brink of doing it he felt –

'They've stolen the book! The Rebels have *The Book of Black & White*!'

'They've stolen the key to the Gate! Prepare to fire! Anything that moves, shoot it!'

Temperate Thomas, then the Marshall.

Bruno had no time for further feeling.

'Pace,' he said. 'I—'

'I'll give ye time,' he said. 'Go slow across the strip of Marsh, that's the trick.'

178

'But—'

'None of yer arguing now, Bruno. Just trust yerself up there. Ye've got yer father's way of seeing things, and ye've got the truth now. Trust in that and ye won't be going wrong. Keep the book safe, and that pocket watch too. Do ye understand?'

Bruno nodded.

'Good lad,' he said. A final rest of his hand on Bruno's head and then Pace left him, vanished. The Witherman didn't want Bruno to see him any more. He was alone.

'Be securing the Gate!'

The Temperate and the Marshall were approaching at a run, trailing Enforcers, but before anyone could act on anything the darkway was swamped with Cat-Sentries. From roofs they fell as though chasing something – someone? – unseen, crying their recorded cries, climbing the legs of Enforcers, pouncing with paws sprouting blades, and the Marshall kicked them away as his Enforcers, no more than boys, squealed. And in the confusion Bruno heard that hot blast, familiar:

'None of yer usual waiting about,' said Louise. He suddenly had a very large, heavy key in his hand. 'When it opens, ye'll have ten ticks, so don't be hanging about! Go on, for *Pitch* sake!'

Bruno ran, slipping-almost-falling, then stopped. He took slow steps, feeling the Marsh churn beneath, ready to take him if he moved too swift. He turned to look –

Cat-Sentries still in disarray, leaping, thrown –

Bruno slipped, fell onto his front and grabbed out for the Gate, pulling himself across the last metre of Marsh and then straightening to search the Gate's surface. He found no place for the key to go. Then lightning like a silent scream showed him; he screwed the key into the dark space for it, a loud graze of metal on metal. Cogs, chains, locks awoke. The entire Gate was reanimated, mechanisms spinning, clicking and whirring in one interminable, ancient movement, teeth locking into teeth, chains clattering from one end to the other until, with a jarring prang, the gate sprang open and back. A steady, ticking countdown began. No chance of such a thing going unnoticed –

'The Gate!' cried the Temperate, looming out of the rain, any Cat-Sentry that approached him being thrown back by his Talent. He looked exhausted, Bruno thought. Perhaps what he'd done to Sabitha, using his Talent to steal her youth, had drained him?

Ten ticks.

And then, like the whipping away of a dark sheet, Pace reappeared. But not just for Bruno's eyes –

'There!' cried the Marshall. 'Stop him!'

Bruno, intent on his Talent, not wanting to leave Pace to the mercy of the powers of Pitch End but remembering the insistence of the Witherman and Louise, slipped under the arch of the Passing Gate, and out.

I'm through, thought Bruno. I'm gone. I've left Pitch End.

'Shoot him!' The Marshall ordered.

Bruno turned. A spurt of blood left Pace's kneecap and

he crumpled without a cry. Bruno wanted to cry out, to run back and help. Being shot not enough, another opportunistic Enforcer landed a blow to the Witherman's mouth with his rifle butt.

'We've got him!' shouted the Enforcer who'd taken the shot.

'I helped too!' called the second, the one who'd probably broken Pace's jaw.

'Keep shooting, ye fools!' the Temperate shouted. 'He doesn't have the book, he wasn't alone!'

'Shoot at *what*, Temperate Thomas? There int nothing there!'

'At the open gateway, ye numbskull! Someone is standing there, I *know* it!'

The Gate continued to tick down, hadn't shut. And Bruno, standing beyond the wall, outside Pitch End, watched the Enforcers focus, taking aim against the empty archway. Already to Bruno they had the appearance of ghosts, or the Shadows from *The Tall Tale of the Dishonest Elder*. He was beyond them now, set apart. He didn't move. Any twitch might reveal him, darkness itself peeling back to show, betray him.

All the mechanisms on the gate began to churn back, to slide home –

'*Stop!*' Temperate Thomas bellowed and he rushed forwards, his eyes locked on the key Bruno had left in the Gate. A Cat-Sentry leapt (or was thrown?) into his path and he stumbled, fell into the Marsh –

181

Bruno darted back towards the gate –

The Temperate crushed the Sentry with a snap of his Talent and rushed on, sinking to the knees but still coming –

The Gate shut. Bruno snatched the key from the lock. He was locked out, Temperate Thomas and the Enforcers locked in.

The Temperate came so close to the Gate that Bruno backed away. He thought that it might merely surrender itself, come apart under fear, the presence of the Head of the Elders enough to wither it. The same eyes that had shamed every conscience at the town meeting were fixed on the dark. But Bruno couldn't be sure if he was being seen or merely sought. Still he didn't want to move. Once again – hardly dared breathe.

The Passing Gate shook, and Bruno knew Temperate Thomas was trying to move the thing with his Talent. Only moments and then it ceased; the Temperate leaned against the Gate, breathing deeply. He had no energy left, thought Bruno. Or perhaps – as Bruno was learning himself – he couldn't summon enough of the emotion needed, enough power and concentration to fire his Talent.

'Open it,' muttered the Temperate, breathless but still looking at the space where Bruno stood.

The Enforcers looked to one another behind the Temperate's back. Bruno saw fear transmit amongst them – they'd been schooled for ten turns on the evils of the world outside the wall, beyond the Gate.

'But how?' said one, the youngest present, stepping into the Marsh, falling over himself to be helpful.

'Don't ask me how,' Temperate Thomas told him, 'just do it.'

'But we dunno how to be opening the Passing Gate without a key,' said the same Enforcer. 'I thought that *you* would know, seeing as ye closed it. I mean' (he began to dig) 'I have Forgotten everything like ye said we should so I don't remember right-well.'

Said with an embarrassing truthfulness, no malice intended. Just what the Elders preached: honesty, subservience, Forgetting. But that didn't stop the Temperate from interpreting it otherwise, from sweeping around and slapping the boy across the jaw, hard.

'*Never* speak to me like that again,' he said. 'Ye understand me well?'

The Enforcer could do nothing but assure him. Yes, he understood.

'Good. Now, I want this gate open. I don't care how ye do it. Just do. And I want a horde of Enforcers to head into the forest.' The Temperate pointed to the mass of trees rippling with storm on the slope of Mount Tome.

The struck Enforcer, now dabbing a bubble of blood on his split lip, looked unsure. But under the gaze of the Temperate, he could again do nothing but nod in agreement and promise in a mumble that yes, it would be done.

The Temperate walked, half-waded, back through the Marsh.

'Sir,' said the Marshall, when Temperate Thomas had rejoined him, 'with all due respect, my men have captured the Witherman.'

The Temperate snatched a lantern from the Marshall's hands, held it high and said in a whisper fierce enough to carry through the gush of rain: 'He wasn't alone, Marshall. It's clear as anything . . .'

He lifted the lantern higher. A rush of light showed two sets of tracks in the Marsh – Temperate Thomas's and Bruno's.

The Marshall said nothing.

'The Atlas boy,' said Temperate Thomas.

'My men will be rightly-fearful,' said the Marshall, glancing at the Enforcers. 'They've heard the stories, like all of us. Tales of whispers in the mountains. Phantasms, the dead left there, cursed children wandering through the forest and in the dark places under the earth.'

'*Children?*' repeated the Temperate. 'This is the greatest fear of the Head of the Pitch End Enforcers – *children?*'

The Marshall didn't reply.

'If that is yer men's greatest fear,' said Temperate Thomas, 'then that is what they'll have to be facing. We must stamp out this rebellion before it gets wind in its sails.'

'Ye will try,' said Pace then, words crackling from a broken jaw. 'And ye'll get yer lesson, Ignatius Thomas. Ye've taken too much, tried too rightly-hard, treated too many people too badly. Not just anger and fear can be used to power a Talent. But ye wouldn't know that, being the sanctimonious sod that ye are.'

Temperate Thomas turned to Pace. 'Ye have something,' said the Temperate. 'Something I'm wanting to claim, *Wither*. Let's see if I can use my Talent – humble as it is. Let's see if I can be taking it.'

Bruno watched Temperate Thomas's Talent find new purpose. And Pace watched as his own fingers – plucked as though by a breeze, like emptying gloves – began to dissolve, a stream of ash peeling away from them. Bruno noticed the intense working of Temperate Thomas's digits, working as though bound together and he was trying to free them.

Enforcers all around looked to one another, transfixed, terrified.

'The Rebels,' said Temperate Thomas, his voice as low as it had been in the chamber beneath the Clocktower, his tone as gently explanatory as when he'd addressed Sabitha. 'And all who are for following them will soon be forgotten, Witherman. Soon, they'll be nothing more than dust.'

A final, swift rush of the Temperate's Talent consumed Pace, unpicking him furiously, particle by particle: feet first, legs, torso, chest, charring without fire, humanity evaporating. Last of all the face. Disbelief widened the Witherman's eyes, taking their last look at Bruno.

The leaves of the Faerie Fort, thought Bruno, ridiculously, before the end.

Pace was there, and then not, survived only by Dr Bloom's addition, the old, battered clock without hands falling with a dull clatter to the cobbles. And the last glimpse Bruno took before he turned, ran – Temperate Thomas, hand on one knee, crouching for the pocket watch, on his face such a satisfaction, such a stretching smile that the dark couldn't disguise it.

PART THREE

THE REBELS

XVII
Boy and Blade

The mountainside was softening to sludge, every step becoming a lunge, almost impossible to advance. Behind Bruno, the shouts of Enforcers rigging explosives. Ahead, a rustling darkness he knew in daylight as the forest that wound itself around the middle of the Elm Tree Mountains, trees falling just short of the three main peaks that formed Pitch End's other horizon. He looked high and saw – as Pace had told him – Mount Tome, central peak, his apparent destination, its tip as jagged as the shattered neck of a bottle.

A single cry from the Marshall: '*Back!* Stand yerselves back!'

Bruno powered on, legs lifting higher, trees surely closer, aware that his track through the mud – faltering, gouging footsteps – was as clear on the mountainside as the wake of a fishing boat on a placid sea. But total darkness was near enough, the leaves frantic in the wind.

Then an explosion –

Heat felt first, sound later, Bruno was catapulting upwards and forwards, slope rushing towards him. The landing was soft. Soft to the point of yielding to the point of swallowing; as soon as he landed he tried to keep moving, lift himself clear of the mud, but the ground embraced hands, his fingers splayed and already submerged to the wrists.

'Follow the track in the mud! Just like the Temperate said!'

They were stupid, Bruno decided then. Nothing but stupid. And he'd feel even more stupidity in himself if he was caught by them. Why hadn't he taken another route? Skulked by the wall and waited till they'd left?

He'd stopped struggling, was sinking slower but still sinking. Then more pain – his scalp! Bruno looked up and saw a figure with hand outstretched, tugging on his hair, trying to pull him from the mud. He couldn't see a face. Bruno offered his hand as a better option and whoever it was released the hair and took the hand. From below, Bruno thought this figure looked no taller than himself (someone about to Come-Of-Age?) but he had as much strength as a man and freed Bruno from the mud with a great heave and a churning squelch.

Lantern light skimmed the ground, touching on Bruno. He froze like a spooked hare.

An Enforcer cried, 'This way! Track's towards the trees now!'

'Do ye have the book?' said the voice of whoever had

pulled Bruno to safety. A boy, thought Bruno but, like Louise at first, the boy wasn't entirely, decidedly there.

Bruno nodded.

'Well do ye?' asked the voice again, giving Bruno a dig in the side with something sharp.

'*Yes*,' said Bruno.

'Good.' And then the boy became clear, as seeable as anyone could be in the dark. 'Those Enforcers better not be coming into our wood,' the boy said. 'They'll be regretting that, I can tell ye now. Let's go. Quick-smart.'

The boy dragged Bruno on. By the hand thankfully, not the hair. On the mud, the boy didn't slip or falter once. But Bruno could see a problem in this boy –

'They'll see ye!' Bruno told him desperately.

'They won't,' the boy said right back. 'I'm unseeable to them. We've all the Talent – all the Rebels. I'm just letting ye see me now. Understand?'

Bruno understood but didn't reply, just kept going; struggling, still falling more than advancing.

'Take em off,' the boy said. 'Those big oul shoes of yers!'

'No,' Bruno said, then added, meaning it – 'I need them.'

'Ye'd be surprised what ye don't need when ye get rid of it,' said the boy. 'Suppose ye'll be needing them rightly though when ye're walking to see the Temperate. Ye'll look rightly-presentable.'

Bruno sighed. He balanced with one hand against a tree, tugging at the laces in turn and letting his father's old shoes fall away. Once again he was just in socks in mud and rain and night.

'Don't just be leaving them!' said the boy, who ducked for Bruno's shoes, tied the laces together and flung them into the air like a slingshot. They thudded far off. The attention of most Enforcers followed.

'Good job,' the boy told himself, watching lantern light veer away.

They didn't move. Bruno could see no expression on the boy's face, had only a sense of two wide, watchful eyes overhung with thick, curled hair.

They waited.

'Go!' cried the boy suddenly, loud as a gunshot, pushing Bruno on as though this were all an entertainment, that being caught would mean only bringing the end of the game. And a pair of Enforcers of course heard, saw and ('This way here!') followed.

Bruno found it only a bit easier in his sock-soles to negotiate the slope, the boy still leading him by the hand; the Enforcers in the forest now, cracking branches. Bruno imagined what they must be seeing, following: the boughs ahead being swept aside of their own volition.

'Up here,' said the boy, a little quieter.

He cupped his hands, laced his fingers together and took Bruno's socked foot in the sudden stirrup, heaving him up towards a low-hanging branch. Bruno remembered his climbing attempts in Old Town and tried to do better. But his fingers only clawed, legs pedalling like a dozing dog, and he just about dangled and no more. The branch was a lucky choice though, strong enough to hold his scrambling body. The boy's support vanished suddenly from beneath him as he scaled the tree too, though more expertly than Bruno – grasping a branch with both hands and slipping feet first and upside down into the tangle of branches and coming to rest, flat, just as Bruno managed to achieve something like stability.

The Enforcers ran out of trail just below. Neither Enforcer spoke, just directed their rifles ahead, lantern beams stabbing the dark. They stood, waiting for a clue to visit them.

A few moments passed.

Bruno could hear other Enforcers, somewhere else –

'Any sign? Any sound?'

Rain leaked from above, one branch to another, touching Bruno's hair, ears, toes. His foot jerked, the branch beneath him creaked and the Enforcers shared a look with one another, infinitesimal, before aiming upwards and firing off a shot each. The first struck high into the tree, scattering birds, and the second snapped against the branch supporting Bruno who couldn't help but cry out as it gave way. He fell, landing and rolling across the mud –

'What's doing that?' said one of the Enforcers, eyes wide, seeing nothing but the long graze caused by Bruno's unseeable body.

'Some kinda phantasm,' replied the other. 'I knew these woods were rightly-haunted. Just shoot at it!'

Bruno willed himself to be seen, even held up his hands like it would do any good but the boy who'd pulled him free of the mud acted first –

He leapt, unseen by anyone but Bruno but surely heard as he gave a guttering war cry and pulled a dagger with a warped blade from his belt. No delay, no time for the Enforcers to react, he wrapped his forearm around one of their necks and dragged the blade across – a snap, a jerk in the dark.

Bruno looked away.

The second Enforcer took off, lantern falling and blinking out, his rifle rattling useless at his side, abandoning his comrade without hesitation. Bruno knew they wouldn't have long before more came. He still didn't look. He'd seen death before, murder even, but that had been ten turns ago. He couldn't rid himself of the vision of the blade, scoring his sight – the tug of the boy's arm, the flash across the neck, something about it so easy, perfunctory.

'Ye're just gonna lie about in the muck then, are ye?' said the boy, his bare foot falling beside Bruno's face, looking inhuman, like a slab of compacted mud. 'Hardly Michael Atlas's son, if ye're gonna be a cowardly boat-jumper when things get tough.' He offered his hand. 'We've not got a whole bag of time, ye know!'

Sure enough, the alarm had been raised – more Enforcers were penetrating the forest, would soon find the body. Bruno took the boy's hand against any good judgement and was dizzied by the abrupt wrench to his feet. He wanted badly to puke, but didn't have time; like after he'd punched Sabitha, he felt contaminated by violence.

'I know a place,' the boy told him. 'It's safe enough. Before that though . . .'

He left Bruno's hand to hover, ducking down to the dark heap of the Enforcer. He undid buttons, forced his hand into the Enforcer's tunic and came away with a small box.

'We'll need these for later, calm the oul nerves,' he told Bruno, and on they went.

More lantern light, casting shadows like lightning rods, and Bruno saw the boy's hand – he'd stolen a pack of cigarettes. He felt closer to retching.

Not much farther on there was a fresh sound – the scramble of paws and pant and growl of hounds, joining the chase.

'They want ye right badly. In here,' said the boy suddenly, and he pointed to the base of a tree. Bruno stopped, reaching out, feeling a deep knot in the trunk.

'*In!*' the boy insisted.

Bruno, willed by the boy's hands, pushed on, finding the knot ready to stretch, to accommodate, and he slipped – pointed hands and bowed head, legs, ankles, socked feet and all, satchel catching a bit – into a tunnel that bored downwards like a fall, through cold and wet, roots snatching at his clothes, into the heart of the mountain. The tunnel left his sides and he braced his arms across his face just as he collided with hard ground, forehead taking the brunt of the landing. Not a tick later, the boy landed beside-almost-on-top of him, though he managed to find his feet quicker.

The boy cried out again, the same holler of elation as above when he'd leapt on the Enforcer. 'Now that's the way to get round an Enforcer!' he shouted.

Bruno emptied his stomach finally, easily.

When he was done, he concentrated only on breathing, fingers searching his face for any wound. But he was so saturated with rain he couldn't tell what might've been blood. He needed to know where he was but couldn't see anything. Listened, but there was nothing much to hear except his own breathing and a steady dripping sound, like he was surrounded by dribbling taps. He sneezed and heard an echo.

There was a spark of light so close Bruno whimpered. It was the boy striking a match, lighting one of his stolen cigarettes. He sucked on it, its light giving a brief impression of a face; Bruno registered again a ragged mass of curls, then a glitter of stubble on the chin and two eyes dominating – even by the temporary light, Bruno knew they were bright blue.

'Is Louise safe?' the boy asked.

'I think so,' said Bruno, still not getting to his feet. To his own ears his voice sounded too big for his battered body. 'She gave me the key to the Passing Gate, then I got out. And I think—'

'Ye *think*?' said the boy. 'Well, good thing she can take care of herself.'

'She told me to leave,' said Bruno, feeling the need to explain. 'I didn't just run off.'

'I know ye didn't,' said the boy. 'She can be pushy at the best of times. And what about Pace-the-Witherman, how was he when ye left him?'

Bruno could say nothing. How could he explain it? Explain what he'd seen, what he'd felt at what he'd seen. His silence said too much.

'So that's one less on our side,' said the boy.

'He didn't give in,' said Bruno, feeling again he needed to make clear. 'Even at the end, he wasn't for just giving in to the Temperate.'

'Stood by and just watched, did ye?' said the boy. He hadn't returned to the cigarette. 'Again – not a bit like yer father.'

'Ye knew him?' Bruno asked.

'I did indeed,' said the boy. He sucked again on the cigarette, finally, the light conjuring the same view – hair, stubble, wide eyes . . .

'Then ye know who I am,' said Bruno, trying to make it sound a statement, not a hopeful question.

'I do indeed,' said the boy. 'Thing is – do ye know *me*?'

Bruno felt something squirm at the back of his mind, something close to memory, but closer still to experience. Truth was, he felt as though he *should* know who this boy was. But the knowledge didn't arrive with him.

'No,' he had to say. 'Except that ye're one of the Rebels?'

Another drag – slow this time.

'Indeed I am,' said the boy, varying his response only the slightest. 'Son of a Rebel, now a Rebel meself. Just like you.' He took the deepest drag yet. This time the light swelled to reveal something of the ground: crude formations – rock, mud? – surrounded them, things that Bruno's imagination was keen to interpret as crouching animals or cowering children, his eyes darting from shape to shape, trying to take them all in. Then gone. The cigarette fell and its light was squeezed under the boy's bare foot.

Dark again, and the impression of unknown space all around.

'Here.'

Something soft struck Bruno's face.

'Lie on that there,' said the boy. 'Ye look like ye haven't slept in a long while. I'll wake ye when it's time to head on up the mountain. There's some food in there, a match too, case ye need some light.'

'I'm not afeared of the dark,' said Bruno.

'Didn't say ye were,' said the boy. 'I was thinking more if ye needed to take a piss or something.'

The boy's last words receded. Bruno listened and heard the faint peel and slap of bare feet on stone, moving away.

'What's yer name?' Bruno called, standing up at last, needing something certain before he could rest or sleep, neither of which seemed probable.

In the wake of his question he felt a tension like the tautening of a fiddle string – a connecting line between himself and the boy, long-established, now winding tight.

The boy's footsteps stopped. Then he spoke, proud and unhurried: 'I am Nicholas M. Delby Junior. And my da was the man who, so they've always been saying in Pitch End, murdered yer father.'

XVIII
Cavern of the Forgotten

It was a familiar nightmare for him: Bruno screaming but no one hearing, no sound even coming out. In the Discussion Chamber he was crying for justice, raging against the Temperate but with no one who cared. All the faces of the Pitch Enders watched. And where their eyes should've been were mouths, toothless, contorting, keenly condemning. And where their mouths should've been were pocket watches running backwards at sickening speed. Their legs were deep-rooted . . . then roots proper that squirmed for purchase, inching forwards for him with fingers dark twigs, nails dull needles, scalps disgorging boughs like the broken roofs of Old Town, their mouths widening to shriek, a righteous roar, deafening –

Bruno woke and sat up, gasping, rapping his elbow against stone. Sweat beetled down his back. Stone, not mattress? It took him a few moments to remember where he was, who he was with, and what he had stolen. He rubbed his eyes and looked about.

The place he'd slept in was lighter, perhaps. Morning must've arrived, he thought, and somehow managed to enter even this place, allowing less than a total dark. The stone shapes he'd glimpsed the night before were clearer, slimed with moisture, hunched like boils on skin and not so much resembling things from life above.

'Awake, are we?'

Bruno turned, breath catching, inhaling and coughing on a serpent of blueish cigarette smoke; Nicholas M. Delby Junior was leaning against the wall of the cavern, watching.

The son of the man they say murdered my father, remembered Bruno.

'Ye could have that food now,' said Nicholas.

Bruno didn't want to do just as directed, but he was hungry. He dragged his legs closer to his chest, found the package and opened it. Inside was a fist of hearth bread, a small and flat, sweet-smelling griddle cake, a fawn-coloured apple and the remains of a catfish. He cracked the bread against rock, ripped and tried to eat, but could hardly swallow it was so tough. He switched to fish, discovering bones with each nibble, dragging them from between his teeth. And all the time Bruno examined Nicholas in sideways looks, trying to work him out.

The boy's face was so engrained with filth it looked as though it'd been tattooed there. A shift – a threadbare vest stitched and re-stitched, mended with wool and thread across the chest and under the arms – was all he wore for a top, a pair of torn trousers on his lower half. Then back to the eyes – blue, as Bruno had thought the night before, and brimful with whatever he was thinking, like two flooded saucers. Now he looked only calm and watchful. And despite the wildness of his appearance, Nicholas didn't seem remotely abashed. One hand remained fixed around the hilt of a dagger that was fastened to his belt, the warped blade clean of what it had recently done. There were other things alongside the blade, but it was still too dim for Bruno to be sure what they were, except that they all had a burnished look that declined light.

Finished with what he could of the fish, Bruno got up, adding the apple to his pocket. He only realised then that (apart from the one nightmare he'd woken from) he'd probably had his most undisturbed night of sleep in many months, countless turns.

Nicholas took another drag, smoked the cigarette as though it were an entitlement. He offered the box to Bruno, who shook his head.

'Are we going on?' said Bruno. He settled the hearth bread and griddle cake in the blanket he'd been given and folded it up. Then he said, felt he should add, '*Nicholas.*'

'*Nic*,' came the reply. 'Call me Nic. Ye'll be the odd one out if ye don't.'

'Right,' replied Bruno.

He kept his back to Nic as he unfastened the flap of his satchel, briefly, to check on the book, the pocket watch – still there. He buckled it tightly and lifted it onto his shoulders.

'Ye have yer father's pocket watch,' said Nic.

Bruno didn't turn.

'Yes,' said Bruno. 'Why?'

'And tell me this,' said Nic, 'does the Temperate have Pace's pocket watch?'

'Yes,' said Bruno. He felt that Nic already knew the answer. 'And Gumbly-the-Witherman's was taken out so he—'

'Has all the Withermen's pocket watches now,' Nic finished.

Bruno turned, and saw that Nic held a pocket watch of his own on his palm.

'Me da's,' said Nic. 'Left it to me, same as yer father left his to you.' A click, a sombre whirr, and the lid of Nic's pocket watch flowered. He allowed Bruno to see: not a clock face beneath, instead the full, gaping face of the moon, a pale coin of light in Nic's hand. 'That Temperate has been searching ever since the end of the Single Season War for all eight pocket watches.'

'That's why he did it,' said Bruno suddenly, voice echoing, realisation sending a shiver through his words. 'All the clocks and everything – that's why he Elder-Ordered to collect them all ten turns ago?'

But Nic didn't seem to see a point in answering. Instead, pocket watch refastened to his belt, more questions of his own – 'What else do ye know about the Elders? About that book ye're carrying on yer back?'

Bruno hesitated. He knew this boy was a Rebel – knew he was suddenly an ally he needed to accept, knew they were linked already through their fathers, part of the same side – but still he felt unsure.

'Ye're a deep one, aren't ye?' said Nic. He smiled. 'Tell me this then: what did ye see?'

Bruno cleared his throat. 'I saw what they're going to be doing,' he said at last.

'Ye mean,' said Nic, 'what they've *already* been doing.'

Bruno nodded. 'Under the Clocktower,' he said, 'they took a girl I went to Hedge School with and made her old. And the Temperate became younger.'

'Who was this girl?' asked Nic.

'The Marshall's daughter,' said Bruno.

'Is that right?' said Nic. 'They're getting more desperate if they're risking upsetting their own supporters.'

'They're planning to do it to more,' said Bruno. 'The Elders are gonna take all the youth from the children in Pitch End, keep themselves young and still in power.'

Bruno thought he heard Nic swear, low and breathless, the cigarette in his fingers continuing to burn low, sending smoke.

Bruno went on: 'The Temperate said something else. Something about restarting the Clocktower, needing the pocket watches, and *The Book of Black & White*.'

'Aye, Dr Bloom said that the Temperate would try do that,' said Nic.

'Why?' asked Bruno.

'Dunno,' said Nic quickly, and this time he turned away. 'But if the Elders are after the pocket watches then we have to keep them safe. Dr Bloom said someday we'd need the watches to defeat the Elders. A day that'll be coming very soon.'

Nic took one last suck from the cigarette, then flicked it away.

'We need to be going, quick-smart,' said Nic. 'Temperate will be making plans – we need to be doing the same.'

Nic took up a bag of his own – a fold of sacking that might've held spuds once, bound with a loop of twine that he slipped his arm through. He said, 'Good to have ye with us, Bruno,' and he clapped Bruno between the shoulder blades, like they were very old, very dear friends. He took the blanket from Bruno's arms, food still inside, and stuffed it into his bag as he started across the cavern.

'Come on!' shouted Nic.

Bruno followed but had taken only a few steps; a single drop of water fell from the ceiling of the cavern and the ground itself rippled a response.

'What's this?' he fired at Nic.

'*That*,' Nic said, the word tremulous with echoes, 'is something ye shouldn't have to see.'

Bruno thought this was no kind of answer so he edged closer, each foot balanced on a mound of rock. Another drop, another ripple. He realised what he was looking at –

'A lake,' he murmured.

Then he saw faces in the water –

'What are they?' he cried, recoiling but almost toppling in too, the sight magnetic.

'What are what?' said Nic.

'Ye know what – the faces in the water!'

'They're not *in* the water,' said Nic, and his voice this time quivered with more than echoes.

'But . . .' Bruno began, then understood.

He looked up. Fastened to the ceiling of the cavern, their bodies wrapped in swaddling, everything covered but their faces, some with eyes pinned open – the dead. The *Forgotten*. Some were easier to recognise as bodies than others. Some looked as though they'd long since fused with the cavern itself, were no more than limb, bone; protruding from the ceiling like the barren, jointed roots of something above. Many of them, Bruno noticed, were the size of children.

He watched the slow *drip-drip* of moisture from above to below, and shivered. He could never have slept a wink, not even stayed there, if he'd known what was above.

'Cavern of the Forgotten,' said Nic, suddenly closer. He had a way of creeping up, remaining unseen and unheard even without Talent.

'This is where . . .' said Bruno, with an added revelation to follow the rest, 'where they've been taking and storing them, instead of the sea burials?'

Nic didn't nod or agree. Instead he dipped down, found a stone on the ground and hurled out into the water. Only then did Bruno get the truest sense of how wide and deep the lake was. The surface crinkled, reflected faces wavering, mouths ruffling like silenced laughter.

'And this is where,' said Nic, 'they've been hiding all the children.'

Bruno's understanding took a moment. But then truth, a horror, came to him: the children the Elders had been stealing youth from, stealing from the town. Small bodies, faces old. His breathing grew louder, hurt his heart. He swallowed and the sound was massive. And eyes more accepting, more willing to see, other things appeared to him – pale, near-silver, like delinquent fragments of moon swapping night sky for seclusion, a cache of objects beneath the water, in the shallows. He moved closer, kneeled to see: a knife with an ivory handle, blade bent in two; a silver Birth Bracelet, the wishes of the inscription lost to age; a doll's face, porcelain smeared with mud, eyes cracked, sulking and longing for the rest of its body; and picto-frames, many, one in particular double-sided and hinged, two portraits on either side with their gaze meant for one another. Their eyes had been scratched away.

'Objects they usually send off with them to sea,' said Nic. 'Or things the Enforcers go and collect after they die so they can be properly Forgotten. All reminders got dumped here too. Precious things to these people. Don't look like much now though, do they? Just things, no meaning.' He sighed. 'Leave the dead where they are' (spat on his fingers and blessed himself, briefly) 'and the living, take with ye. On we go.'

Nic moved off.

Bruno stared a while longer into the lake, till the surface was composed. Then he turned away, watching where Nic placed his feet, in what way he curved his soles to fit the curve of the rocks, following exactly in his shadow, and not once wanting to look back.

XIX

The Tall Tale of the Miner's Fiery Heart

Nic led Bruno through passages child-sized – narrow crevasses littered with scraps of light, so cramped they were made to move sidelong in careful steps, grazing knees and elbows. Bruno kept as far behind Nic as he could without losing him. They didn't speak much, except for some brief exchanges of courtesy, which suited Bruno well – he wanted to think. So much needed dissecting, examining, everything upset by his escape from Pitch End. What had been left behind, what had he set going? What schemes had Temperate Thomas fallen into, what plans? And his mother – what might she now be enduring, because of him?

A long time of journeying, thinking – Bruno feeling exhausted but determined not to show it – and then a deep rolling sound rose.

The tunnel widened, the walls laced with white and shimmer, and they took a final corner and were shown a pool polished with light. A tall shaft above told Bruno how far underground they must be, the roaring a bright cascade, dropping, exploding on stone and peppering them with drops like instant diamonds. Bruno found the very sight of it refreshing.

Nic cast his bag aside, stuck his head under the fall and slipped the ragged shift from his body. He raked his fingers across his scalp, dragging out twigs, tufts of moss, whatever else clung there. The skin covering his chest was drum-taut, the ladder of his ribs clear to be counted, sharp edges at the bottom like a pair of wings itching to tear through and unfurl. The rush of water relieved so much dirt Bruno thought him transformed.

'How long have ye been up here?' Bruno had to shout. 'Hiding in the mountain?'

'Do for another while,' said Nic to himself, stepping out from under the flow, ignoring or just not hearing Bruno's question. He ran his hands across his head once more, then snatched up his shift from the ground. He didn't put it on though, just tucked it into his waistband.

'Time to move on,' he said, bending again for his potato-sack bag.

'How much further?' asked Bruno.

But Nic had passed through the water – a shimmer, then gone.

Wants to avoid questions, Bruno thought. He followed

though, ducking under the water, moving quickly but still getting a soaking, a shock of cold on his scalp and shoulders. He saw Nic far ahead and had to hurry after him.

Only minutes later and they came to a meeting of tunnels – three ways ahead.

Nic stopped.

'Which way do we—'

Bruno began but couldn't finish. Something he took first for the still-roaring fall of water behind them was following. He turned as sound blasted like a gale through the passage, noise that wanted to move them on, warn them. Bruno stumbled as though shoved, falling against the wall of the tunnel. Then it left, the silence around them like the quivering calm after a storm.

Bruno turned on Nic. 'Tell me what that was,' he said, feeling that no answer was likely, knowing Nic as he did so far.

'Echoes,' said Nic. 'We go this way here.'

He took the passageway right.

Bruno followed again, demanding, 'Of what? Who?'

'People who lived in the mountain long ago,' Nic shouted back, not stopping, not turning. 'From before Pitch End was even created. Dr Bloom called them the Undying Voices. Things said, memories still bouncing around inside the mountains.'

Bruno felt suddenly colder. He said no more, but moved faster.

Only minutes further into the tunnel Nic stopped and

turned. He had a chunk of griddle-cake in his fingers, the rest bulging in one cheek. He swallowed his mouthful, then dropped the remainder of the cake and shouted, '*Get down!*'

Bruno fell to the ground just a blink before an arrow would've shattered his forehead, striking instead the rock behind. Bruno stayed down, didn't know whether to crawl or curl up for most protection –

'*Stop!* Stop it!'

Nic was shouting – adding his voice to the echoes, the Undying Voices, thought Bruno – still naked on his top half, hands not pulling his dagger from his belt as Bruno would've expected (and wanted) but waving above his head.

'He's a Rebel!' he shouted. Like an indictment the word repeated and repeated by the echoes: *Rebel! Rebel! Rebel!*

'It's fine,' he told Bruno. 'Don't be worrying.'

Bruno tried not to cower. He followed the direction of Nic's gaze upward and scanned the half-dark there, but saw no one.

'He has *The Book of Black & White* with him!' Nic added. No more arrows came.

The laboured heave of their breathing, both in perfect, anguished time, was the only sound. Nic tugged his shift from his belt, ran it across his forehead, then waved it with limp surrender. Bruno wondered then if he should run. Had they strayed into a waiting group of Enforcers?

Then Nic called: 'Dave! Come down and show yerself for *Pitch* sake!'

They waited.

Small, clammy moments passed, and then Bruno heard footsteps – a crunch of stone, a figure moving fast towards him. Bruno got to his feet, weakness bleeding into every bone. Nic didn't move, didn't pull his dagger from his belt and Bruno felt a desire to reach out for him, stand behind him even –

It was another boy, as different to Nic in appearance as Mr Pace had been to the Temperate: hair parted neatly to one side, shirt clean and buttoned to the neck, more adult than child, but with a crossbow in his arms. He made Bruno his target. Bruno thought of Louise, the same way she'd approached, confronted, and he thought this boy may not stop at all, just storm on through him as though he were mist.

An inch from Bruno's face the boy halted, pushing Bruno against the wall, the swell of their chests touching. The boy glared.

'He's Michael Atlas's son alright!' cried the boy, voice as loud and harsh as a hammer blow. 'Look at that sulky oul face on him, just the very same!'

'Steady on, Dave,' said Nic, settling another cigarette between his lips.

'*David*,' said the boy, 'not *Dave*. I've been telling ye that for how many turns now? Still it doesn't sink in.'

Bruno glanced at Nic, repeating to himself: How many turns now?

'Right,' said Nic, looking away. 'Well, now ye've almost

killed him with an arrow and eyeballed him enough – we need to get into the chapel, keep the book safe.'

'Just like that?' said David, still not looking at Nic, still letting his scrutiny travel over Bruno's face as though trying to detect a crack, a flaw. 'Thankfully, yer say-so isn't the only test for letting someone new into the Rebel Chapel. We'll be needing more than just a name. No offence, *Atlas*.'

'Then how're ye gonna check?' asked Nic, snapping the cigarette from his mouth, unlit. 'Slice him open, check the colour of his blood?'

Nic laughed. Bruno tried not to shudder. Then he had a thought he was pleased with and said, 'I have this.' He reached into his shirt and brought to David's sight the Rebel medallion.

David might've given it half a moment's consideration, then said, 'Ye know, that's just what a rightly-devious person would do: show the medallion quick-smart and think that makes everything good. Well it doesn't. Not with me anyway.' He glanced at Nic. 'Sure, he could've stolen that!'

Bruno closed his hand around the medallion, for the first time feeling it as worthless. 'I didn't steal it,' he said. 'It was my father's.'

'I'm gonna ask him some of the Knowledge,' said David.

'Fine,' said Nic. 'Just be quick-smart about it.'

David shut his eyes.

Bruno thought of sidestepping away. He didn't like being

214

discussed as though he had no words to say for himself. Nic gave him a look though: a roll of both eyes that said plainly that they should let David have his time, his questions.

Then David opened his eyes and told Bruno: 'If ye've any notion of the Knowledge, then ye might know some stories, Atlas. Stories only the Rebels knew about, that were passed on from fathers to sons to keep the truth alive under the lies of the Elders. We all know the *Tall Tales* inside out. And so should you, if ye've not been Forgetting like the Elders say, if ye've been a true Rebel in Pitch End, searching out things other than what them Elders tell ye. If ye were a good little pupil then ye'll only have in yer head the rubbish the Elders filled it with. So I'll make it rightly-easy for ye. Tell me this and no more: in *The Tall Tale of the Miner's Fiery Heart,* what creature did that miner meet below Pitch End, and why did he give his heart so easily to it?'

'Rightly-stupid waste of time,' said Nic.

'Don't worry, Delby,' said David, 'he'll prove hisself less than stupid. Wouldn't want to be letting ye down, the son of yer father's best mate and all.'

'Stop,' said Bruno then. 'Stop speaking for me. I know the answer.' He took a breath, and then told David: 'The miner encountered not a creature but a woman, the Lady of Lamplight, who had in place of her own heart a small, faltering, flickering flame. She explained that she was dying. Explained that her heart was about to be extinguished forever and that she had a beloved waiting in the world above who she wished to return to, but had fled from because of the dwindling, shameful nature of her heart.' Bruno paused for a moment, then continued with more confidence:

'The Lady offered an exchange: her heart for his, and she would give him one kiss for his sacrifice. The miner had a beloved of his own in Pitch End but was so enamoured and bewitched by the Lady that when she offered him the exchange, he took the kiss without reservation or hesitation, and he gave his heart to the Lady of Lamplight, taking for his own her small, meagre flame. And so she departed, returning to the world above to seek her beloved, the miner remaining in that tunnel. And it is said he remains there still, waiting for someone to encounter so that he might regain a heart and return to the surface, to his own true love.'

Could've been word-perfect, Bruno thought, straight from the pages of *Tall Tales from Pitch End*. He hadn't realised he remembered it, not until then.

Then the (growing familiar) slap on his back from Nic, and words: 'Well done, Bruno!' Nic looked to David. 'All good, present and correct, Mr Gatekeeper! Now let's go.'

Nic fastened his arm around Bruno's shoulders.

'Wait,' said David.

He looked at Bruno.

David's hand shot out, so sudden Bruno flinched, and

216

then looked down – an offer of a handshake. Bruno took it, and felt his hand squeezed too tight.

'Hope ye're ready,' said David. 'Ready to fight. We've got a struggle ahead, difficult choices, sacrifices even. But I say warmest welcome to ye, on behalf of all Rebels here and gone. And outta curiosity – how did ye know that *Tall Tale*?'

'I read the book of them when I was ten turns,' said Bruno. 'I remember things.'

David released Bruno's hand. Nic, his arm still across Bruno's shoulders, pushed him on.

'It's almost time!' shouted David. 'Almost time to finish what our fathers started!'

And then David was left behind.

Nic kept his arm around Bruno. If he hadn't, if he'd abandoned him for just a moment, Bruno imagined he would have been instantly lost – deeper into the mountain, all light quickly gone. He could see nothing and feel nothing but the inflexible guidance of Nic's arm and the rub of rock against his body. Then there was an ending.

'Where now?' Bruno asked.

He felt Nic move away, but bringing him along.

'Should be,' Nic said, 'just about . . . *here*.'

He felt Nic descend as though the ground had taken him in one gulp. Then Bruno was pulled down too. A match flared in Nic's fingers revealing the wall and a small, circular wooden door. Spun threads of thinnest brass branched across the surface, delicate and intricate as web, half embedded and half raised, all with their fine beginnings in a brass lock on the right of the door. Bruno shifted his bare feet, soles getting a grazing but he didn't mind – excitement was obscuring everything else. He looked closer – chipped into a stone arch curved over the doorway were words:

THE REBEL CHAPEL

FOUNDED BY DR JONATHAN BLOOM, YEAR +287

FOR THE PRESERVATION OF TRUTH AND

KNOWLEDGE

AND THE REBEL WAY

Bruno didn't speak.

'Wait till ye see this,' said Nic, taking a key from his belt. '*Genius*, that's what Dr Bloom was.'

Nic inserted the key, wound it tight, and then let go. The tapestry of brass threads began to tug and shiver, the key slowly unwinding as a collection of locks and bolts clattered inside the door, the sound reminiscent of the Passing Gate. The opening took minutes but Bruno could've watched longer, burning to see inside but enjoying the anticipation. Because in those moments, there was nothing to contradict his hopes. Behind the door could be anything he imagined: an army primed to challenge the Elders; dozens of Rebels in waiting, armed with all the resources needed for battle . . . and as many copies of *Tall Tales from Pitch End* as he wanted . . .

The door eased back. Nic smiled, blew the match out and on his belly squirmed through the gap, blackened and bare soles vanishing inside with Bruno following behind, as close as he could get.

XX

Fathers

Ahead, Bruno saw Nic stand. Moments after he stood too, and in the darkness, in a firm whisper, Nic told him, 'One wee minute, don't be moving. I'll show ye what we'll be using to defeat those Elders,' and then left his side.

Alone then. But Bruno had the surest feeling of being far from by himself; the dark held things, he could feel their waiting. And as the slow creep of anticipation reached its peak there was a widening of light from many sources like many waking eyes – a thrum of energy that shook Bruno's nerves.

On the edge of a cavern, Bruno stood and saw things above and below as light everywhere graced metal. The scene rose like a returning wreck: domed and angled heads, open mouths, teeth and claws, eyes and ears, limbs and yet more limbs – wings and spines and horns and tails. Metallic animals numbering hundreds, some species known to Bruno but more not; most he thought must be imagined, couldn't possibly exist anywhere.

'*Sentries*,' said Bruno, to himself. And then he remembered what Pace has asked Louise – '*How's the army coming along?*' 'An army of Sentries,' he murmured.

Nic was back beside him. He was breathless, saying nothing but smiles.

Bruno's eyes watered against the brightness. Not since he'd read *Tall Tales from Pitch End* had he felt such a desire to absorb, to note and remember and relish each detail as though at any moment the spectacle and reality of it all might leave him.

Bruno swallowed.

'I don't recognise some of them,' he whispered.

'Dr Bloom travelled rightly-far,' said Nic. 'Probably made these when he was remembering creatures he'd seen elsewhere. He had a great imagination on him too though. I reckon it'll scare the *Pitch* clean outta those Elders when they see all these heading for them. Come.'

A rough slope led them into the midst of the clockwork army.

Bruno saw lamps with three gnarled branches, each topped with a naked bulb.

'Miner's lamps,' said Nic. 'Me da was down the mines, before they all got flooded in +277.'

Bruno moved faster, further into the assembly, soon leaving Nic and looking up to see figures stacked high on circular chandeliers ascending into darkness, tier on tier bearing Bird-Sentries. Bruno recognised a raven, an owl and something smaller, maybe finch or robin. Then storm-petrels, in unaccountable numbers.

His foot struck something. A Fox-Sentry? Stoat? Rat? Then a thing like a pheasant with needles down its back, then a hare, then a rabbit. Open caskets were packed, the small circle on the head of each Sentry where its winding key should be, empty.

'We've been working on them for ages,' said Nic. 'Most were just bits and pieces after the last battle they had ten turns ago, had to use whatever we could be finding or nicking – metal scraps we had to beat at and cut down to make clockwork. Me and Louise got lots of them back together. Should be good to go rightly-soon. Well, they'll need to be now, after what's happened.'

Bruno noticed Nic's eyes flicker to his satchel.

'We like to think,' said Nic, still staring at the satchel, though with eyes glazed, 'that they're all just only sleeping. But soon we'll be for wakening them up.'

Bruno saw one Sentry then that attracted him more than any, which dwarfed all others. He moved towards it, reached for it with caution. But what was it? A feline form, but not like the bandy-legged Cat-Sentries used by Elders. Size of a small horse. Bruno set his own human proportions against it: a mouth packed with teeth twice as long as his hand, paws twice as long and many times broader than Bruno's own feet when settled alongside. Its eyes were on the same level as his, colour the kale-green of a summer sea. And Bruno at that moment felt sure of Nic's words: '*only sleeping . . . soon to be wakening . . .*'

'That's the best one of all,' said Nic, and he crushed his eyes shut for a moment, as if searching his memory. 'It's like a cat. Now what did he call it? A . . . *tiger*!'

The word resounded, the cavern in unanimous agreement.

Nic added, 'Yer da used to ride that one into fights with the Enforcers, would ye believe it?'

Bruno didn't immediately believe anything, usually. But with this army around him, Nic beside, and out of Pitch End, part of the Rebel movement opposed to the Elders, for the first time he wanted to believe in everything.

Nic said, 'There's something else ye need to be seeing.'

He moved off fast, picking a path between Sentries.

At the farthest end of the cavern a platform had been hacked from the wall, high, with steep, uneven steps rising to meet it. Nic had already bounded up and stood, looking down. 'Come on!' he shouted to Bruno.

Bruno began to climb, the steps sharp and with no support. He looked down: the army of Sentries wavered like sunspots, the cavern rippling in miners' lamplight.

'Come on, Atlas!' shouted Nic, and Bruno moved quicker. At the top he stood straight, and stared into the face of Dr Jonathan Bloom.

'Impressive, int it?' said Nic. 'And not a bad likeness of the man hisself.'

A good likeness right enough, thought Bruno. A clockwork statue, face just similar enough to the face depicted in the posters Bruno had seen in Old Town to be recognisable – the leader of the Rebels had been rendered in brass. Bruno examined – Dr Jonathan Bloom's nose here was a faultless, tapered slope, brow considerable, but unlike his posters in Old Town it boasted intelligence, not animalism. A mane of fine brass filaments – not wild but pinched at the back – was snaking over a broad shoulder. Bruno looked to the eyes: they were directed up and out, and were not quite lifeless. On his chest was the Rebel symbol, inlaid in bright silver.

'Genius of a man,' said Nic, again.

But Bruno had gone beyond the statue of Dr Bloom. Passing more rough wounds to the wall he counted ten, fifteen more Sentries in the form of clockwork men, all with the Rebel symbol on their chest. He glanced at faces, dismissing, moving quickly along to the next, in anticipation of one figure, one face –

'He's the last one!' he heard Nic shout behind. 'Right beside me own da!'

But Bruno was already there. He'd found his father.

Like Bloom, the likeness was sharp and true. He stepped closer, wanting to touch and scrutinise. But he stopped himself, and tried to be content with just looking.

Nic arrived beside him at a run.

'They don't move,' he said. 'Don't think they were designed to, not like the animals. But they do one thing.'

He stepped forwards and reached a hand up behind the

head of Bruno's father, biting his lip with effort, straining on grubby toes. After a few moments, a sharp click made Bruno and Nic step back. The mouth of Bruno's father opened. Slowly though, and with so much grinding and creaking it gave Bruno unexpected pain to hear and see. The jaw eased down. Bruno's heart raced him into new places, wild wonders of his father alive again (or close to). With him once more, guiding, protecting . . .

A crackle of static, words buried in a cloud of white noise, and his father's recorded voice went: '*Remember the first virtue of the Rebels: Fight, even when believing ye're rightly being beaten. Fight, and ye'll never know such a thing as a shameful death.*'

The static ceased.

Bruno didn't know what to feel, except that he needed to hear more. And then he did; Bruno's father set conversation spinning and all the Rebel statues – all fathers? – began to relate Rebel Virtues:

'*Never betray a Rebel. Not under torture, coercion, blackmail nor barter. Never, ever, never!*'

'*Sacrifice sets us apart – we would die for one another. Treat all Rebels like brothers, fathers, as though the self-same blood rushes through our veins!*'

'*Never forget a thing, never give in, never be forgetting yer kin!*'

Continuous and on, in a clamour that reminded Bruno of the Discussion Chamber, words flung, sentences lapping at one another . . .

'. . . *forgetting* . . .'

'. . . *brothers, fathers* . . .'

'. . . *blood* . . .'

Bruno had to shut his eyes.

Minutes, and then one after another the statues quietened, a final voice consoling itself with – '*Never be forgetting yer kin!*'

A silence like sound.

Bruno opened his eyes. His own voice feeling worthless, too weak, he asked Nic, 'Is that all they say?'

'Dr Bloom says more,' said Nic. 'Sometimes he says so much it's like he's still here, speaking to us, helping and telling. It's good having their bits of wisdom. Keeps the Rebel way living on. Comforting.'

Bruno looked at him, wanting to know what Nic was really thinking, whether he really believed in his own words.

He turned back to his father. Bruno reached out at last and touched – the metal was the coldest thing.

In the hush of the chapel, Nic said, too loudly, 'Louise should be back soon!'

Then another realisation came for Bruno, sudden and undeniable –

'It's just us,' said Bruno. 'Me and you, David and Louise. We're the only Rebels left, aren't we?'

Nic nodded.

'And what do numbers matter? Doesn't stop ye if ye have a rightly-strong heart! It's the fight *in* us, not how many of us there *are*!'

226

Bruno turned to see David marching towards them, bypassing Sentries as though they were unseeable to him, crossbow close in his arms. His words were like some piece of Elder rhetoric, thought Bruno. No – *Rebel* rhetoric, if any.

'Has anyone been checking what's going on down in Pitch End?' David asked, reaching the steps to the platform, taking himself to the top in three long strides. He stopped, and almost grinned. 'With Atlas here with that book, we won't be safe for much longer.' Another pause, then – 'I want to see it. I wanna see *The Book of Black & White.*'

'When Louise comes back,' said Nic, 'then we can be looking at it together.'

'No!' said David.

Bruno looked to Nic, but he offered no support.

'Here,' said Bruno, thinking he didn't mind who looked at the book; better to let David have his way. He took the satchel from his shoulders and enjoyed some relief in its removal. He crouched, undid the buckles and with both hands lifted the book free.

David moved closer but didn't take it.

'Just want to look,' said David.

Bruno felt an urge to fling it from his hands.

'Ye hear so much about a thing,' said David, wetting his lips. ''Bout how rightly-nasty and evil and all it is, and soon ye want to see it in the flesh to be rightly-sure. Dr Bloom said it was the most impressive, powerful thing he'd ever come across. And the most indecent thing he'd ever come across too.'

227

'That's what Temperate Thomas said about it as well,' said Bruno.

Same as other times, Bruno couldn't stop the words leaving him. David looked up. Moments later, every sound amplified to alarm in the cavern, another voice arrived –

'I'm here!'

Louise Green materialised out of a dark pocket between miner's lamps.

Bruno saw David shut his eyes and keep them that way, like they'd been injured by the sight of *The Book of Black & White*. Bruno returned the book to his satchel and hauled it to his shoulder once more. Once more sank under it.

'How did ye escape?' Nic called down. 'What's going on?'

'Took the track past the wall,' shouted Louise, running towards them. 'Went east, through Mickleward Marsh, across the sloggs and then left em far behind me! Most Enforcers went into the mountains after the two of ye, but they got rightly afeared when they saw one of their own dead. Turned back then. It was quite funny actually, I—'

'What else, Louise?' asked Nic.

She remained at the bottom of the steps, eyes bright, possessed of the same energy Bruno had seen in her in Pitch End. Something different though, he thought (and Nic must've thought too): her energy all in a twisting of hands, feet fumbling on top of one another. He couldn't say why, but it worried Bruno. He had to ask, 'Are they looking for me still?'

228

Louise took her emerald cloak in her hands, balled it up.

'What's happening down there, for *Pitch* sake!' cried David. 'Tell us!'

Louise swallowed, then formed the words: 'I went back into Old Town to spy. Saw the Marshall giving a report to that Temperate. Temperate wasn't happy. Said that the Enforcers were all children themselves, too wet behind the ears. Said more rightly-drastic things needed to be done to get at the heart of things – "*the black heart*". Aye, that's what he said. Said an example needed sending to the lower parts of Pitch End, the lower life. Then he organised to send one group of Enforcers into the Elm Tree Mountains, to come after Bruno.'

'Never worry,' said Nic. 'They'll never find this place. Not a body knows how to get in except us.' Bruno looked at him, thinking Nic's dismissal too careless, too quick.

'And another group,' Louise went on, 'he's keeping in Pitch End. He's gonna use them to search. He was saying he'll stop for nothing till he finds Bruno and that book, and the pocket watches. Even if it means destroying Pitch End in the process . . .'

'All talk,' said Nic, and he half-turned away. 'Usual rubbish.'

Bruno looked to David. Both were perched on the brink of the platform and Bruno knew their thoughts weren't far from the same thing, from knowing there was more in

229

Louise to be discovered. It was Bruno who asked, 'What else? What is he going to do first, Louise?'

Nic turned back to face her. Bruno and David remained still.

'I heard Temperate Thomas giving the Elder Order,' said Louise, her voice breaking. 'Tonight, they're going to set fire to Old Town.'

XXI

The Tall Tale of the Locksmith's Sanguine Son

'Won't anyone stop him?' asked Bruno.

'No one cares about Old Town,' said Nic. 'Temperate'll just tell everyone he thinks the Rebels are hiding there, being kept safe by gypsies or whoever, and no one will give a damn if it burns.'

'Either that or he'll just be saying the Rebels started the fire,' said Louise. 'He'll tell Pitch End whatever he likes, just like last time.'

Last time, wondered Bruno.

'Ten turns ago,' explained Nic, staring at Bruno. 'Did it then too. Kept the Pitch Enders scared, on edge.'

Bruno thought back – the Marshall shouting to neighbours whilst Bruno's home burned, ordering them back indoors, that the blaze needed to be left as a reminder of what the Rebels were doing, of the ongoing war. Left, or

231

else. Bruno felt fear even at the recollection of it: he knew what it was to obey, too frightened for any disagreement. But he had known anger that night, remembered too that feeling – rushing at the Marshall with childish fists, childish passion propelling him forwards.

'Very clever of him,' said David.

'*Clever?*' shouted Louise.

'*Very* clever,' said David, his voice level. 'No wonder we couldn't get him beat ten turns ago.'

'I'll beat him alright,' said Louise. 'Put a few bullets in him!'

'If we're ever gonna get the better of Temperate Thomas II,' David continued, almost maddening in his calmness, 'we'll have to be smarter than him, not be shooting more bullets than him.'

Louise didn't reply. Bruno silently agreed.

Nic looked to him and said, 'Don't worry, Bruno. We'll soon be at the mouth, then we'll be seeing things better.'

They were rising, had been for a long time and still no light above, moving upward through a narrow shaft Bruno thought like a throat, a passage from belly to 'the mouth', as Nic had called it. They'd climbed each into a harness of knotted twine and leather, each easing back, Nic tugging on a lever, starting clockwork that wheezed as it took their weight, protesting but lifting them slowly, leaving the cavern of Sentries deep below. Bruno kept adjusting his position but couldn't find comfort – the shaft was so narrow their legs kept striking the walls or one another. He focused on above, wishing for the top and an end to it.

Louise began to sing to herself, and Bruno was surprised at the softness in her voice, as low and gentle as a lullaby –

> *'When times are raging,*
> *And lights go dim;*
> *When prayers, when pennies*
> *Are dropped on the whim.*
>
> *When tide and time,*
> *Takes trouble to come;*
> *When memories are stubborn*
> *And babbies struck dumb.*
>
> *There'll be a sure way,*
> *From foul to free;*
> *Clear as the stars,*
> *And bright as the sea.'*

'We're there,' said Nic.

They were lifted into an evening clean and cold. Their ropes stopped, Nic and David reaching for the walls, pulling themselves clear of the drop then undoing their harnesses. Louise tried to copy but needed helping –

'Here,' said David, offering a hand to her. 'How long have ye been doing this, Louise, and still ye can't manage it yerself?'

'Shut up and just be helping me,' said Louise.

Bruno saw both of them smile, though only to themselves.

Nic reeled Bruno in and helped him free. His feet were numb after so long suspended, and he had to walk some feeling back into them – through a cavern open to the world, to the edge of the mouth.

'Careful,' said Nic, but Bruno didn't want to hear.

He had a view he'd never had, the entirety of Pitch End, the whole of the town seen from somewhere not within its walls. Looking down on familiar things all made small, Bruno found it difficult to imagine himself in such a place: so crammed tight, all the disorder of the buildings like they'd been dropped, all at odds; all scoured rough by the elements, all the lunatic tilt and lean of the place. He felt larger than it all, and at the same time smaller – his world, the one he'd known always, was almost nothing, and within it he was one of the smallest things.

Nic stepped up beside him. From his belt he took and shook out a spyglass.

'What ye see?' asked Louise, venturing even closer than Bruno to the edge of the mouth.

'Pyres,' said Nic. 'Inkpot Lane, Whalebone Slope, the Squeeze-By . . .'

'The people in those houses won't be getting out if they light fires down the Squeeze-By,' said David, stepping between Bruno and Nic.

'*Squeeze-By?*' said Bruno. 'Do ye mean the Rat-Run?'

Nic, David and Louise stopped, all looking at him as though he'd insulted.

'We don't call them that,' said David. 'We use the old names for Old Town, not those names the Elders gave them.'

'Ye might call it the Rat-Run,' said Nic, tone softer than David's. 'But we know them as they used to be.'

'And rightly should be!' added Louise.

'We'll have to head in tonight,' said Nic, turning to David. 'If they're searching so high and low, and burning too, we might not get another chance.'

'Agreed,' said David.

'Head where?' asked Bruno.

Nic didn't answer right away. Instead from his belt he detached his pocket watch and opened it; Bruno saw that the moon inside was almost entirely in shadow.

'Not long to wait,' said Nic.

'One hour till sundown to be rightly-precise,' said David. Bruno saw a coin in David's hand – a Pitch, tarnished and commonplace as any. David saw Bruno looking. His thumb slid one side of the coin away and a small clock face was uncovered. 'One hour,' he said, 'so we better decide things good and fast.'

'Aye, one hour,' said Louise, quickly consulting her own pocket watch – one with deep grooves and swells, its casing like the whorl of a seashell.

'But where are we going to?' asked Bruno again.

'Town hall,' said Nic, and took his blade from his belt,

turning it, examining its edge, running a finger along it. 'Ten turns back, when Temperate Thomas was trying to stop the Rebels, when he stole all time, he turned Pitch End upside down looking for anything "indecent". All books were taken. Pictos, maps, papers, anything he liked. Ended up confiscating lots more stuff than just Rebel things, anything he didn't like the look of. One thing he discovered and stole were the winding keys for the Sentry army.'

The blade drew blood. Nic pressed his finger to his lip and sucked it clean, then returned the blade to his belt.

'But,' said Bruno (aware of being too disagreeable but unable to resist), 'how do ye know they're in the town hall? He could've moved them. It's been ten turns.'

'I have one other bother too,' said David. 'Does Louise even know where in the town hall the winding keys are hidden?'

'I towl ye last week,' said Louise and she stepped towards David, though couldn't look him in the eye. 'I haven't managed to get a proper look inside all the town hall, not the whole way. I've been trying, following the Elders and everything. But we were supposed to have more time than this!'

'Told ye I should've went,' said David.

'Shut up!' cried Louise.

'What did ye find out, Louise?' said Nic.

Louise took a breath and shut her eyes. 'I just know,' she said, hands moving in the air, as though feeling her way somewhere, through darkness, 'there's this small door on the right at the back of the hall, behind the Faerie Fort.

After that there's some stairs ye go down and it brings you into a tunnel.'

'Sounds easy enough,' said Nic.

'How many ways are there to go when ye get into this tunnel?' asked David.

Louise's eyes opened, flickered, looked away. Bruno saw her fingers touching one another, counting silently. 'I think,' she said, 'maybe, about at least six . . . *maybe* . . .'

Nic said nothing. David shook his head. But Bruno suddenly spoke words he hadn't known were coming – 'I know the way to go from there.'

They all looked at him.

'Explain,' said David.

'My da told me,' said Bruno. 'When I was four, just before he . . . before he went, he used to tell me this same story every night. It was about a boy, a locksmith's son, who was looking for his father's lost keys.'

'*The Tall Tale of the Locksmith's Sanguine Son*,' said David.

'Ye know it?' asked Nic.

'I know *of* it,' said David. 'It's a more recent one. Don't think Dr Bloom ever wrote it down so must've not been worth much.'

'Be quiet,' said Louise. 'Just coz ye don't know it doesn't mean it means nothing.' She moved towards Bruno. 'Some were just used at bedtime and not written down, like the songs ye sing to children . . . my da used to tell me some too.'

Silence for many moments, and then Nic said, 'Bruno, do ye remember it?'

All three looked at Bruno. He shut his eyes and imagined himself in bed, his father close, a stuttering light at the bedside, a storm beyond, and in a low voice Bruno began –

'*There once was a locksmith's son, an only child who worked all hours of light and dark, all year, all three seasons. But the boy was not miserable, nor self-pitying nor hopeless – he was a sanguine child who arrived at all things with much enthusiasm. His teacher called him a dreamer, and that was true. But dreaming is no bad thing, and you should be mistrustful of those who say otherwise.*'

'I remember it too I think!' said Louise.

'What happens next?' asked David, ignoring Louise.

Bruno opened his eyes, looked to David and tried to see sarcasm. But there was none. Bruno cleared his throat, and went on –

'*One day, after the locksmith's son had spent the morning in his father's shop – courteous, cheerful and rightly-helpful to all customers, taking orders and writing out receipts and giving exact change to the penny – the locksmith said that he had a job for his son to do. He told him a box of keys had been stolen from him. A box of keys that would unlock doors that some in Pitch End wouldn't want opened. He had an idea (he said), a wee notion of where they might be hidden – in the passageways below the ruin of a home. The home of the founder of Pitch End, George Pitch.*

238

'*Hungry for adventure, always willing to help his father, the boy agreed, and so set off at once to track down the lost keys.*'

'It's not the town hall,' said Louise. 'He doesn't go to the town hall, so how does that help? Maybe I don't remember this one.'

Bruno said, 'Perhaps it's not meant to be rightly-identical. The story says George Pitch's old house, but maybe it's really the town hall?'

'No,' said David. 'Dr Bloom would be rightly-exact about it.'

'No,' said Nic, who had held his silence for a long time. He was looking out over Pitch End, watching shadow invade. He turned to face Bruno. 'It is rightly-exact,' he said. 'The town hall is built where George Pitch's old house used to be.'

Excitement made Bruno stand taller, made Louise leap up and down and giggle. Made David fold his arms and ask, 'Are ye sure? We need to be rightly sure.'

'I am,' said Nic. He looked just at Bruno. 'Are *you*, Bruno? Do ye remember the rest of the story? How he got to the keys?'

Bruno wanted to say yes. But truth stoppered him; the *Tall Tale* would only unfurl when told, the words feeling inevitable as he said them. So he had to hope – wish and believe – that he held enough in his head to lead them, take them safely to the end.

'I will remember it,' he settled for saying.

'Then that's good enough for me,' Nic said.

'And me!' said Louise.

'But how are we gonna be getting down into town?' asked Bruno.

Nic smiled. He strolled away from them. When he reached the back of the mouth, he said, 'This is how.' He took hold of the dark and tore it down. A crackle of material descending and a reveal – two things lurking, metal and canvas. Not Sentries, but what?

'We call them the Cleggs,' said Nic, and he slammed a hand against one. There was a sound like a struck dustbin.

'*Cleggs?*' said Bruno.

'Ye know,' said Louise, 'like them big oul flies in the eastern fields that bite ye and get all fat on the blood, make ye come out in big itchy lumps that sting like anything!'

Bruno had never been in the eastern fields, so couldn't sympathise. But he left Louise and David and moved closer to see.

The pair of gliders – *Cleggs* – had been slopped with pitch, their surfaces dulled, metal parts just visible beneath; rusted undersides, a testament to past battles in the wide, ragged tears and the dents Bruno could've fitted his head into. In the gloom of the mouth, this was all Bruno was allowed, struggling and failing to see where they began and ended, or began again. And he felt just as strong an urge to keep his distance as explore. Something in their presence threatened energy barely contained, sharp joints primed, looking ready to snap. Each had eight long, skinny legs that kept them standing.

'They've not been used much is the only thing,' said Nic. 'But we'll be grand. Dr Bloom hasn't let us down. Yet.'

Bruno looked at him.

Nic cleared his throat, and continued: 'We'll take this one Bruno, you and me. David and Louise, the happy couple, on the other one.'

'I'm not flying one of those gliders with her on it behind me,' said David.

'Get stuffed!' said Louise. 'And *I'm* flying it!'

'And certainly not if she's flying. She's too unstable.'

'I'm not mad keen on being on a glider with you either, *Dave*!'

'If she flew she'd be all over the place, we need a calm approach.'

'I can be calm!'

'Ye're a storm in a thimble, ye wouldn't know calm if it slapped ye.'

'What did ye say to me?'

'I'll go with Atlas. He's a quiet one. I'll not hear so much disagreeing from him.'

Bruno felt he should speak. 'What about my satchel?' asked Bruno. 'Will it be okay with us?'

'We leave *The Book of Black & White* here,' said David. 'If we bring it and it gets lost then—'

'And if we're leaving it,' said Nic, 'and they attack the chapel when we're away, they'll get it. It stays with Bruno.'

David opened his mouth to offer new argument but –

'*Stop!*' said Louise. 'What does Bruno himself think? He's the one has to carry it.'

Bruno looked at them all. But looked most to Nic.

'I'll be keeping it with me,' he said.

Nic nodded. David held his hands up, then let them fall, muttering some further protest.

'Decided!' Louise shouted.

'Let's get ready, quick-smart,' said Nic. 'We might only have one go at this. Let's make sure it's our best.'

XXII

Flight

Bruno watched as Nic's foot found a pedal, no more than a shard but when kicked it woke the Clegg. Against Bruno's legs the glider trembled, thundered like it wanted to throw him off and would soon do something about it. Smoke streamed from everywhere, stars were dampened and David and Louise (on their Clegg, after all the protests) were lost to sight.

On the edge of the mouth, Bruno looked out – below all was dark, but with small buds of flame beginning in Old Town.

'Ready?' he heard Nic shout over the noise.

Bruno had no time to reply, only adjust the straps of his satchel that harboured so many things, contained so much of importance.

'Hold on to yerself!' Nic said.

And then they tilted, lunged, the Clegg intent on entry into night sky, and Nic released a holler, same as he let out in the Cavern of the Forgotten, Bruno feeling his whole self clench as they left mountain behind –

They dropped.

Bruno shut his eyes, holding Nic tighter as they fell. Without promise of being stopped or saved, Bruno kept his eyes shut, not screaming, not shouting, only awaiting sudden end and thinking: this is it and I'll be gone soon. I'll not be here any more. I'm going to die.

Thought it and thought it in tightening circles until he felt Nic's foot twitch, kick. At once the engine cut, the heat scorching Bruno's legs cooling, the stench of smoke dissipating and there was a sound to either side like two blows to the chest. They slowed, and Bruno needed to open his eyes to see –

Canvas wings, ribbed with steel, had opened and filled with air. They were no longer dropping. Most important thing to Bruno: he wasn't on his way to dying.

The Clegg eased left and Bruno found himself leaning into the turn. He had a glimpse of Pitch End, the Clocktower the only thing he focused on – four-sided face held above the rising tide of smoke like a victim treading water – then gone as they whirled. Another snap and the Clegg's wings returned to its side. They were back into a plunge, one Bruno guessed must have been begun by Nic. He clutched tighter still.

Nic cried over the rush: 'I'll not kill ye if I can help it! Don't be such a worrier, Bruno!'

Bruno couldn't be anything other than what he felt – scared but trying to master it. But he decided he'd keep his eyes open no matter what came next.

Down, lower, closer, and again came the hard punch of wind against canvas, wings of the glider thrown wide. Then higher, rising, lifting –

'Want to let go of me a wee bit there?' said Nic. 'Ye'll have me in bits by the time we land!'

Bruno did as he was told, and felt better for it. He was cold, but not the same cold that he felt in bed on endless Ever-Winter nights, or in Hedge School when frost spread pale tendrils across glass, water barrel in the playground losing reflections, puddles solid as stone. This was cold he could bear. And after many more moments, as Bruno straightened his back, he experienced the realisation, the thrill, of flight. Like the window of the world thrown wide, dark sky and sea surrounded him, enormous, no slip between to part them. Pitch End had shrunk smaller even than when he'd seen it from the mouth of the cavern; grubby thumbprint on a dark pane, all around blank and silent and terrifying. Exciting.

A few moments later Nic asked, 'Ye alright or what?'

Bruno replied without a lie, 'I'm alright.'

David and Louise appeared beside them, silent in flight. Both looked unhappy.

'Is this a scenic flight now?' asked David. 'Down and up and all over the place. I know ye're showing off for

Atlas, but I'd be preferring not to be flying around all night.'

'Me neither!' said Louise.

Nic shouted to them, 'Just circle a bit out over the bay, once or twice at least, check things. Then we'll think about maybe—'

'*Think about*?' shouted David. 'Atlas is rubbing off on ye, Delby! We've no time for thinking, we have to just *do*!'

David kicked a pedal on his own glider: one wing folded and they fell away to the right, steeply and not circling but dropping, and not towards the bay but towards Pitch End's centre.

Bruno heard Nic curse, and then follow.

'How are we gonna get into the town hall?' asked Bruno. 'The doors, they'll be locked for definite.'

'There's other ways,' replied Nic.

They flew over Old Town. Bruno saw flame on gnarled fingers – the trees reaching from Old Town's shattered roofs, fire flourishing, their crackle and sputter filling Bruno's hearing. Then on but through smoke, landmarks looming like things just thought of: Clocktower, empty town square, town hall . . .

The glider's wings tilted back, Bruno marvelling at how little sound they were making. 'Get ready,' he heard Nic say.

Bruno pressed his legs tight to the barrel-body of the Clegg as Nic's feet and hands tugged and kicked at levers and pedals, wings almost vertical at either side then arching, glider slowing as its insect legs flicked – *snap-spasm* – and touched stone.

Bruno inhaled familiar Pitch End. Tasted sea, smoke, suspicion. He looked around. They'd landed on the roof of the town hall.

XXIII

The Dark, the Banshee and the Giant's Staircase

'Don't forget yer Talent,' said Nic.

Good thing he reminded him – Bruno struggled to catch the thread of it, the thoughts of nothing and being no one, being forgotten, unseeable . . .

Nic leapt from the Clegg and with head down ran, surrounded quickly by rising smoke. Bruno took longer to dismount, and when he did had to put all effort into not coughing or retching. He pressed both hands to his mouth and stood, trying to see. A breeze was dragging smoke from the Old Town fires, east to west. He could see nothing. Nothing, and then had to shift himself quick – David and Louise appeared, landing alongside the first glider with less noise and even more ease than Nic had managed.

'How are we gonna—' began Bruno.

'Quiet,' said David, voice muffled behind a tied

handkerchief, him and Louise slipping from their Clegg. David held his crossbow, Louise her short shotgun.

They waited for Nic, then watched the smoke disclose him.

'I see no one about,' Nic said, though he didn't sound convinced.

'Well ye wouldn't see anyone in this, would ye?' said David.

They waited again, and Bruno held the same question in his head still: how were they going to get inside?

'Do ye think they'll have traps set?' asked Louise.

Without a word, Nic left them again. David and Louise followed quickly, Bruno behind. *The Book of Black & White* was like granite on his back, like something gaining weight.

Light appeared ahead, hovering, then dividing – a trio of small orbs, white. Bruno realised that Nic must've brought a miner's lamp with him. Towards it he ran.

Shortened by smoke, Bruno noticed Nic and David were only thighs and everything up, himself and Louise not even this. They all moved close to Nic, who crouched to examine a space between his feet. Bruno had the faint, uncertain impression of glass. 'Only way in,' said Nic. 'Dave and Louise, stay out here and keep watch for us. Use the signal if ye need to.' Nic held up his pocket watch, and Louise and David did the same with theirs.

Nic took his blade, raised it for a moment, then down – a crunch of metal, glass, then an opening, an untainted space for smoke to pour into and explore. There was a momentary clearing and Bruno saw Nic pull a rope from his bag, a crooked tooth of metal bound to the end, and latch it to the edge of the opening, feeding it in and down. David and Louise kneeled, held it there.

'Go,' said Nic. He was looking to Bruno.

Bruno wished he could have no doubt, could throw himself into whatever situation without fear or thinking, just knowing on instinct what to do (climb a tree, fly a glider, fire a gun) and not be stymied by imagining what could go wrong, what might happen for the worse. But didn't say a word as he kneeled beside the other remaining Rebels and manoeuvred himself around, rope loose in his hands. He felt Nic grip his shoulder. 'Ye'll be alright,' he said. 'Clamp yer feet around the rope good and tight, keep a good distance between the hands. Go slow. I'll be right after ye. Trust me.'

Bruno held the guidance in his head like he held his Talent. He began his descent.

The Faerie Fort was a blush below. Bruno remembered the din of the Discussion Chamber, cages holding insults, the shame at being summoned to the stage, his escape . . . But the town hall held no trace of what had happened. There was placid peacefulness everywhere, only crimson leaves for light, but fading, surrounded by a determined dark.

Bruno's bare feet touched the floor, and cold shot to the ends of him.

250

He expected to be seized. How could he not? Alone, his Talent felt like a petty, fragile thing, easy to see through, whip away. He stepped back from the rope and held himself. A sound like a razor on wire and Nic arrived beside him in a blink, sliding the length from roof to floor without stopping.

'This way,' said Nic. 'Let's be seeing if Louise was right.'

They moved away from the Faerie Fort, to the right and the back, the rope inching upwards behind, being retrieved by David and Louise.

The miner's lamp was unlit in one of Nic's hands, curved blade in the other.

'Here,' breathed Nic, pulling Bruno close. 'See it?'

He blinked, did see: a door, tall, wider at the top than the bottom, no handle or knocker or keyhole. Bruno had a feeling; no more than an idea, but he grasped the door and pushed. It opened without protest.

They looked at each other. Both sets of eyes spoke – a trap?

But they couldn't turn back. No choice but to accept good fortune and move in. Bruno and Nic's shoulders brushed one another in the narrowness. They let the door close by itself.

Nic's fingers fiddled with the dial at the base of the miner's lamp and it woke, its light a bleary company. He shook it to rouse fully – they were at the top of the stone staircase Louise had reported. Bruno tried not to think of the junction that would come soon below, the moment when Louise's information would stop and his memory of the *Tall Tale*, his father's long-ago whispered words, would have to lead.

Down then, walls narrowing as though behind the stone on either side there pushed forces determined to stop them, squeezing so tightly before the end that Nic had to shuffle sidelong and Bruno had to squeeze, be prised free, head and arms first, legs and feet after.

Bruno wanted something other than what Louise had told them but the passageway ahead indeed splintered into six, each way heavy with darkness, walls leaning like they'd been animal-dug. Nothing distinguished them, cold air a long slow sigh from each.

Nic looked to Bruno. Nothing needed saying. Now me, thought Bruno. He shut his eyes, needing to remember –

'*When the locksmith's sanguine son stepped into George Pitch's house, he saw that there were many ways and rooms. George Pitch wasn't a man who loved luxury or prized pennies (he'd a habit, in fact, of giving all he could to his people, to his town!), but he needed a large home to welcome people into. It was a place of inclusion, comfort, joy, unlike so many places in Pitch End.*'

No, thought Bruno, need to get past these bits. It felt not like his father's voice but like the voice of the writer, Dr Jonathan Bloom, trying to educate, preach even. Bruno breathed, trying with delicate, intangible movements to slip ahead . . . Something more returned to him:

'Below, in the darkness, in the space beneath the house, he came to six ways. Six choices, and the locksmith's son made the best and bravest decision, taking the way that looked darkest.'

'They're all rightly-dark, Bruno,' said Nic.

Bruno opened his eyes. He'd been speaking aloud.

'One has to be darker than all the others,' said Bruno, speaking more to himself than Nic. He stepped forwards.

'*Darker, darkest,*' Bruno whispered, then said, 'Let me have the lamp.'

He turned, and hated the doubt he saw in Nic's eyes.

'Ye have to trust *me* now,' Bruno found himself saying.

'Ye're to be careful with it,' said Nic. 'This one was me da's own.'

Nic held the lamp out, Bruno moving halfway to meet him, to take it.

Bruno confronted the tunnels, left to right, holding the miner's lamp high, letting light crawl into each. None promised an end, just continuing long past any relief offered by the lamp. At the final opening, the same darkness. Or *darkest*? Bruno could see five feet of ground then nothing else. He moved back to the previous passageway, holding the lamp high – more than five feet, maybe twice that before the light stopped.

'Isn't a passageway,' said Bruno.

'What?' asked Nic.

'It's this way here,' said Bruno.

He moved into the last passage with Nic close behind

and within moments they were stopped. Bruno reached, touched stone.

'Can't be this way,' said Nic, and Bruno heard frustration in his voice. Only a small, niggling note, but not nothing.

'It is,' said Bruno, and he recited for Nic:

'The darkest way, darkness so dark it turned solid before the eyes of the locksmith's son and he had to push against it, fight the dark, before it allowed him to continue.'

Nic sighed and said, 'Best get pushing then.'

Shoulders to it they pressed and after long minutes of refusal, feet rasping the ground, it moved. Continued to move. Strength spawned strength – the more it shifted, the more Bruno felt he could push it.

'Almost there,' said Nic.

A gap wide enough to slip through and Bruno went first, miner's lamp throbbing in his hand and blessed words still unspooling in his mind:

'A banshee with a gaping mouth stood barring the way. The locksmith's son thought of what his grandmother had told him once: "Banshees just like attention with all that keening and nicking people's babbies! And Pitch End banshees are worst of all for the wailing on and on and taking what isn't there's. But like all Pitch Enders, if ye give em a penny they soon shut their yap!"'

Bruno faced himself many times over from all angles; mirrors were fitted, floor to ceiling, all points of the compass, rust wreathing their contents. Bruno stepped forwards and watched his body twist, contorting into many question and exclamation marks.

'What is that?' asked Nic, stepping up beside him.

A banshee, in sculpted black stone, was crouched on a narrow stone pillar, fingers and feet boasting long, pointed nails. Between its toes like hawk talons was clutched a small bundle of deep-ridged stone. Bruno moved closer, looked and saw a small face within – an infant, eye sockets clogged with dust.

'Now what?' said Nic, again in frustration, anxiety.

But Bruno felt calm, didn't panic, because he could feel understanding rising. He moved closer again to the banshee. Her mouth gaped with silent screaming. Bruno thought – if ye give em a penny they soon shut their yaps! – and then remembered.

He returned the miner's lamp to Nic. His hand fell against his pocket. But would he still have it? From that dull morning, that world to this with so much changed – Pace's black penny, given moments before everything altered?

Bruno's fingers moved into his pocket and felt nothing. Nothing, and then solid something – his fingers snatched at it, like a penny was a thing that could vanish with too much seeking and not enough seizing. He brought it out, pinched between finger and thumb.

'Thank you, Mr Pace,' he said.

'What are ye . . . ?' asked Nic.

Bruno stepped up to the banshee and slipped the penny past her tongue.

It joined others in a stone belly, a hollow clash against earlier offerings.

For a long time, worse than nothing: pressing silence. Bruno was left to thinking he'd not remembered right at all, Nic watching him, and the miner's lamp too, with its low, thoughtful and (to Bruno) sceptical-sounding hum.

Then a scream that sent hands to ears, worry striking against their hearts – we'll not go unnoticed now, thought Bruno – and a crack was flung into one of the mirrors. A cascade of glass and behind was a new opening. The screaming stopped but its echo thrived long after.

'Good,' said Nic. 'Now hurry.'

Bruno saw the desperation in Nic. Not fear (he couldn't imagine fear ever showing itself in Nic) but a need, after so many turns of rebuilding an army, of waiting and work, a need for the final thing to set it going. Bruno took care through the new way that had opened behind the shattered mirror but Nic leapt, shards blanked by miner's lamplight.

Sooner than Bruno would've expected, wanted, came a shout somewhere behind them, and heavy footfalls.

'Definitely a bit quicker now,' said Nic.

Bruno nodded.

They ran. Into a long, straight passageway, Bruno in a desperate murmur to himself:

'The longest tunnel, one that the locksmith's sanguine son thought could've rightly taken him around the world twice and back again. And all along the route, the dead

*who had perished in the tunnel, unable to find their way
back to the surface, their hearts neither as true nor as
genuine as that of the locksmith's son.'*

Bruno saw statues like slumbering bodies, so lifelike,
tucked into niches with legends chipped above. He grabbed
names in glances:

TEMPERATE BODLE – +167 TO +174

TEMPERATE WALLINGS – +175 TO +186

TEMPERATE HIGGINBOTTOM – +187 TO +200

They stopped and had a choice, left or right. Bruno decided
on no more than instinct: 'This way,' he said, turning left,
not wanting to slow but still exhausted.

He heard Nic behind him: 'I hope ye're right, Bruno
Atlas.'

More shouts, more feet – were they being pursued as
close as it sounded?

A curve that they had to take so sharp it turned them to
face the way they'd come; a lowering of the ceiling, a crouch
and then a crawl needed to make it through:

*'The locksmith's son had to shrink, scramble slow like an
infant, had to think himself smaller . . . and when that
wouldn't work he tried to think himself younger, more child-
like, remember bygone days that lived in him still – no worries
about his father's shop and its business, no concern over why
his mam had died when she did, or over what the neighbours
would think of the holes in his shoes, what the other children*

*in Hedge School thought of his torn trousers. All this he had
to shed, weight he had to shrug off . . . and then, barely, just
about, he managed to pass through.'*

Through and then standing, Bruno and Nic came to a
single, towering step that curved away out of sight on both
sides.

'The Giant's Staircase,' said Bruno.

'Taking a wild guess that the locksmith's son climbed,'
said Nic, 'and quick-smart.'

He handed Bruno the lamp and attacked the step with
a leap, chest slamming against the edge, fingers clawing
stone. Bruno rushed to support him, push his soles up and
clear. Nic turned and reached down, taking the miner's
lamp, settling it on the step beside and then hauling Bruno
up. They knelt there, turned and looked up – a dozen more
steps. And still behind (though closer, without question
nearer) the following of Enforcers or Elders? Marshall or
Temperate?

'Up,' was all Nic said, and he threw himself onto the
next step.

'Wait,' Bruno tried to tell him, but too breathless.
Something was in his mind, some part of the *Tall Tale*, no
more than a throw of words, but important. 'Wait,' he said
again.

'No time,' said Nic, reaching down for Bruno once more.

'There's an easier way,' said Bruno, and then it arrived
with him, words he told Nic:

'After only one step, the locksmith's son – without breath,

258

without energy – collapsed upon the Giant's Staircase, defeated. And perhaps he would've stayed there, never completing his father's task, were it not for a companion. The boy's Shadow – best friend, true self, that part that would survive him and live on in memory and time, never fading so long as someone lived who remembered him – looked down on the boy and knew he must help. With a great wrench he tore himself free of the boy's fallen body, conquered the Giant's Staircase in mere moments, and looked down. He saw what the boy could not see from his place at the bottom: the curve of the staircase was not as wide as it seemed, but instead at its furthest edge grew shallow, steps more easy to be taken. Knowledge flowed like shared dreams from Shadow to boy, and the locksmith's son awoke and knew without worry what to do.'

A clear voice behind Bruno then –

'I hear someone talking up ahead! Come on!'

Bruno and Nic looked at one another.

'I hope this works,' said Nic.

Again they ran, following the curve of the Giant's Staircase to the left, Nic a step above Bruno until the stairs began to shrink, Bruno rising, Nic sinking –

'I see it,' said Nic. 'I see the steps getting smaller.'

And soon they were alongside one another again, same height at the edge of the staircase. They turned right onto shallower steps, each with a hand pressed to the wall and faster, more easily, towards the summit and onto a landing, a final tunnel, the final choice –

Three low doors, a Cat-Sentry surmounting each.

Bruno listened to their slow whine, the twist of their winding keys.

'Which one?' demanded Nic. 'Which way? What does the story say happens?'

'Wait,' said Bruno, looking to each in turn. 'I need to think.'

'Can't wait or think,' said Nic. 'They'll be here soon.'

The *Tall Tale* whispered in his mind, but like someone moving away, a fading voice –

'Now, a cat is always a troublesome, flighty thing, to be sure, and should never be trusted. The boy knew this as well as anyone in Pitch End. But he knew too how to get their secrets and . . . and . . .'

And that was all.

'What happens next, Bruno?' asked Nic.

Bruno shut his eyes. He'd known this, seen it approaching. The memory, the past and its voices had been drowned by more recent storms. He was incapable of more.

'Bruno,' said Nic. '*Speak!*'

Bruno swallowed, opened his eyes and confessed: 'I don't know. I can't remember.'

XXIV
Knowledge

'What do ye mean ye can't remember?' said Nic.

Bruno cleared his throat for words but spoke none.

Nic faced him fully, toes pointed, miner's lamp listing in his hand.

'Ye have to, Bruno,' said Nic. He moved closer, his eyes bright, mouth parted, top lip shivering. Only the two of them, for that moment. 'Ye have to,' he said again. 'We can't be getting beaten now, not this close. Ye must remember.'

Bruno thought, maybe I can move beyond the story, finish things myself?

Voices below –

'We can't get through this gap, Marshall!'

'Then the smaller ones of ye – Tonner, Tidsell – be crawling under there!'

Not maybe, thought Bruno – *must*, like Nic said.

He moved towards the three doors, steps small, barely

stirring sound. But stirring something else – the Cat-Sentry above the door furthest left twitched. A fuzz of static, and then came a divulging of recorded words in a deep male voice Bruno knew. The Temperate said –

'The demise of lighthouse number four was as a result of a rightly-nasty and opportunistic attempt on the Mayor's life by one of the Rebels.

'The bullet from a Rebel rifle ricocheted off one of the pillars of the town hall, hit the back of a jellyfish in the Sea of Apparitions and struck the lighthouse, shattering its glass.'

Quickly – response triggered by words from the first – the second Cat-Sentry over the second door protested. A different recorded voice, all passion and exclamation –

'No! It was destroyed by an Elder!

'Elder Dishonest, killing that farmer cos he was lusting after the man's wife!

'Then he lied and lied and tried to cover it up. But he was got in the end.

'Things don't just go away.'

And the third Sentry threw more words into the debate, yet another side to things, yet another voice –

'Should never've been made outta glass anyway.

'Could've been shattered by any number of things.

'Storm, hail, expanding in the cold of Ever-Winter, then contracting in the heat of the Swelter Season.

'Poor work by the glaziers or short-sightedness by the brainless Mayor at the time . . .

'*And on and on and on.*

'*Some things just can't be known for sure.*'

'Second one,' said Nic. 'Let's go.'

He took a step but Bruno held him back with words –
'Wait.'

'Why?' said Nic. 'Don't be disagreeing, not now.'

'No,' said Bruno. 'I'm not gonna rush just coz ye think
the Rebel version is the right one.'

'I don't *think*,' said Nic, teeth tight together. 'I *know* it's
right.'

'How?'

'Because, and that's enough to be knowing.'

'Because *why*?'

'Because . . . the voice that said it just now was my da.
And he never told a lie in his life.'

Bruno could conjure no argument. And still the shouts
behind them –

'This way! To the left-hand side – the steps are smaller!
Hurry!'

'It's the last one,' was all Bruno said.

'What?' asked Nic. 'That wishy-washy, on-the-fence
answer?'

'Yes,' said Bruno, and he moved towards the door, but
this time Nic took him by the arm and held him.

'Tell me how ye know,' he said.

'Because it's the least sure of itself,' said Bruno. 'It's not
the Elder version or the Rebel one. It's the one the Temperate

263

would never expect a Rebel or anyone in Pitch End to go for.'

They stared at one another, Bruno seeing the strain, the effort it would cost Nic to believe Bruno over himself, over his own father, over the Rebels. Stared, brow taut. Then Nic nodded.

'There they are! Shoot!'

They ran to the door together as gunshots clipped stone at their heels. The door opened onto darkness. Bruno threw himself forwards, Nic slammed the door shut, Bruno leapt for a bolt on the inside, snapping it home.

Fists and boots beat unseen on the other side, words came – 'There's another way in there, the Marshall said so. Head back down them steps!'

Only a small time stolen then, but enough to search further. Bruno turned to the dark, listened. Wherever they were was full of an agitated *tick-tick-ticking*. Nic spun the dial of the miner's lamp to its loosest. Bruno heard the low hiss of gas, light brightening.

They were surrounded by clock faces. All of Pitch End's collected time was packed around them, stockpiled, in a room with unknown ends, storms of dust churning in the lamplight.

Tick, tick, tick . . .

More beats to a moment than needed, clocks not in time together but against one another. Bruno walked to the nearest clock, hands reaching out –

'No,' said Nic, grabbing him. 'We're here for one thing. And the lamp won't last long at this strength.'

Bruno's arms fell, attention too falling to the ground; he saw circular stone plates no bigger than bicycle wheels. He crouched and began to explore the surface with his fingers. Engraved were things Bruno struggled to see.

Nic joined him with their dwindling light.

'We have to check them all,' said Bruno.

'What for?' asked Nic. 'How do ye even know—'

'I'll know,' said Bruno.

Bruno blew dust from the first and saw words –

THE ARRIVAL OF THE ELDERS

His fingers gouged engrained filth, stubborn history, and he saw depicted ten tall figures, behind them a vast circle – a sun with broad spokes. Elders, their divine arrival; a gift, a blessing to Pitch End.

'Bloody sicken ye, wouldn't it,' said Nic.

'Next one,' said Bruno, crawling to the next, awaiting Nic, needing light however little.

SILENCE AND SEEING

The second of the Eleven Decent Ways written by the Elders: '*Rightly-obedient silence and rightly-diligent seeing are a Pitch Ender's greatest virtues, especially if what you*

265

don't say or what you see would be to the continuing support of the Elders.'

No matter how many times he heard or read it, Bruno could never fathom meaning in it.

'That it?' asked Nic, so much hope in his voice it hurt Bruno to shake his head no.

But did he even know what he was looking for? He had to hope he would know it when he saw it. If guessing, he would think a stone plate that had some link to the Rebels, something they did that Definitive History tied them to, gave them blame for – that was what they needed to discover.

And all the while, still the frantic chorus of *tick, tick, ticking . . .*

THE RUINING OF MOUNT TOME

Bruno's gasp drained him.

He fell beside the circle of stone and final (he thought forgotten) words returned, which he said aloud:

'Beneath a painting of Mount Tome – a place where any Pitch Ender can seek safety, seclusion, peace – the locksmith's sanguine son found a box, and knew it as his father's from the symbol upon it. And he knew that inside would be what his father had lost, what he would soon rejoice at being reunited with.'

'Is it . . . ?' asked Nic. He awaited Bruno's consent. Bruno nodded. Nic drove his knife downwards, blade sinking to the hilt into the rim of the stone plate.

'Wait,' said Bruno. 'I want to see it properly.'

'Why?' asked Nic.

'Because,' said Bruno, 'I just need to know.'

Fingers working to remove more dirt and dust, the scene below THE RUINING OF MOUNT TOME: a sharp, jagged blade of lightning striking from a storm cloud, leaving the familiar sharp, jagged summit . . . the cloud bore the word REBELS.

'Ye think that's true?' said Nic, working to pry the stone circle free. 'Only made-up lies.'

'The *Tall Tale* that got us here is made up too,' said Bruno.

'Not the same,' said Nic.

Bruno didn't disagree. Instead he moved, letting Nic work.

'Help me,' said Nic, as the circle of stone lifted a little, then Bruno helped to push it aside.

No surprise – darkness below.

Nic unscrewed a bulb from the miner's lamp and let it fall – down a drop like a well, losing light as it tumbled, casting swift shadows on packed walls. Bruno counted slow, reaching ten before he heard a splash.

'Must be right down to the old mines,' said Nic.

They looked at each other.

Nic found another rope in his satchel, another crook of metal on the end that he fastened to the stone lid, the other end around the stem of the miner's lamp. He lowered it in, two bulbs left.

'Go,' he told Bruno.

From the descent before, Bruno remembered Nic's advice – hands apart, hold tight – and was better able now. He edged down the rope, lamp at his feet, eyes examining the contents of the well. Deep stone shelves surrounded him, curving with the wall. Everywhere were loose papers folded, not just yellowed but browned, green, even, with the creep of mould; books denied covers, edges singed like escapees from a blaze; much more paper in rolls, bundled away like obsolete maps of forgotten countries, string noosed around.

Bruno turned and the miner's lamp flicked its gaze onto copies of the *Pitch End Journal*, its light carelessly browsing, touching past headlines, whole shelves devoted to storing and not destroying like Pitch End had been told.

The rope shuddered, Bruno looked up – Nic was descending too.

'It should have the Rebel symbol on it!' Nic called down.

Bruno's fingers found his father's medallion and he pressed it between thumb and forefinger to impress its image on his mind. He had to focus on the winding keys, wrench attention from all else – all that he wanted to read and know, pluck from the shelves and devour, learning what was hidden, what was denied every eye in Pitch End on Elder Orders.

'See it anywhere?' asked Nic.

Then an explosion above –

Bruno and Nic stopped, listening to the advance of time – *tick-tick, tick-tick* . . .

Shouts, an order of, 'Another load of explosives!'

'Is there not a key for this other way in?' they heard an Enforcer ask.

'Temperate Thomas has it and we've no time for going to get it. Now pile up those explosives good and tight!'

How many more minutes?

Then something –

Bruno's attention snagged, not on the Rebel symbol, not on a box, but a book, the title in a familiar hand, silver on black –

Without Time
The End of Ageing – A Proposal
By Dr Jonathan Bloom

'Did ye find it?' Nic demanded, rope conveying upwards Bruno's stopping, his sudden attentiveness.

Bruno reached for the book. He dragged it free, one-handed, cobwebs clinging. He thought of adding it to his satchel, thought of tucking it under his arm, into the waistband of his trousers, any way he could bring it. It opened in his hand like a mind heavy with secrets, showing Bruno a meticulous, hand-drawn diagram: the Clocktower, eight smaller clock faces sketched in and around. Handwritten beside in a hurry was –

Talent & Time, most powerful thing (so said Arthur Pitch)

Time in physical form will aid in the imagining of it?

Pocket watch for a heart?

Bruno sought more words but the page was darkening, lamp almost empty and Nic crying above, 'What are ye doing? Do ye see it anywhere?'

Another explosion, not muffled now, and the Marshall's voice clear – 'Move the wreckage outta the way, be getting in there!'

Bruno turned the page and on the back saw more words –

have already identified a number of bright, healthy young subjects of on which experiments can be carried out. Rebel parents more than willing to

'*Bruno!*'

Nic's bare feet struck Bruno's head and Bloom's book was knocked from his hands –

'*There!*' cried Nic, pointing towards the shelf where Bloom's book had been; a dark box, Rebel symbol embossed in dull silver. Bruno reached for it, took it on fingertips, in one hand –

The shelf cracked, spat dust and Bruno thought of the whole place failing without Bloom's book, crumbling like a bridge with the keystone snatched.

Another crack to the shelf above –

Bruno looked up, saw dark faces around the circle like numbers on a clock, aiming, firing –

Nic shouted, '*Drop!*'

Bruno loosened his grip and let the rope rush through his hands. Torn skin, papers fleeing shelves like leaf fall –

Nic's feet slammed again against Bruno's scalp and then deep cold as he hit water, Nic a tick later, grabbing for Bruno and bringing them both to the surface. Like pennies dropped in a good-luck well – *I wish, I wish, I want* – the water popped around them with gunshots.

Nic said, 'Under. Follow me.'

But Bruno didn't. Knew he couldn't. Holding his breath and not knowing when he'd have another?

'Bruno,' said Nic, and he took Bruno's face in his hands. 'Ye have to. Can't let them win, remember?'

Bruno looked at him, and didn't know how to prepare himself.

More gunfire and Nic jerked forwards, shoulder struck –

And it was Bruno who acted. He took Nic's hand and pulled him under, plunging together with the box of winding keys tight under his arm, Dr Bloom's book nowhere in sight but dominating Bruno's thoughts, looming in the dark, wondering space behind his eyes.

XXV

Blood and Fire

All of Bruno was grazing stone, his bare feet insensible, his satchel anchoring him, the box with the symbol of the Rebels under his arm another weight. Forwards in the water a little but downwards more, with all Bruno's thoughts on how little longer he could hold his breath and how far off the surface might be. Then Nic helped – he kicked out hard. The water around them clouded. Bruno tried to see the extent of the wound in Nic's shoulder.

Soon Bruno could go no further, and his mouth itched open, lungs burning, and he saw Nic's mouth open too in exclamation, bubbles exploding from his lips as he took Bruno under the arms and kicked as both throats flooded with water –

Bruno returned to air and spat, retched, Nic still with a hold on him and demanding from somewhere close but sounding distant – 'Ye okay?'

Bruno didn't answer. He was trying to bring himself back. Eventually, he nodded. He looked up and saw flames imprisoned, heard a sound like laundry wild in a gale. He wiped water from his eyes – a drain above, a way out, fire beyond.

'We're in Old Town,' Bruno managed.

He noticed beams bracing the walls around them, bloated, and tools studding the surface of rough rock – axes, picks, their handles, all abandoned there mid-work. Bruno remembered, having heard (how else but in whispers in the Hedge School playground?) of sudden floods that had ended mining in Pitch End. He'd listened to Sabitha tell with relish of the drowning, bodies never found, men lost and families incomplete above ground. The Rebels had been responsible, she'd put about. More lies in life, he thought, and anger made Bruno shake himself out of reminiscence, focus on what needed to be done presently.

'We need to climb,' said Bruno, firelight fingering metal rods fixed to the walls.

Nic looked up, slowly, then nodded. 'Gimme the box,' he said.

'But I can—' he started, but Nic's hands went out for it and Bruno had to give. Nic lifted his bag around it, tugged the twine to tighten and began his climb, one-handed, the other arm loose, dark with blood. Bruno was close behind, clothes worse than a weight, all of him dripping like something being wrung.

Bruno felt a prickle of heat, and his scalp warmed and face tightened at the flames overhead. Memory took him again, ruthlessly, as he saw himself at four-going-on-five turns, the house in a rage around him . . .

Nic flung back the grating. The fire bellowed and he vanished upwards. Bruno pulled himself out, crawling and staying that way; fire was the source of the smoke but Bruno saw barely a light. He knew he was inside though. He half-stood, stumbled alone until his hands were reunited with Nic's, and with heads low, together they searched for their way out.

A wall came and they followed, awaiting a door – when it was touched it crumbled, falling to ash. Out into the street and there was more light to dazzle – fire snatching for stars, flames high and higher the farther Bruno looked, the more he watched . . .

He saw frantic shadows. The families of Old Town? Would Conn and his Cinder-Folk family escape? Go anywhere at all or just perish in the fire that tomorrow they'd be blamed for alongside returning Rebels and gypsies and all lower sorts the Elders bemoaned as the enduring blight on Pitch End?

'*Move*,' said Nic, and then he coughed so deep it doubled him over. Bruno gave him support and the pair of them turned as one but still there was nothing to see, no way to know where they needed to go. They could only stay close to one another, hope for something.

The Cinder-Folk, thought Bruno, again. Then he remembered the coal, the one Conn had given him. Help (he'd said) for whenever Bruno needed it. If that time was any –

'Wait,' Bruno said.

He eased Nic down, twisted out from under his satchel and kneeled to open it.

'Bruno,' said Nic. 'We can't wait.'

Bruno's fingers met shingle, the sharp edge of a pictograph – he let everything go, even this last. Only finding the Cinder-Folk's gift was of any consequence.

'Bruno,' repeated Nic, his voice faint. '*Please*.'

It came to him at last. Bruno held the coal in blackened fingers, both his gaze and Nic's resting on it.

Blood. It would work when blood was added, was that what Conn had told him? Without a thought Bruno pressed the coal to the wound on Nic's arm.

At first nothing; the flames of Old Town skulking, edging towards them, and the coal remaining dark in Bruno's hand. Then the touch of blood began to glow, burned white and white-hot but Bruno couldn't release it, had to hold it as white flame leapt high, a flare that rose and twisted through smoke, one way then another, exploring the air above and finally blossoming, spreading long tentacles. Unlike any flare Bruno had seen fishermen use, it continued its blaze, its disjointed trail like a frozen branch of lightning, its source Bruno and Nic below. Old Town was bleached with its light. Bruno was sure Enforcers would see, but hoped that Conn and his family would see first. But in the end, it was neither –

'*Clegg*,' said Nic, and Bruno was shocked at how weak he sounded.

And then a splutter-grumble that Bruno had already grown to recognise. The smoke was parted as one of the gliders tore through, swooping low, a shout falling from Louise – '*Get yerselves to higher up ground!*'

Then shadows with heavy footfalls approached, that could only be Enforcers. They gave no warning – just began to fire.

Bruno lifted Nic and turned; darkways everywhere.

Words reached for them from behind – 'There they are! Just ahead!'

Hopeless, thought Bruno. And as he imagined being caught, he saw a single silhouette ahead.

'Bruno,' said Nic, trying to press onto him the bag, the box with the Rebel symbol inside. 'Take it. Leave me and go.'

But Bruno stayed focused on the figure ahead. 'No,' he said. 'We're not running.'

'Too right,' said the voice of the shadow. Conn of the final Cinder-Folk family stepped from smoke. 'Stay close to me,' he said. He moved in front of Bruno and Nic, facing the Enforcers.

'Back!' one shouted, who must've thought himself braver than the shake in his rifle. 'I said back into yer rotten hole, on the Elder Order! I have a rifle, I'll shoot it!'

Conn took a step forwards, definite with defiance.

'I will!' shouted the Enforcer. 'I'll have no choice!'

Coward, thought Bruno. He'll not mind killing if he thinks he was pushed to it, needs to uphold the 'Elder Order'.

'We all will!' the Enforcer added, hoping for support, reminding Conn he wasn't alone. 'We aren't afeared to fight ye know, not against scum like yerself!'

'Good,' Bruno heard Conn say. 'Coz Cinder-Folk aren't afeared of a fight either.'

And he moved – a snap of the hand and flame from the nearest building was torn from its devouring and fell across the Enforcers' path, looping and enclosing them, its movement guided by Conn's Talent.

'Now, boys!' Conn called.

Bruno saw two low, swift shadows race from darkways on either side and fling coils of fire into the air, lashing the rifles from the Enforcers' hands. Bruno heard the Enforcers cry out, leap free of the circle of flames and run back into smoke, upwards, towards the town square. Conn didn't try to stop them. He would've had every right to destroy them, thought Bruno, after all that had been done to the Cinder-Folk. But on he let them go, just a low, crackling laugh for a farewell.

Suddenly Bruno felt less afraid of the flames. He held the white coal tighter in his hand. Dominic and Donal appeared beside, both grinning, both having to shout to make themselves heard over the flames.

'Did good, Da, dint we?' said Dominic.

'See them Enforcers running!' said Donal. 'They won't mess with us again.'

'Let's not be too proud,' Conn told them. 'But ye did well, boys, no doubt there.'

Their mouths widened all the more, feasting on their father's approval.

'Now,' said Conn, turning to Bruno. 'Ye need to be going.' He looked at Nic, took in his injuries. 'But first . . .'

Without being told to, the twins lowered themselves on either side of Nic. Both took small parcels from their belts and opened them, Donal rubbing something thick against the wound in Nic's shoulder, Dominic pressing small seeds between his lips.

'It'll help him,' said Conn.

'Yer father,' said Bruno. 'Is he alright?'

'He's grand,' said Conn. 'Would take more than this to end him.'

'The other people,' said Bruno. 'Families, won't they—'

'All safe,' said Conn. 'Got everyone to safety quick-smart, soon as we saw them making their pyres. They were getting ready, and so were we. We have our own ways and means under Pitch End.'

Dominic placed a final seed on a finger, pushing it deep into Nic's mouth, Donal still prodding Nic's shoulder, then both smiled, satisfied.

'That's him,' said Donal.

'He'll be grand for now,' said Dominic.

Conn cocked his head. Had he heard more voices?

'Somewhere high we need to get to,' said Bruno, helping Nic to stand.

Conn paused, then said, 'This way.'

As they walked, any threatening flame was sent slithering, cowering behind cracked windows, clearing a way ahead. 'Why don't ye just stop the flames?' asked Bruno, feeling Nic's legs reclaim the weight of his body, strengthening.

'Can't stop a thing when it gets going,' said Conn. 'This is the rage of Temperate Thomas, his Talent keeping it going. And that can't be disappeared in a tick, even by one of the Cinder-Folk. All we can do is try and tame it.'

Conn stopped. Bruno faced a building with wooden stairs clinging to its side and, like all things in Old Town, already crumbling, keen to collapse.

'Hold that coal high,' said Conn, 'and yer friend on the flying contraption will see.'

'Thank you,' said Bruno. 'That's a second time ye've been saving me. I—'

'Being alive is thanks enough for me,' said Conn.

Then a thought came to Bruno. 'Ye said ye know ways under Pitch End. Do ye know a way under the Clocktower?'

Conn said, 'Yes, but—'

'There's a girl under there,' said Bruno. 'If ye can, then help her. She was taken by the Elders. She's the Marshall's daughter. If we can get her to safety, show Pitch End . . .'

Conn looked at him, and understood. 'I'll try my best,' he said. 'Now go.'

Bruno took to the steps and gradually conquered them, Nic walking taller but still slowing him.

'Ye should've been leaving me,' said Nic.

'Shut up,' Bruno told him. 'Stop trying to be a martyr.'

He saw Nic smile, then grimace with it.

And when they finally stepped out onto a sagging flat roof and looked out over Old Town, Bruno saw a world unravelling, ribbons of smoke drawn taut by rising winds. He held Nic close and the Cinder-Folk's coal high, waved it, its own bright trail curling into the sky.

They waited, and he wondered if anyone could see them in such chaos and ruin.

'Will they come?' he heard Nic ask. 'Will they have waited for us?'

Bruno saw David (in his worst imagining) leaving them, deciding they were a necessary casualty of the continuance of the Rebels. A sacrifice. Regrettable, but unavoidable. He shook himself free of it and said, 'They'll come.'

As though summoned by resolve, Bruno saw the Clegg. It charged from the smoke, Louise flying, a rope trailing below, David just behind on the second glider.

The ground beneath Bruno and Nic dipped, began to fold –

'Grab it!' shouted Louise.

The rope touched Bruno's hands and, still holding Nic, he wondered if it would take them both, but Nic recovered enough of himself, clutched the rope as well and they left, the roof collapsing as they were lifted free of Old Town. They swung wild and wide. Bruno noticed Nic's hand curled tight around his bag, the box inside. Bruno allowed himself to think, we did it.

Gunshots followed them, distinct from snapping flame, small bursts of white.

Bruno shouted up to Louise, 'Get us away, quick-smart!'

He didn't hear Louise's response, only felt the swerve of the glider as they turned towards the Elm Tree Mountains.

Then Nic, with sudden aggression, shouted, '*David!*'

Bruno turned and saw flames feathering the wings of David's Clegg, racing along ribbed frames. A gunshot from below struck the belly of the glider, a stream of fuel catching, liquid becoming fire –

Again Nic shouted, '*David!*'

But Bruno knew there was nothing they could do. David was too far behind to leap to their glider, too high to throw himself to safety.

David looked to all sides, rising to half-standing, then sinking. His last look reached Bruno. Despite what had gone before, Bruno felt a rush of respect for David then. Quick-thinking, knowing the extent of the situation and making a decision free of panic or emotion or pride – this was David. And the calm expression he always wore didn't falter, even as he kicked a pedal and the fiery wings of his Clegg snapped closed and dropped him into darkness.

XXVI
Dr Bloom's Gift

How well Mount Tome held its secrets, Bruno thought. If he'd been flying the Clegg he wouldn't have known where to aim for. The mouth, the cavern, the home they needed to return to – all were invisible, Tome widening till it was everything Bruno could see.

But through habit or practice, Louise could direct them arrow-straight and Bruno recognised the mouth only moments before the glider – rattling and shuddering like it wanted to explode under them – deigned to enter and land, spindle-legs scraping stone.

Nic was off without hesitation, his injury not forgotten but reduced – the box with the Rebel symbol and its contents was all that mattered to him.

Bruno knew there was David to think of. But he knew also how much the loss of David was bound up in the success of their mission. He thought: please let the box contain the winding keys, or what has David been lost for?

Nic ran to the edge of the mouth and fell to his knees.

Bruno needed to see too. He looked at Louise, and they both leapt from the Clegg and went to Nic's side, Louise dropping her gun, Bruno his satchel.

All three were crouched.

'Yer arm,' breathed Bruno, eyes on the small, dark point in Nic's shoulder, slapped over with what Donal had done – a yellowish membrane, transparent. 'Is it—'

'Leave it,' snapped Nic. 'Stop fussing.'

From his belt Nic took a small dark key. He pressed it to his lips, mouth muttering a silent prayer around it, and then added it to the small lock. Bruno heard a low whirr of clockwork. The lid of the box opened on its own.

Nic shivered. Louise held both hands to her mouth. Bruno leaned closer.

Winding keys.

Nic sighed, smiled.

Bruno looked closer: some were as large as his hand, some smaller – some fingernail-sized – but all dark. He saw his curiosity reflected: water from the mine had entered and made a mirror the keys were stranded in. Dark water, and not just reflecting night, Bruno thought. He saw his own worry there, a face full of a mind full of the usual series of doubts – what if . . . ?

Nic smiled wider. He reached into the box.

The first key held together in Nic's fingers for so long Bruno's worry receded, a little . . . Then the key crumbled as though a hand, unseen, had denied it, with iron intent crushed it, wanted it dust and memory.

'No.' The word left Nic in a whimper, but he took up another key without waiting.

Bruno saw a small carving, embossed metal shaped like a fox, telling the key's Sentry counterpart. And it crumbled too. And the next, and again, Nic breathless as though trying to outrun disappointment, Louise too realising their calamity and disagreeing – 'No, no, no' – both hands leaving her mouth to cover her ears, her eyes snapped shut, denying.

But Bruno watched. Saw each key taken, saw each disintegrate. It had been too long, he thought. The winding keys had waited, weakening, for ten turns. The water had been the last blow. Bruno might've wept himself if it weren't for Nic and Louise. Same as after his father had gone – his mother steeped in black and permanent grief – he felt his own upset too small for consideration. At home, he'd needed to continue, his mother the one to stop living. He felt the same with Nic and Louise – he needed to be stronger.

'Leave them,' he told Nic, reaching in and taking one key for himself. Somehow it held. The largest, heaviest one, it carried the embossed form of the Tiger-Sentry. 'Wait,' said Bruno, and he removed others, slowly, and laid them aside. 'Some are okay.'

But Nic had turned away.

After minutes of delicate rescue, Bruno had twelve whole

keys salvaged, and bits of others. 'We have some,' he said, watching the side of Nic's face.

Nic looked at him, desperation edging into anger, same as Bruno had seen in the labyrinth beneath the town hall. 'How would ye know?' he said. His teeth were tight together. 'How would Bruno Atlas who's been in Pitch End all rightly-comfortable and well fed and well kept for ten turns – how would he know how much this meant?'

Bruno wasn't supposed to answer, he knew. He'd heard enough lectures – from Miss Hope, the Temperate, his mother when she'd been bothered – to know he was to provide an audience only. To be the person Nic could rage against; just a person to be angry with.

'Ye think this is a game?' said Nic. 'Do ye? Just all playtime and whether we defeat Elders or not doesn't matter, one way or the other?'

'I never said that,' said Bruno.

'Ye don't *say* anything!' cried Nic. 'Nothing useful anyway!'

Bruno didn't reply. He said to himself: he's just angry. Doesn't mean it.

Nic slumped against stone, arms slithering around his knees. Louise stood, sobbing, pacing the mouth end to end.

'We can still fight on,' said Bruno, his voice not feeling like his own – too loud, too alone in the silence dictated by Nic and Louise's disappointment. 'We might not need Sentries to fight with, we can think of another plan or—'

'Or what?' said Nic. 'Dr Bloom left us that army to fight with.'

'Maybe he left more things,' said Bruno. 'Maybe in the *Tall Tales* he—'

'For *Pitch* sake, *Tall Tales* are for children, not us!'

Something in the statement made Bruno stall, look at Nic more clearly. Nic looked away, rose again but went nowhere. Louise had stopped.

'We are children,' said Bruno. 'Aren't we?'

'*You* might be,' said Nic. 'Still just for daydreaming, just like yer da.'

'*Tall Tales* helped us find our way to the keys,' said Bruno, and he rose too, slowly. 'And they helped me when I was ten turns, gave me something else to think about than what the Elders were saying. Even David, he believed in them.'

'And look where it got him,' said Nic.

'He died fighting for what we're meant to be believing in,' said Bruno. 'Isn't that the point of the Rebels?'

Nic sighed, and spoke slowly. 'Look, maybe it's all too complicated for ye, Bruno. Being a Rebel isn't rightly-easy, but Dr Bloom always told us—'

'Maybe Dr Bloom isn't the bloody beginning and end of everything!' shouted Bruno, and he felt as though some deep anger, long-waiting, had been tapped. 'Maybe he wasn't this genius that ye all thought he was!'

'Right,' said Nic, and he turned away. 'And where did ye get that bit of good wisdom from? The Elders? Temperate Thomas hisself?'

'I saw something,' said Bruno. 'When we were in the town hall.'

Nic said nothing.

'Another book by Dr Bloom,' Bruno continued. 'Not *Tall Tales*.'

He looked to Louise. She was staring at Nic, and she was shaking.

'It had a picture of the Clocktower,' said Bruno.

'Dr Bloom designed it,' said Nic. 'Thought ye might've worked that out already. No big news there.'

'And our pocket watches were beside it,' said Bruno.

'He made them too. So?'

'And some writing. Some writing about – about experimenting on children.'

Nic had nothing then. Louise looked on the verge of collapse.

'He came up with the Clocktower and the pocket watches,' said Bruno. He swallowed. 'But it was him that came up with the idea of taking youth from the children too, wasn't it?'

Still no reply, so Bruno advanced –

'He did it first, or planned on doing. And now the Temperate is for seeing it through.'

Still no answer. But each moment of silence, each word unspoken, made Bruno feel more right, closer to the truth.

'We should tell him,' said Louise. She'd stopped crying, stopped shaking. Bruno thought she looked relieved. 'Nic, we should tell him the truth.'

But Nic didn't move.

Bruno looked between them, and then realised aloud. 'It was the two of you, and David. You were the children he experimented on.'

There was no disagreement.

'How come ye're not old?' Bruno asked, moving towards Nic. 'Sabitha, the girl I saw him do it to, she went older as Temperate Thomas got younger.'

Nic sighed. And at last he turned, face not to Bruno but out to the night.

'Because he abandoned it when he knew what he'd created,' he said, in a voice barely heard. Bruno waited, sensing that Nic would start the story where he wanted, where it made sense to him, and out it would furl like the memory of a *Tall Tale*. Nic cleared his throat, and then began –

'Before Dr Bloom started up the Rebels he was a Trainee Elder. Temperate Thomas's best pupil, all in Pitch End said. Was well on his way to becoming Temperate hisself one day. But he was different – he read more than any of them oul fools. Studied, designed things, made them. Made anything he could out of clockwork, like the Cat-Sentries that the Elders use. He looked for things, deeper than anyone had gone, into the places under the town hall. He found *The Book of Black & White*. Became rightly-obsessed by it. Ye see, Dr Bloom had this fear of getting old. Not dying, he told me once, but just being old.'

'The shame of it,' said Louise, and then went quiet again, sinking to the ground.

'Aye, the *shame*,' said Nic. His fingers crept to his shoulder, to the wound given temporary repair by the Cinder-Folk boys. He began to pick at it. 'And he thought that the ideas Arthur Pitch wrote about in *The Book of Black & White* – about Talent and what people could do if they put their mind to it, how if ye think a thing and yer Talent is strong enough, if ye have enough feeling behind it and imagination, ye can be doing anything – he thought he could use it all to stop time dead.'

Nic swallowed. Bruno waited. Felt he would've waited forever for the rest –

'So Dr Bloom started to plan,' continued Nic. 'A way to keep all of Pitch End young forever. He planned to build a Clocktower with eight pocket watches that would be given to eight key people in Pitch End: a fisherman, a farmer, shopkeeper, street-sweeper, market-seller, lamp-lighter, Widow, and the present lighthouse-keeper – yer father, Bruno. And with the pocket watches they'd be able to start the Clocktower. But only all together, all united. When they needed it, Dr Bloom planned, then Pitch End could come together as one to use the Clocktower, like he'd learned in *The Book of Black & White*, to channel their Talent and keep everyone in the town young. It was a *gift*. Something he'd be remembered for. Or was supposed to be. Everything changed when he told Temperate Thomas about his plan.

'The Temperate agreed, to begin with. Only thing, he was wanting the eight pocket watches to remain with

289

the Elders, not just common Pitch Enders. And then he said that maybe only the Elders should benefit, keep young, them being the people who looked after the Pitch Enders. They needed to stay young more than any, so they could continue ruling Pitch End. Dr Bloom didn't agree, but he was given permission anyway to start his experiment. But on the condition that he test it on children.'

Nic stopped again, but not for lack of remembering, Bruno knew. From a lack of . . . what? Courage? Determination? Or a surfeit of pain?

'The first children he tried to make younger died,' said Nic. 'Dr Bloom realised he'd misread Arthur Pitch's book, misread his own feelings, he'd said. Youth couldn't be taken or given out just like that. He needed to take from one and give to another. Straightaway he gave up his plan.'

Nic began to pace, fingers still scratching at the shoulder wound and powered (Bruno thought) by familiar, firm feelings: Dr Bloom and Rebels good, Temperate Thomas and Elders bad.

'But that Temperate,' said Nic, 'he already knew and wanted to continue on. The Clocktower was nearly finished, it'd taken nearly two years to be built and that couldn't be undone. So Dr Bloom left the Elders and began to gather followers for a Rebellion. He started to build a clockwork army. He hid the pocket watches, putting four into the chests of the Withermen, thinking that even Temperate Thomas wouldn't be for taking them out of a man's chest, not the men who deal with the dead. And the others he gave to our fathers.'

Nic stopped – pacing, picking – and leaned against the wall, spent, as though he'd travelled a great distance. 'The Rebels were never going to be winning,' he said. 'We all knew that. Dr Bloom needed to a way to keep the cause going, hope that someday the Elders would be weak enough to beat. So he used *The Book of Black & White* and his Talent on me, Louise and David. Instead of making us old, he gave us his own youth. Wanted us to be young forever so we could keep on the fighting. Our fathers gave their youth too. And then they left.'

'Where did they go?' asked Bruno.

'Dunno,' said Nic. 'On a boat, taking *The Book of Black & White* with them. And we came up here to stay, to get ready to fight again.'

Bruno waited. Held his silence as long as he could before he asked his final question –

'Ye've been here for ten turns?'

Nic nodded. 'I suppose I'm something like twenty-five turns old,' he said. 'Inside anyway.'

'I'm younger than that,' said Louise, quickly. She looked immediately baffled at her own words. She examined her own hands, her whole self, wondering.

'It was a *gift*,' said Nic, and he clenched his fists on the word. 'It was the Elders who've been doing the wrong thing. Dr Bloom was in the right. He gave up his plan when he knew what would happen, tried to make it *right*.'

291

'Just coz the Elders are wrong doesn't mean Dr Bloom and our fathers were right,' said Bruno, and he felt somehow weighted by the notion. But he went on: 'Doing a thing just so ye can last, hold onto power and keep on fighting, that's what Bloom wanted. And it's what the Elders want too.'

'He tried,' said Nic, finally. 'Dr Bloom left us the army, the pocket watches.'

'The pocket watches restart the Clocktower,' said Bruno, throwing a glance at his satchel. 'If anything we should be destroying them.'

'He said they'd help us too in some way,' said Nic.

'How?' asked Bruno.

'I—' said Nic, and said no more. A final scratch at the wound. Blood escaped, drawing a line as dark as charcoal on his arm. Nic ignored it, returning to the ground to sit on the same spot he'd occupied earlier.

'If the watches were meant to help,' said Bruno, 'he should've just been telling ye how, clear as anything, and not playing his games.'

A moment, multiplying into many. Silence and then the rain, like a new voice in the conversation. It began like it would never stop, sharp and straight and silvered by moon, a torrent of dropped needles.

Bruno turned away from Nic and Louise, the winding key for the Tiger-Sentry being turned over and over in his hand. Somehow he felt older. Older on the inside than out. No wiser, but lonelier. He sank too, in the end, eyes closing, and within the minute drifted, exhaustion a welcome sleep.

XXVII
The Tall Tale of the Clockwork Boy

'Are ye ever gonna bloody wake up?'

'I will,' said Bruno, eyes still shut, forgetful of where he was. 'Will be waking up soon, Mam.'

'I'm not yer mam!'

Bruno opened his eyes. He saw Louise, cross-legged and close.

He moved and found he still had the winding key for the Tiger-Sentry in his hand. Then everything – all he'd learned, listened to from Nic – returned in a rush.

'I'm awake,' he said.

Bruno put the Tiger-Sentry's key into his pocket and eased himself up.

Rain was still a racket, but was the world lighter, brighter? Perhaps (thought Bruno) the darkness was less deep. He shut his eyes, hard, then sat up a little straighter.

And then he noticed – Louise was reading *The Book of Black & White*. The clasp that had held it shut was broken, in pieces by Louise's feet.

'What are ye—' Bruno began.

'I'm trying to learn,' said Louise. 'My da always said to learn what others are rightly afraid of. And I'm not gonna sit around moping. Boys are so rightly-keen for feeling sorry for themselves. If we're gonna be beating that Temperate then I want to know why him and Dr Bloom thought this book was so bloody great.'

Bruno had an instinct to tell her no – shut the book, put it aside. But a moment's thought made him realise he would be betraying himself – he wanted to see as much as (maybe more than) Louise. He was afraid, but knew fear stopped things being discovered. If he'd obeyed fear, he'd never have found *Tall Tales from Pitch End*. He moved in a crawl towards Louise, and sat beside.

Like the single page the Elders had hidden under the Clocktower for ten turns and used to leech youth from children, the inside of the book was black. Rough ridges, raised like raw wounds, marked the paper. Bruno thought first that it might be another language, then that it might not be language at all.

'Can ye read it?' he asked Louise.

She was leaning – elbows on knees, fists pressed into her cheeks – close to the book, eyes narrowed. Louise took a long moment to say, 'No. But if I sit and stare long enough, force all my feeling to thinking about the book

– like when I use Talent – then I start to feel things. See things.'

Bruno looked to the page too. His fingertips itched against one another. He made a decision, took a breath, and placed his fingers on the top of the page nearest him.

His eyes shut themselves.

Louise said, 'Be careful.'

Like he'd seen Temperate Thomas do, Bruno dragged down; his fingers felt things sharp on the surface that pained and caught, holding his progress, and then allowing them to pass. And behind his eyes Bruno felt a rising, an oncoming sensation, same as when he thought of being unseeable and knew he'd achieved it. But not pleasurable, not liberating like a Talent.

His fingers moved on, like wanderers through a maze, down and across, from one ridge to the next, faster, easier. And then he saw things. Like scenes lit by lightning, possibilities for his Talent were glimpsed. He saw fire become ice, earth rising in sharp spikes to form whatever he desired, imagined. Bruno realised: I'm not just reading this book, the book is reading me. It knows what I want, and how to achieve it.

Memories came, then – the old house burning, in Hedge School striking Sabitha, bodies scattered on Diamond Beach, his mother weeping, Temperate's face losing old age – mingled with imagining, wishing: Bruno and his parents together still, on Diamond Beach, in their old house, on South Street. And then other, darker wishes: Pitch End split, breaking open, destroyed as Elders tumbled into the void, the entire town swallowed by the sea . . .

'*Bruno!*'

Louise's shout, her snatching away of his hand, brought him back.

Bruno opened his eyes. The world felt drab, poor, after where he'd been. He was shaking but felt stronger than ever. He looked at Louise. Her eyes were glistening, fearful. Then he looked to his hand, the one she was holding – blood stained his fingertips like ink.

'What did ye see?' she asked him.

When Bruno spoke he felt stronger still. 'Things that Talent can do. It's not just feeling that fires a Talent, it's imagining too. If ye can think of something, then it'll happen.' He remembered written words – *Time in physical form will aid in the imagining of it*. 'It was what Dr Bloom imagined, what he wanted – must've been what he saw when he read this book. He built the Clocktower coz he knew it'd help him to keep Pitch End young. It'd help him to imagine it, help his Talent to do it.'

He looked down and saw blood, a track crossing the page through rough complications. Louise slammed the book shut.

'It'll be doing us no good,' she said. 'We keep to Dr Bloom's plan: keep the book away from that Temperate, along with our pocket watches.'

'And that's it?' said Bruno, eyes still on *The Book of Black & White*. 'Just stay here for another ten turns?'

'Yes,' she said, and the determination in her voice, the speed with which she spoke, left Bruno weak and trailing to catch up. 'Have to keep going and keep the eyes open and the mind thinking and the heart *tick-ticking*, that's what my da used to say. His name was Edgar Green, best sign-painter in Pitch End, always in demand, used to paint at home these amazing pictures! "*Keep the heart tick-ticking.*" Have ye ever heard that *Tall Tale*? It's the best one!' Before Bruno could reply she went on: '*The Tall Tale of the Clockwork Boy*. My da used to tell it to me. I can remember it word for word –

'*Not too many turns ago, on the narrowest street in Old Town, in the narrowest house with the narrowest rooms and the narrowest doors and the narrowest halls, there lived an old couple with the narrowest minds. This man and woman – narrow-shouldered, narrow-faced, narrow-eyed and narrow-mouthed – owned a clock-making business. One day, contemplating their oncoming age, and worrying for how they'd look after themselves (as they had no children and no family who liked them), they decided to build themselves a son. A clockwork boy.*

'*Once completed, he was almost in every way like a usual boy, except for a dark, empty place in his chest – he had been denied a heart by the narrow-minded couple (they didn't pay much attention to such a detail) and so every day he had to be wound tight to get him going.*

'*Although he lived with the narrow man and woman in their narrow house, the clockwork boy did not have the* same narrow mind. He was kept in the narrowest room at the narrowest part of the house, at the very, very tip, and the boy spent much time gazing through the tall, narrow window out over Pitch End, to sea and sky and mountains. The boy had an urge he couldn't trace – a need, like breathing, for adventure. But his narrow old parents viewed him as more a servant than a son, always with demands and scolding, groaning like martyrs and weeping for endless cups of sugary tea or toast dripping with dripping.

'Every morning he would be wound, wake with his chest crackling, arms and legs stirring and in his recorded voice he would say, all sprightly: "Good morning! Would you like some breakfast?"

'The man and woman would order, "Yes! This very minute!"

'"Right away!" the clockwork boy would reply.

'His clockwork limbs sent him sprinting into the kitchen where his clockwork hands would set to work, cracking eggs, flipping bacon, churning butter, kneading bread, boiling water. The old couple would smile at one another, lazy and content. And every morning, they would sit down and eat their fill of a sumptuous breakfast.

'The clockwork boy cooked and cleaned from morning till after dark. And the old, narrow couple would always retire to bed early, taking care to wind the boy up before they did so, or risk him running down and stopping before the day's work was done.

'For days, months, for many long turns, the clockwork

boy continued without complaint, being wound so tight that he never stopped, day or night. Until one morning, his usual enquiry met with no response – the clockwork boy stood over the narrow bed of the narrow couple and asked: "Would you like some breakfast?" The couple's lips did not part. They did not stir. The clockwork boy asked again, and again and again . . . He stood over them for the entire morning, asking and asking. But still they did not move, did not answer.

'With no work to do, no order to follow, the clockwork boy had no clue how to pass time. But he quickly became aware that if he wasn't being wound up, then very soon he would stop moving altogether. Would stop thinking, stop doing. He decided then that he would try and see as much as he could of the town before that happened.

'He stepped out into Old Town, and had taken no more than a few steps along the cobbles when he saw a girl nearby. She had long, blond, curly hair that stood up like a brush, and a long emerald cloak around her shoulders. The girl was crying.

'The clockwork boy approached her and asked, "Would you like some breakfast?" for these were all the words he knew.

'The girl looked at him and said, "Ye can see me? Ye knew I was here?"

'Small cogs in his head churning, the clockwork boy thought about the girl's words. Her answer wasn't something he recognised, it sounded more like a question, not the commands he was used to. He wanted to say one thing but ended up saying another – "Would you like milk in your tea?"

'The girl laughed. She quickly forgot her tears and stood up.

'"My name is the Emerald Ghost," said the girl. "I'm called that coz not everyone wants to see me or listen to me."

'The clockwork boy didn't reply, knowing he had no words to properly reply with. He settled for shaking a hand that the Emerald Ghost had offered.

'"I'm trying to find my father," said the girl. "Do ye want to help me look? He wears an emerald hat, same colour as my cloak."

'The clockwork boy nodded, saying, "I'm sure today's weather is going to be grand indeed," which (although still not what he wanted to say exactly) felt close enough to what he meant.

'The girl laughed, took him by the hand and off they ran together, him clattering on his clockwork feet, her laughing to herself with delight.

'They searched for the girl's father. High and low, and then higher and lower – slopes and street corners, rooftops and mines . . . but he was nowhere to be found. The hours of the day grew shorter, darkness crept in and the clockwork boy felt sure he was going to soon wind down completely. Unable to find words to tell the girl what he needed though, he continued to follow her – from the fields of barley and corn on the east of Pitch End to the rocky head on the west.

'In the end, even the girl lost hope, and on Diamond Beach she fell to her knees and began to weep anew, looking just as she had done that morning when the clockwork boy had first found her.

'The clockwork boy looked out. The sea's surface was scarlet, set alight by the slipping away of the sun. And then he saw a flash of emerald.

'Without words he ran across the sand with his final energy, his feet sinking, his winding key spinning with the effort, and threw himself into the water. He didn't know how to swim, so simply let the tide take him. But it carried him with great speed to a man with an emerald hat on his head who was struggling, was almost drowned. The clockwork boy grabbed hold of the man and, thrashing his metal arms, kicking his metal feet, he dragged him back towards shore.

'It was hard work, hard going, and by the time he regained the beach he was all but wound down, ready to stop, cease moving and thinking and being forever.

'"Thank you!" cried the girl, who had thrown herself on the man with the emerald hat. "It's my da, ye found him!"

'But the clockwork boy couldn't reply – he was unable to speak, unable to move, had only moments left of life. He looked out over the sea, towards the sunset, and felt that even if this was to be his last sight, he would feel contented – he had experienced one day free of chores and orders, and in it he had made a friend and helped reunite

301

her with her father, and surely that should be enough for anyone. What the clockwork boy didn't know was that the man he had just saved was a skilled clockmaker.

'"Any being" (he said) "that shows as much courage as this boy just has deserves better than to live with the constant threat of leaving. Ye need a way to exist on yer own, without having to be wound up by others."

'And from his waistcoat the man took a pocket watch and pressed it into the dark space that had always existed where the clockwork boy's heart should've been.

'The clockwork boy stood, knowing that so long as the pocket watch kept going – his new heart still ticking – then so would he. He would never have to rely on another to be wound. He found the right words then, words he'd learned from the girl. "Thank you," he said.

'And the clockwork boy left them, his new heart tick-ticking with excitement and adventure, with thoughts of where he could go, what he could do alone or, if he became lonely, the people he might see, friends he might be destined to make.'

XXVIII

Wakening

Bruno was on his feet, satchel in hand and moving fast for that opening like a long, jointed throat that would return him to the cavern of Sentries, to the statues of their fathers.

'Where ye going?' asked Louise, standing. 'Come back! Didn't ye recognise me in the story?'

Bruno wriggled into the harness and found the lever that would lower him. He said nothing, couldn't speak. More quickly down than they'd risen, with words in Dr Bloom's hand repeating in his mind – '*Pocket watch for a heart?*' – he landed, shook the harness off and stumbled into the cavern where their erstwhile army was still assembled. He stopped on the edge of things, hearing a voice – '*Ye have to fight on, don't be a coward! Always for acting like a child, Nicholas! Grow up, hold yer head high!*'

Bruno recognised it from the town hall – it was the voice the second Cat-Sentry had spoken in. Nic's father.

He looked to the platform and saw Nic seated on the ground, head down. Bruno moved more slowly, feeling like he had interrupted, was taking from Nic time that needed to be spent between father and son.

Then he heard Nic speak – 'I tried, Da, I really tried.'

'No excuse! No excuse at all for cowardice. A Rebel is never afraid, not of anything!'

Bruno lingered with so much to say.

A rattle of clockwork behind and Louise was deposited too, unpicking her harness. 'I just worked it out!' she said, running to Bruno. 'I worked it out too, from the *Tall Tale*!'

'Worked what out?' asked Nic, voice hollow.

Bruno hesitated. What if I'm wrong? What if I've taken too much from a story? A story intended, as Nic had said, for 'children'?

He swallowed, and then shouted, 'Ye were right. About Dr Bloom, about telling us to use the pocket watches to fight the Elders. We just had to listen to him.'

Nic didn't reply.

And Bruno was suddenly tired of thinking and worrying, tired of words too – he ran forwards, weaving between Sentries, leapt the steps and ran the line of statues to Nic, who stayed seated. Bruno took his pocket watch from his satchel. He faced the clockwork statue of his father, eyes on the Rebel symbol, his chest.

'Is this going to work?' said Louise, arriving behind him.

Bruno said nothing, nor did Nic.

Bruno's fingers went to the catch beneath his pocket watch.

304

He felt it shiver – unseen movements trickling through its insides – and flower on his palm. He had to remember to breathe.

Then Nic stood. A single tear beaded his cheek. His hands came together like prayer.

Bruno reached up and settled a hand on the chest of his father's statue. He felt he should push. The Rebel symbol split, parted like a pair of small doors. And behind was an absence, a darkness, with four radiating, triangular spaces. Bruno settled his pocket watch into the chest of his father. He felt he should turn it. He tried, and was allowed – slowly, and with a sense of many mechanisms within the statue struggling to remember old, intended movements. Turned and turned it until he felt a click so profound it sent shock up his arm, into his own heart.

He stepped away, standing between and slightly in front of Nic and Louise.

All waited. Bruno shut his eyes and hoped and then doubted, hoped anew –

'Look,' said Nic.

Bruno looked and found his father's eyes. They were moving. A slow slide, trying to register strange surroundings. His brass fingers twitched, his head turned.

'It's working!' shouted Louise, her words bouncing around the cavern. But anything else was set aside, banished by more words –

'*Rebels, be warned!*'

Not Bruno's father speaking.

'Who is that?' asked Bruno.

Nic drew in a long breath. 'It's Dr Bloom,' he said.

'*Prepare yerselves!*' Bloom continued from further along the line, calling in a voice not quite human, not quite Sentry. '*Be ready to fight!*'

'What is he—' began Bruno.

But then another voice, one not recorded but alive, that chilled them like biting Ever-Winter, made Bruno, Nic and Louise turn –

'I think we'll be doing without the fighting, don't you? After all, it's a great sin to be defying the Head of the Elders.'

They were found. Temperate Thomas had entered the Rebel Chapel.

XXIX
Masked

'Rightly-nice of Dr Bloom to put that informative little notice outside,' said Temperate Thomas. 'But it gives rather too much of a clue, didn't ye ever think? But he never was the most modest or rightly-retiring sort of man. Though we did have our helpful little guide.' He lifted his hand. Between finger and thumb the Temperate held a pitch, but one like no other: one of his fingers slid across its surface, showing the clock face hidden inside. Then the Marshall and two Enforcers appeared, and one other –

'*David!*' Louise stood on tip toe, straining towards the edge of the platform and hurling the name. 'Ye two-faced, bloody—'

'He's been rightly-useful,' said the Temperate, and he didn't need to shout, to fire words, voice flitting across the cavern without effort. 'Rightly-obedient. Says he's seen the error of his ways.'

Silence, and then David's voice, calm as ever: 'He's right. It's over. We can't fight on any more.'

Bruno looked to Nic and saw the same thought: why had David done this? They got an answer –

'I don't want to be in this mountain forever!' roared David across the distance. 'I want a normal life!'

Bruno didn't know what to believe, what to allow himself to think. But Louise allowed herself anger – she swore, cursed, and Temperate Thomas chided, 'Now, now, none of that foul talk. Let's just be stopping this game. It's gone far enough. Time to end this and come back to Pitch End.'

'Not a bloody game!' Louise shouted. 'It's a war! Rebels against Elders!'

The Temperate's laughter was a torment that Bruno cringed at.

'A *war*?' he repeated. 'And what will ye be fighting with? This collection of rightly-curious but broken, battered, rusted toys?'

'Other things,' said Nic, and Bruno saw some of the old Nic return, some of the same resolve that had sent him leaping on an Enforcer, killing. He saw him whip his pocket watch from his belt, press his hand to his father's chest, watch it open as Bruno's father's had done, then add the watch to the dark space, Louise observing then doing the same.

'Other things?' said Temperate Thomas, who had begun a slow descent of the slope on the far side of the cavern.

The Marshall was close behind, hand on pistol, David held by the Enforcers.

'*Such as us.*'

The reply not from Bruno or Nic or Louise, but from Dr Bloom. The statue of the Rebel leader stepped forwards and Bruno couldn't help his spirits lifting, hoping, wondering if they might have a chance. He wondered though, how can Bloom move without a pocket watch in his chest?

'*Rebels!*' boomed Dr Bloom. '*Prepare yerselves!*'

The statue of Bruno's father stepped forwards, clockwork working furiously in battered legs. Then Nic's father, then Louise's, both ungainly, arms outstretched like incorrigible dreamers.

Temperate Thomas stopped halfway across the cavern.

'One more chance,' he said, holding up a finger. 'One more, and then I end this nonsense.'

Not even a moment for reflection. Dr Bloom shouted – '*Now!*'

Michael Atlas, Nicholas M. Delby Senior, Edgar Green and Dr Jonathan Bloom leapt – a solitary bound that took them high into darkness, reduced them to faint glimmers, faint hopes, Bruno's head dizzy with the sight. Then down to face the Marshall and the Enforcers who fired as David was forced to the ground, bullets sparking off brass, the sound of metal against metal terrorising the cavern –

But Temperate Thomas did nothing. Not fight, not flee, only waited, watching the approach of the Rebel statues.

'What do we do?' asked Bruno, having to raise his voice but keep his words between the three of them.

'We need to get David,' said Nic.

'Too right!' said Louise. 'And once we get him I'll be beating the living *Pitch* outta him!'

'No,' said Nic. 'We get him, we save him.'

'*Why?*' said Louise. 'He bloody betrayed us!'

'No,' said Nic. A pause, then, 'He wouldn't do that.'

Louise looked to Bruno, who realised he was being asked, silently, for his opinion. 'I agree with Nic,' he said. 'We have to move quick.'

But Bruno wasn't thinking of swift rescue for David – he was almost as torn about David's motives as Louise – but instead of the Temperate. The sight of the man so impassive, so unconcerned, filled him with a need for action.

'We can make ourselves unseeable,' said Bruno. 'We get to David, we escape.'

'No!' said Louise. 'I'm not leaving! We stay and fight, we need to—'

'Bruno's right,' said Nic. 'We need to go.'

Louise folded her arms, didn't move.

'*Bring down the Head of the Elders!*'

Dr Bloom's fresh shout made Bruno turn and watch as the statue of Louise's father charged at the Temperate. Temperate Thomas worried only a hand – he sliced the air and Edgar Green's head was removed. Louise's folded arms loosened, watching as her father lumbered, clashing against Sentries, blind, and then fell, legs kicking but finding no ground, arms a pitiful paddle. Then still.

It was enough to give the Marshall and Enforcers nerve – their shots entered the heads of the remaining statues as Bruno told Nic and Louise, 'Now or we'll never.'

He focused his Talent, thought himself free of the cavern – imagined it, as *The Book of Black & White* had instructed – and knew within moments that he was unsee-able. He watched Nic and Louise, then heard the Marshall cry, 'The children have vanished! They'll be escaping!'

'They'll be going nowhere, Marshall,' Temperate Thomas replied. 'Don't worry yerself.'

Bruno, Nic and Louise left the platform, moving quick to the edge of the cavern, in a creep, clinging close to the wall, avoiding but still watching –

'Bring down the Head of the Elders!'

Again Dr Bloom's cry, but it was nothing. Too futile, too wishful for Bruno to bear – too much, too loud, too late. But biddable to the end, Bruno saw his father and Nic's turn, still reeling under gunfire, and stagger in the wake of Dr Bloom as he crossed the cavern. Bruno, Nic and Louise had to watch too –

Michael Atlas and Nic Delby Senior met the Temperate first. They attempted attack but each blow was matched by another, mirrored as Temperate Thomas cast his hand – still so very unworried – left and right. And as he'd done with Louise's father, each flash of Talent removed a limb, a cog, some small but vital piece from the statues. Fingers, then whole hands, then arms. Blunted but still fighting on, blades snapped out to replace hands, but still they were being dismantled by the careful diligence of the Temperate's Talent.

Bruno knew it was almost over. He moved on, taking Nic's sleeve, Louise the most unwilling to move but following too. They came to the slope that could lead them free. David was close, face a bruise, his expression distorted.

Then Bruno and Nic's fathers fell, their final acts to tear off their own heads and hurl them at the Temperate. In moments they were no more than metal and daydreams, disintegrating into recorded voices, spluttering unintelligible noise.

Dr Bloom cried out, more a plea than an assertion: '*Rebels don't run!*'

'Perhaps not,' Bruno heard Temperate Thomas say, 'but they do die.'

The Temperate raised one hand. He clenched it. Slowly, carefully, he tightened his fist, Dr Bloom's mechanical head collapsing, last sentiments squeezed through the statue's tightening mouth –

'*. . . fight . . . ending . . . Forgetting . . .*'

'Quiet now,' said the Temperate, his tone gentle. 'Quiet, and rest yerself amongst all the filth and broken decency of the other Rebels. Quiet, and be gone.'

A crack, Bloom shattered, and he was no more than dust.

The Temperate gasped, staggering for support against

312

the Tiger-Sentry. The effort of destroying the statues had exhausted him, thought Bruno. Louise thought the same thing – 'Now us.'

Seeable, she charged from their hiding place, shotgun in hand, scream in her mouth, Nic too on his feet and running, dagger raised –

'Stop!'

The word from Bruno but the action from the Temperate; exhausted but not powerless, Nic and Louise were seized by Temperate Thomas's Talent.

Bruno watched, still unseeable, unmoving.

'No use in fighting any more,' said Temperate Thomas. He breathed deep. 'Just be good, decent children and we'll have no more trouble. And Bruno too. Bruno Atlas? Hiding, are ye? We have yer mother, I'm sure ye know.'

Bruno crept, careful, towards David, towards the way out. Any image of escaping was slipping from him though; he could scarcely conceive success. He had no weapon but his Talent, and even that was fading as doubt attacked it. He tried not to look at the Temperate, felt that if their eyes met he would falter, be seen as he was in the chamber beneath the Clocktower. Bruno looked to the Tiger-Sentry, like it might help. Instinct took his hand to his pocket and he found its winding key. He clung to it like something talismanic.

'Oh yes,' Temperate Thomas went on. 'Yer mother was most eager to protect her wayward son. Most well speaking of his decency, bravery and so on. If she could see ye now – *hiding*. Rebels fight, do they not, Marshall?'

'They do,' said the Marshall. 'Brutal and rough as animals.' His middle finger touched the scar on his face.

Bruno stopped. By his feet was a blade from his father's statue.

'No Rebel in Bruno Atlas,' said the Temperate, and Bruno knew what the Head of the Elders was trying at. 'No bravery in his actions, no courage or decency. Ye're a shame, Atlas! To yer mother, to yerself, and to yer no good father. To think that yer indecent mother screamed yer name like a blessing when she was tortured.'

As Temperate Thomas wanted him to, Bruno did what he couldn't resist doing: he showed himself to cry out, 'I'm here!' and charged forwards as Louise and Nic had done, as his father had done, cavern a blur, no fear, winding key in one hand, blade in the other –

Feet from the Temperate he stalled. The blade was whipped from his hand, fell somewhere distant. As in the town hall, Temperate Thomas had him in his Talent.

'That's better,' said the Temperate, running eyes over Bruno, Nic and Louise. 'Marshall, have yer men collect the hearts of the Rebels.'

The Marshall passed the command to his men, who picked their way towards remains, toes turning over hollow chests, kneeling to pluck out the pocket watches.

'And *The Book of Black & White*,' said Temperate Thomas, 'is, I'm guessing—'

He tore Bruno's satchel, the book sailing out and into his waiting hands.

314

'And to think,' the Temperate said, fingers running over the cover, 'I was almost afeared of the Rebels all over again. Afeared of this Atlas boy being as much of a fighter as his father.'

'What do we do with them?' asked the Marshall.

'Atlas and Delby Junior,' said Temperate Thomas, 'will come with us.'

'And the other two?' said the Marshall, throwing looks on Louise and David.

Temperate Thomas examined them.

'Leave them,' he said.

The Marshall blinked.

'Leave them to rot,' said the Temperate. 'Ye see, Marshall, these so-called Rebels don't have that sense of solidarity that we have. They bicker, they blame each other. They're broken now. As useless as these clockwork toys.'

Bruno looked to Louise, and saw in her eyes all that Temperate Thomas had seen – she blamed David, and the anger she'd shown too freely was being used against them. Without Nic, without Bruno, Louise and David would have no chance to reconcile. And the Temperate knew it.

One of the Enforcers said, 'This one here – Bloom – he hasn't got a watch in him.'

Temperate Thomas smiled. 'He wouldn't do,' he said. 'Knowing him as I did, I'd guess Dr Bloom would've wanted a statue of himself rightly-free of such a dependency as a pocket watch or winding key. He'd have wanted something that could be living on without any help, without a heart even.'

Bruno saw the truth of this, saw the arrogance of Dr Bloom. Saw, felt, mourned. Grieved a little, ashamed of his own naivety.

'Leave them,' said the Temperate, again, turning away. 'And let us return to Pitch End quickly. We don't want to be missing the three-hundredth year celebrations.' He slapped a hand to the Marshall's shoulder. Something in the gesture made Bruno bristle and, unable to move, with only words as weapons, he cried, 'Where's yer daughter, Marshall? Where's Sabitha?'

The Marshall looked at Bruno.

'She's missing, isn't she?' said Bruno. 'Since the night I escaped from Pitch End. It was *him* that took her, he took her youth, he—'

Talent struck Bruno, made blood rush from his nose.

'*Liar*,' said Temperate Thomas, rubbing his whitened knuckles like he'd struck Bruno with a hand. And then he smiled. 'I say let them be permanently silenced. Let them have what they want so badly. Let them truly be their father's sons.'

His hand, so adept, moved once more, and the statues of Bruno and Nic's fathers stirred. A snapping, a wrenching, and the brass faces of the statues – dented, torn, defeated – rushed at Bruno and Nic.

Bruno had a moment of protest, looking to David and telling him, 'Ye haven't given up! I know it!' before the masks of Michael Atlas and Nicholas M. Delby Senior forced expressionless appearances on their sons. A snap, a tightening around the jaw and Bruno couldn't speak or think. He saw through his father's eyes, through small spaces, sight shrunk to two slits. Had to breathe in a low hiss. Behind the face of his father, Bruno was glad the Temperate couldn't see his weeping.

Then long threads of brass that served as Dr Bloom's hair were ripped from the crushed shell of his scalp, lashing themselves across and around Bruno and Nic's wrists. Bruno heard Nic's whimper above his own.

Then Bruno felt the Enforcers lift them, taking them.

He glimpsed David, untied by the Marshall, pushed forwards to fall.

Bruno heard Louise say, 'I can't believe ye did it, David.' But she sounded as though she'd forsaken anger for heartbreak, clenched fists for tears. David looked away from her, looked to Bruno. Though reduced by his father's mask, Bruno crammed so much into that look, directed all he had at David and held it as, unseen by Temperate, Marshall or Enforcers, he opened his hand and dropped the winding key for the Tiger-Sentry at David's feet.

David saw but didn't speak.

Before they left, the final words were reserved, as always, for Temperate Thomas –

'*Long live the Elders!*' he cried.

But the cavern stayed silent, reeling with no known reply.

317

PART FOUR

THE WIDOWS

XXX
The Ways Back

Bruno was somewhere between the Rebel Chapel and Pitch End, between sleep and painful waking, when he heard the Enforcer carrying him mutter to the other, 'Obvious why we were brought along, int it? Traipsing up a bloody mountain, through caves and all, and then back having to carry these two. And meantime, himself and the Marshall get to go above ground, get to be going back quicker to town.'

So they were alone? thought Bruno. Himself, Nic and the two Enforcers?

Bruno thought the voice familiar, thought it was one he might come to recognise if he hadn't been behind his father's mask.

Then the Enforcer went further – 'Why doesn't *himself* do it?'

'Would ye be quiet,' said the other, the one bearing Nic. 'Ye saw what he did to them statues? That'll be *yer* head if ye're not careful.'

But, Bruno on his back, the Enforcer went on with, 'He can't hear ye!'

'Ye don't know that.'

Small pause.

'So bloody *heavy*.'

'Heavy for *you*, Dennis,' said the other. 'Not me. I could carry anything.'

Dennis Wire? thought Bruno.

'Oh aye,' said Dennis. 'Sure ye could. Always acting the big man, eh?'

They laughed a little.

'That one ye're carrying is skin and bone – try carrying stupid bloody Atlas,' hissed Dennis.

Definitely Dennis Wire. Is the Temperate so needful, Bruno thought, that he's recruiting from those not even Come-Of-Age?

Dennis swore, adjusting Bruno on his back who was given a glimpse ahead – a choice of tunnels three. Bruno remembered this crossroads; he and Nic had come from the way in the middle, that lead to the cascade, and then on to the Cavern of the Forgotten . . .

Dennis made a decision – 'No further' – and Bruno was dropped, head striking rock, mask biting into his face. 'Wait here five minutes,' he heard Dennis say. 'A wee break just.'

'That weren't the Marshall's orders,' said the other Enforcer, looking ahead. 'I'm keeping going, not getting left behind here. I don't wanna be—'

The Enforcer's words ended.

Bruno felt a shudder beneath him and he squirmed onto his back, facing the wall. He watched as a crack began there, small shoot, then snaking, arcing up and over and he struggled more to turn and see – it widened, watched by the Enforcers. They looked at each other, and then raced towards the passageway on the right –

'*Quick-smart!*' cried the Enforcer with Nic, and he dived into the opening as rock fell, closing the tunnel behind him. Dust ballooned and trickled through the gaps of Bruno's mask, applying rough kisses to his lips, eyes.

He listened to Dennis cough, swear again and then revert to complaint: 'How the hell are we gonna find a way back into town now?'

The single sense Bruno had was hearing – he listened, and heard something other than Dennis's harsh breathing. Voices, some furtive movement?

'Who's there?' asked Dennis. 'Atlas, that you muttering?'

But Bruno couldn't reply, jaw screwed so tight behind brass. He attempted to struggle, testing the bonds around his wrists, but immediately came pain, sure bleeding. Then things began to clear, some seeing allowed in the space they occupied.

'If that's ye talking, Atlas, ye better be stopping,' said Dennis. 'I'll be bloody putting a few bullets in ye, don't think I won't!'

'Excuse me, son, but we'll be having none of that.'

Dennis's head snapped around and he stumbled on stone,

looking for the source of the voice, rifle flapping on its strap, evading his hands.

'Who's there?' he said. 'I'll shoot if ye don't show yerself!'

'I said there'll be no need for that,' said the voice. A female voice.

'Show yerself!' shouted Dennis.

Bruno tried to move, see more, but couldn't. He couldn't help but think of the Undying Voices . . . Then once more the threat, and the answer –

Dennis: 'I said bloody well come out or I'll start shooting!'

Voice: 'No need. Not for the sake of a lowly, rightly-obedient Widow.'

Curiosity pushed Bruno onto his front. He looked up and saw a figure in black.

'*Back!*' shouted Dennis, but he stumbled back himself, hand going to the wall. 'Ye're supposed to be locked up,' he said.

'Seems we've escaped.'

This was another voice Dennis twisted on the spot to see. Another Widow, standing in the passageway to the left.

'Ye think ye can be scaring?' said Dennis. He wiped his top lip. 'Is that what ye think?'

'Yes,' said a third voice, another appearing Widow. 'It is indeed.'

'Well,' said Dennis. 'I'll tell ye how it'll be going: come quietly and I'll say ye were rightly-decent and gave yerselves up without a fight. Either that, or . . .' He cocked the rifle.

'Oh dear,' said the Widow who'd first appeared, 'this isn't working out as we'd hoped at all, is it, ladies?'

As though they'd been hewn, each stepped from blank stone, five Widows emerging from all passageways, surrounding Dennis, all agreeing with the first Widow: 'Indeed, not as we'd hoped.'

'Thank you for yer rightly-decent offer,' said the Widow who'd first appeared, 'but under the present circumstances, we'll have to be on our way.'

'Fine,' said Dennis, and Bruno heard a satisfaction. 'Ye asked for it.'

Dennis aimed at the first Widow, shut one eye and tightened his finger around the trigger.

Behind his father's mask Bruno tried to cry out as the Widow lifted her hand, free of its traditional lace bindings. The bullet that left the barrel of Dennis's rifle went barely an inch before it was reduced. In a tick it was dust, the memory of any threat coiling in the air like a failed insult.

She used her Talent, thought Bruno.

'Ye devious hag,' said Dennis, but any venom in his voice was diluted. 'If ye think I'm bloody well gonna let some stupid Widow get the better of me then by *Pitch* ye've another thing coming to ye, so ye better just—'

A thud. Dennis fell beside Bruno, who looked up and saw a Widow standing with a large rock in her hand.

'Widow Yeats,' said the Widow who'd ended the bullet from Dennis's rifle. 'Was that rightly-necessary?'

'My apologies,' replied the Widow holding the rock. 'But he was really starting to hack me off.'

Bruno heard a murmur from the Widows – it took him a moment to know it as laughter. Then he felt hands lift him, settling him against the wall.

'What have they done to ye?' said one Widow that kneeled before him. Bruno wanted recognition of a voice – there were five Widows, not six, so was one of these his mother?

'Help undo the bonds, Widow Grafter,' the Widow in front of him said. 'Widow Bowen, Widow Friel – keep watch at the tunnels. Widow Yeats, tie that Enforcer up.'

Wordless agreement. Widow Grafter crouched behind Bruno and he felt not fingers but surely a careful Talent working to unpick the brass threads that held him. Bruno felt her soft breath on the back of his neck, and words – 'I meant to trap them both in here. What are we gonna do about the other one that got away?'

'That'll have to wait,' said the Widow in front of Bruno, the evident leader. 'But this mask can't be waiting.'

Then something – some small weakening in the Widow's tone that told of concern close to hurt. Was this her behind the veil? He watched her shake the sleeves of her robes down, wrists revealed – a white too delicate in the gloom – and she began to search the edge of the mask for some release.

326

Bruno waited. Had never felt less like waiting.

'I think,' said the Widow, 'this might be it.'

A momentary tightening around the jaw and Bruno tensed, mask squeezing until he would've shouted *Stop!* if he could. Then his father's face fell away, two halves landing hollow on stone, at the same moment the brass threads leaving his wrists.

'It's alright, son,' the Widow who'd removed the mask told him. 'It's all going to be alright now.' She held her arms open.

Bruno opened his mouth, wanting to shout but settling instead for falling into the embrace of his mother.

'Ye're safe,' she said, laying a hand on his forehead. 'I have ye.'

Bruno's first word – '*Nic*.'

'He'll be long gone now with that other Enforcer,' said his mother. 'But don't be worrying. We can leave now, get outta Pitch End forever and never be coming back.'

Bruno eased away from his mother. His second word – '*No*.'

His mother rose, stood tall above him – the forbidding, unknowable presence of a Pitch End Widow returned.

'We must leave,' she said. 'Perhaps ye don't understand. We had to fight our way out of the town hall where they'd been holding us. One of us, Widow Beckett,' she paused, breathed in, 'was killed in the escape. We can't ever go back. I know ye feel ye need to help but this Rebel idea is long dead, Bruno.'

327

'No,' said Bruno, again. 'It's not the Rebels.'

His fingers felt for the medallion at his throat, and at his touch it came away in his hand, chain broken. He held it, wondered about it. He felt the presence of the other Widows pressing close.

'Then why?' said his mother.

'Because,' said Bruno.

'*Because* wouldn't be enough for Bruno Atlas,' said his mother. She sighed. 'Not for my son, the boy with all the questions all the time. To be giving up on the chance to leave Pitch End for good? There must be a rightly-proper reason.'

Bruno wondered at her tone: was it pride she was feeling for her disagreeable son? Or disbelief? Wry ridicule?

'Because,' Bruno said again. He paused, and then finally – 'Nic is my friend.'

He looked to his mother then. Her veil didn't shift, didn't indicate.

'He's my only friend,' said Bruno. 'The only one I've ever had.'

And he stood, matching his mother's height.

A last pause, last sigh, and then she lifted her veil. Beneath she was younger than Bruno had come to imagine. And she was smiling. She said, 'Well, that's good enough reason for me. Change of plan,' she told the other Widows. 'We're staying. Staying to fight.'

More murmuring from the veils, but not laughter.

'Bruno,' said his mother. 'It's time ye met the other Widows

328

of Pitch End – Widow Yeats, Widow Grafter, Widow Bowen and Widow Friel.'

'Widow Atlas,' said the one called Widow Grafter, immediately drawing closer, 'how on earth do ye propose we move against the Temperate?'

'*Ha!*' went Widow Bowen. 'How can we be planning anything against that man?'

'Oh don't,' said Widow Friel. 'We can be planning plenty – he's nothing but big words and putting-on-airs!'

'That's what I'm worried about,' said Widow Yeats, the one who had knocked out Dennis, and who stood closest to Bruno's mother. 'He has a Talent in him for words, Sara.'

It took Bruno a moment to realise that his mother – so long known just as 'Widow Atlas' – was, before her husband died, called 'Sara'. She said, 'All fair points, ladies.'

Bruno admired the debate of the women – fierce yet respectful; a discussion with fear and worry, but not trite disagreement for its own sake.

'How will we even be getting back into Pitch End is another question,' said Widow Grafter. 'He'll have the whole place covered, every nook and crack.'

'Aye, every crack!' repeated Widow Bowen.

'We can fight well enough,' said Widow Yeats, 'but five Widows and a boy aren't a match for the Elders and who knows how many Enforcers.'

'*Quiet!*' said Bruno.

The word came out of him before he wanted it to, and

loud. He shied a little, but a silence was brought anyway; a kind of attention Bruno had not known since he was ten turns, had stood in a playground ready to read, to be listened to.

His mother was looking at him, waiting.

'It's for the children of Pitch End,' Bruno told them. 'What he's planning to do to them all – that's why we have to do it, no matter how difficult it is.'

The Widows stood, quiet as though chastened, and still waiting.

Bruno swallowed and said, 'I have a plan.'

XXXI

The Imagination of Temperate Thomas

'Why didn't ye tell me that Da was a Rebel?'

'I'm sorry.'

'But why not?'

'Because, Bruno.'

'Not good enough.'

His mother smiled. '*Because*, I knew ye would've wanted to fight. And I wanted to save ye from all that. If I could.'

Bruno held back for a moment, and then had to say: 'Much good it did.'

His mother didn't reply. Her smile subsided.

'It was too dangerous,' she said. 'Ye've no idea how afeared I was about it all coming out. About yer father being a Rebel with his mate Nic Delby. That the two of them had been scheming since before me and yer father married, even long before Saint Jonathan Bloom led them astray.' She shook her head. 'Not that they needed much leading, but they worshipped that man so they did.'

Bruno said nothing. He held the Rebel medallion in his fist and glanced behind – the Widows were their usual single line, Sara Atlas leading, Bruno beside. The tunnel narrowed when it liked. Every step meant they had to move in more of a hunch, the ground rising, sloping towards the surface.

Bruno worried that his time for questions was draining away: 'Were ye ever a Rebel yerself?'

'No,' his mother said.

'Did they not let ye join?'

'I didn't *want* to be,' she said, with such certainty, like each question Bruno put had been long-expected, answers long-prepared. 'I didn't want the Elder way, but didn't see sense in fighting either. Especially not when I had you to think of. But in the end it was yer father and the way of the Rebels, or none.'

In the end, Bruno mouthed. He looked ahead and saw meagre light.

'The last time I saw yer father,' his mother said, the space between them brightening, 'was a week before the fire. It was the last push, Bloom wanting them to fight stronger than ever, try and overthrow the Elders. They knew they were losing, knew they had maybe one last chance. Why else did they prepare so well? Putting that army of Sentries in the mountains, doing what they did to those children.'

'Ye know about all that?' asked Bruno.

'I knew. It was what yer father talked about most in the end, wanting to make sure younger ones could keep on fighting even if they couldn't. He wanted to do it to you.'

His mother stopped before Bruno did. They let the other Widows pass, and waited until they were alone.

'I wouldn't let him do that to ye,' said his mother. 'Sulked like a child about it, then walked out, never came back. I never saw him again.'

Her face might have been veiled again for all the emotion it betrayed. Bruno saw how far his mother had travelled from showing hurt, how she'd distanced herself – the past was a place better left. And there was nothing Bruno could say that would lead her back there.

'I welcomed being a Widow after that,' she said. 'Kept me hidden, safe, and kept everyone in Pitch End out.'

'Including me,' said Bruno, and a spark of anger made him say, 'In the town hall when I was being accused, ye just kept quiet.'

His mother looked away.

'No one can see what a Widow is thinking,' said Sara Atlas. 'Not even those Elders. We kept silent because it was the only thing we had. It's not such a terrible thing sometimes to be ignored – no one expects anything from ye.'

'And what do children do when their mothers ignore them?'

'All the Widows lost their children,' said Bruno's mother. 'That Temperate took them. Don't ask why – ye know the answer, Bruno. He knew that no one would care. And would a Widow ever be for saying?'

'He didn't take me,' said Bruno.

'Because he knew,' said his mother, 'that maybe ye could be put to a use someday. Son of the last man killed by the Rebels – a rightly-powerful symbol. Ye could be a thing of hope for Pitch End. Or not.' And Bruno knew what his mother was thinking, for once: the Discussion Chamber, and what he had been used for, in the end, by the Temperate.

They had a few more moments – silence, stranded – and then Bruno's mother began to move.

'Why did Da leave us?' asked Bruno. He still stood, not following, and then asked, as though somehow they were part of the same riddle, 'Why does that Temperate do these things?'

'Why else?' said his mother, her tone the same – resignation, things already long-decided. 'The same reason all men do foolish things: they think they're making the world a better place.'

Again, she walked. This time Bruno followed. And moments later, when he thought back – when he realised its absence and wondered – he knew that somewhere in the tunnel he had stopped holding his father's Rebel medallion. He had left it behind, and he didn't consider going back to seek it.

Only minutes more underground, and then they were free.

Bruno pulled himself from the tunnel – into a hollow

tree with insides damp and rotten. Then out, and he stepped into morning, but to see the darkest sight –

A single storm cloud was suspended over Pitch End, and it was a nightmare of a thing to Bruno's waking eyes. Swelling, a vast heart furious with noise and threat, it was expanding to the east, west, north and south. He murmured, 'No,' and the storm answered – boasting with black and thunder. Lightning surged inside like excitement. Bruno doubted it could grow any more. And again it answered – towering further, accumulating in peaks and cliffs, towers and spires, claws, teeth – mountain, fortress, monster.

Bruno watched. All they could do was watch, shrouded Widows like snippets of what was above. Bruno noticed they still held their customary Pitch End formation on the mountainside – polite line, polite-looking. The storm roared, and they obediently cowered.

Bruno felt his mother beside him.

'It's him,' said Bruno. He had to raise his voice to hear himself. 'The Temperate is imagining this storm. He has enough Talent in him to make it real. Just like *The Book of Black & White* taught.'

Bruno watched the Widows turn, veils in a fluster of flapping, and he turned too, facing his mother. She'd shut her eyes to it all.

'Mam,' said Bruno. 'We can't leave. Please. We have to stop him.'

He watched his mother breathe in, and then nod. She opened her eyes.

'*Widows!*' she called, and Bruno thought her voice a match for any storm, any Talent. 'We can't be losing heart. What would be the use of fighting at all if it were easy won. That storm is the making of that Temperate and that book. We must cling close to my son's plan, the best hope we have! It is time for us to be plain with one another. Let us have no more shame. Let that Temperate see what he has made!'

A moment of doubt, a turning from left to right, and then the Widows began to tear – as one, veils were removed, faces revealed, eyes that squinted as though into the brightness of a Swelter Season dawn and not into shadow, into storm. Released, the veils whirled – where would they settle, what would they conceal? Bruno didn't follow them, saw only the Widows, truly, for the first time: they were older than he'd imagined, perhaps older than he'd wanted to believe.

'Can they fight?' Bruno asked, words only for his mother.

But she didn't reply, just rallied the women further –

'Remember what we've endured, fellow Widows! All the times we stood by and watched others taken, punished. Husbands lost and lies told. Children stolen. And us standing silent and shuffling by. Remember that when we step into the town square, remember Widow Beckett, and let pain be the feeling that fires yer Talent!'

A gale attacked, flattening grass, chasing shadows, making them stagger but not fall.

'*Remember*,' said Sara Atlas. 'And when we face him we

will not turn. We will not shy or bow our heads. Instead we shall be looking him in the eye and we shall fight until we have no Talent left. Until death if we must, and a battle that no one in Pitch End will ever be Forgetting!'

XXXII

The Demise of the Rebels

Temperate Thomas II was ready to speak. In his town square, aligned with the Clocktower where the eight Rebel pocket watches had been fixed by his hand, each in its particular stone niche, he looked out on his Pitch End – weathered people, weathered place – and was satisfied.

'My fellow Pitch Enders – I extend so many, *many* thanks to you all for attending here today to celebrate our glorious three-hundredth year anniversary celebration! With no rightly-decent Pitch Enders there'd be no rightly-decent Pitch End – I give ye permission to award yerselves some applause!'

Applause indeed went up. Applause that might've been louder maybe – hands held higher, faces happier – if all the townsfolk hadn't been crammed into two large cages that had been taken from the Discussion Chamber and reassembled in the square. The division of Pitch End was simple – adults in one cage, their children in another.

'And to our town itself,' said Temperate Thomas, opening his arms, flexing his fingers, 'let us offer thanks!'

Pitch End had put on its best face – bunting was looped from lamp post to lamp post, fluttering red/black/red, the Pitch End flag above every shopfront, smaller versions on sticks in the hands of children, the breeze doing the waving for them. Largest of all was a banner in shades of soured butter, stretched across the town hall:

HAPPY 300TH ANNIVERSARY –
LONG LIVE THE ELDERS!

The Temperate dropped his hands. Applause died.

Beside the Clocktower were the usual personages, uncaged: the Marshall with pistol in hand, eyes ever restless, a half-circle of Enforcers arranged around – uncomfortable looking lot, rifles held like odd toys, like the officers had snatched their uniforms from 'Da's' wardrobe, trousers swamping shoes, tunics wider than what was beneath. Between the Clocktower and town hall sat the other nine Elders, some already asleep, dreaming on one another's shoulders . . . Then awoken abruptly – the movements of the storm were slow but its discourse loud, its shadow deepening, preventing anything less than total attention, bloodshot Elder eyes wondering at it.

And in the townsfolk there might've ticked a worry, but they didn't show it. They smiled, knowing well how to hide what they really felt.

'Do not fear, Pitch Enders!' the Temperate told them, knowing their true feelings better than they could, for it was he who had created and so dictated their way of feeling. 'This storm is not something that should shake decent hearts – it is a *gift*! A gift from yer Temperate!'

And like the man who had imagined it, the storm was deferred to; every eye in every socket of every Pitch Ender drifted first to the Clocktower, to its immobile hands, and then to the storm. Thunder like tumbling bones. The townsfolk shuddered, cages rattled. Some of the children in their own prison whimpered.

'We are entering a rightly-momentous time!' Temperate Thomas went on. 'On this day we shall accomplish something that no Pitch Ender – not even Jack Pitch himself – could have foreseen. Today, my dear friends, we'll be witnessing the end of two diseases that have blighted our town these many years. First, the demise of the Rebels!'

Perfectly cued, the doors of the town hall opened. Two Enforcers emerged with a figure dragging between. Head low, toes nudging cobble, wearing a shift scarred with stitching and gaudy with blood, with a face trapped behind a brass mask – Nic.

Familiar insults were thrown – 'Rebel dirt!' 'Indecent boy!' 'Filth!' – but not as many or by as many mouths as the Temperate had expected, hoped. Was the outrage of Pitch End dampened? Hadn't he explained fully, clearly? How could they fear at such a time like this? Fools, he decided, and didn't bother to think on it any further.

Ropes were discovered and Nic was tied to the statue of Arthur Pitch (returned to an upright after being toppled by Pace) – his back to the chest of George Pitch's seventh son. The Enforcers didn't choose or care where they lashed rope – around the neck, over ankles, between his legs; knotting and tugging on the bonds until Nic had to react in a cry that was answered from the townsfolk in a hiss ('*Disgusting boy!*') and the storm cloud in a roar.

'Ye notice how even the very elements protest to the existence of this boy!' said Temperate Thomas, his Talent drawing the storm close. 'Ye see how it cheers us on!'

Some Pitch Enders nodded.

The Temperate knew then he needed a lie, something potent enough to keep his audience on his side. He sought to forget about Bruno Atlas, the boy lost on their return from Mount Tome, as he announced: 'This boy is the very last of the Rebels! He has been hiding, concealed, in the dark places of the Elm Tree Mountains, for ten turns. Would ye warrant such a thing, my fellow Pitch Enders? Thinking that he could hide from us behind that despicable mask, spying on our town from his lofty den, plotting and praying for our collective ruin! But now – I reveal yer true face.'

With a wrench of Talent the mask was torn from Nic. It was almost a surprise to the Pitch Enders that beneath there was only a face. The face of a Rebel but also of a boy, so much a child.

Each word the Temperate spoke to Nic he clipped as

341

though speaking to a mind barely developed: 'Ye understand that there is no bettering the Elder ways? Understand how worthless ye've made yerself, child? How none of yer wicked tricks have done any good. That Dr Bloom was a scoundrel who—'

'Ye're a liar!' Nic cried suddenly, words sapping all energy, leaving only gasps. But he recovered quickly: 'Ye've been lying to everyone, stealing the children of Pitch End so ye can—'

Temperate Thomas struck him.

'Silence this monster,' he said.

Enforcers swooped and pried Nic's jaws open, cramming in a foul rag.

The Temperate had a final whisper for Nic: 'I don't know what happened to yer friend Atlas, but rest assured I'll seek him out, and he'll be for the same fate as you.'

Temperate Thomas held up one stiff hand. Talent swirled from it – swirled too in the bald eye of the storm. 'And now the end,' he said. The Temperate's fingers itched, tightened, Talent beginning to choke Nic –

And then other fingers, stone – the statue of Arthur Pitch had awoken and closed one hand around the Temperate's wrist, the other arm reaching across Nic's chest to protect him.

The loudest cry yet from a caged Pitch Ender – '*Mountains protect us!*'

And all – Enforcers, Elders, common townsfolk – looked to the dark entrance of Old Town. The Widows of Pitch

End stood in their line, unveiled, hands loose at their sides, freed of binding. At their centre stood Bruno Atlas and his mother, Sara.

'Ignatius Thomas,' called Bruno Atlas's mother, 'ye better be letting that boy go!'

One of her hands was working the air – her Talent had brought to life the statue of Arthur Pitch. She bid it tighten its grip around the Temperate's wrist. Everyone in Pitch End heard the crackle of bone.

But Temperate Thomas didn't flinch. 'Why not come and be rescuing him?' he called back. 'That's what all this is in aid of, I'm thinking.' And with his own Talent, Temperate Thomas severed the arm of Arthur Pitch and ripped himself free. 'Or perhaps,' he said, 'ye're too rightly-ashamed, too afeared to be stepping out from yer shadows?'

The Marshall barked an order and Enforcers – startled, all elbows, stumbling – tried to form a line, master their weapons, aim.

'Are ye sure of this plan, son?' Bruno's mother asked him.

'I am,' said Bruno, and he spoke to convince himself as much as his mother.

'I don't see *The Book of Black & White*,' she said.

'Doesn't matter,' said Bruno. 'Those pocket watches do something to the Clocktower, that's how Dr Bloom designed it. Something that'll help him take the youth from the children. So if we can get them, destroy them, then we can stop this.'

'Sounds easy enough,' his mother replied. She glanced at him, smiling. 'Get the pocket watches, we'll do the rest.'

'One more chance, Widow Atlas!' said the Temperate. 'Are five rightly-feeble Widows going to be taking on the might of Pitch End?' His laughter was small, its echo large. 'Tell us – what is yer answer?'

Bruno's mother looked to her Widows. As one they tightened fists, set their feet. And she replied in a scream – 'To hell with the Elders! *Long live the Widows!*'

XXXIII
Battle of the Talents

Bruno took a breath and forced all feeling towards his Talent, to make him unseeable to all eyes.

In the next and same moment –

His mother telling him: 'I can't see ye anymore – now go!'

The Marshall telling his men: '*Fire!*'

And Bruno ran as silence was shattered. He wanted to look back, see what was happening to the Widows, to his mother, but he saw only forwards, black smoke bursting from Enforcer rifle barrels, dark exhalations, Temperate Thomas with hands behind his back and the Marshall issuing orders with gaping mouth, face flushed.

No one could hear Bruno – his anguished breathing, his bare feet on cobble – as he arrived at the Clocktower and reached up to snatch the rag from Nic's mouth. The statue of Arthur Pitch was solid lifelessness once more, one-armed and still clutching Nic to his chest. Nic's head had drooped, whole body slumped. Bruno couldn't think how to free him. Then, unable to do anything, needing to know, Bruno turned to see . . .

Bullets were being reduced to dust same as Dennis's had been in the tunnel beneath Mount Tome, rifles crumpling like paper, Enforcers suddenly weaponless, scrambling back as the Widows advanced as one, fists outstretched, Bruno's mother their lead, collected Talent a rippling carapace holding all assault out.

But Temperate Thomas remained beside his Elders, and nothing in his standing spoke of fear or worry.

Bruno looked again to Nic. All he could do was whisper: 'Just be unseeable till I think what to do. Be unseeable to everyone, even me if it's easier.'

He saw Nic's eyes judder beneath bruised lids, but he remained.

'I can still see ye,' said Bruno.

'Coz I want ye to,' Nic told him.

'Shoot them ye bloody cowards!' cried the Marshall.

All Bruno's attention went back to the battle –

Enforcers were continuing to falter, falling back, ammunition shrinking, spaces between gunshots longer, more desperate, the drop in the tumult leaving the Marshall's words heard –

'Attack hand-to-hand if needs be!'

Bruno saw an Enforcer yank a knife from his belt. He ran but had to pause, dodge and crouch, creep close to the Enforcer as the knife was raised (preparing to be thrown, he realised). He snatched it, then away, the knife vanishing as it touched Bruno's fingers. The Enforcer registered shock, fear, and then retreated, screaming, 'To blazes with this!'

Bruno, back at the Clocktower, was distracted by the Marshall – the Head of the Enforcers was sprinting forwards, determined to gain ground, firing shot after shot, some passing further towards Bruno's mother than any yet. But still she advanced with her guard of Widows, indefatigable, almost at the Temperate. But there was one obstacle. They stopped and faced one another, Widow Atlas and the Marshall.

A flick of Sara Atlas's hand. A flash, blue-white, that dazzled Bruno, and the Marshall's pistol was destroyed with a palm-sized explosion that scorched his fingers, hurling him onto his back.

Silence massed. A fine dust decorated the air. Pitch End cowered – townsfolk in their cages, Enforcers with their knives but their Marshall injured, Elders still in their seats but some toppled. Bruno began to hack at the ropes that held Nic to the statue. His hands did this, but his eyes watched his mother . . .

Temperate Thomas stepped forward. He and Bruno's mother were a pair of long strides apart.

'Widow Atlas,' said the Temperate, voice low, shaking his head, 'what is going to be done with ye now? Ye know right-well that the Rebels aren't going to be winning anything today.'

'We seem to be doing well enough,' cried Widow Yeats.

'Too right!' went Widow Bowen.

'We are too,' said Widow Friel.

'Aye!' agreed Widow Grafter.

'Ye're right, Ignatius,' said Widow Atlas. 'The Rebels can't win. But I'm no Rebel.'

Temperate Thomas smiled. 'As the Head of the Elders of Pitch End,' he said, 'I charge you for the offence of refusing to wear a veil, for conspiring against the Elders (and therefore against Pitch End itself and all who live here), for violating all eleven of the Decent Ways, and for addressing me not as ye should – as yer Temperate. As such, I hereby condemn ye' he paused 'to death, and a rightly-swift Forgetting.'

Nic fell free onto Bruno who collapsed under the sudden weight.

A moment more, and then the strongest rush of Talent Bruno had ever experienced – it swept from both sides as his mother and Temperate Thomas threw all emotion at one another, the collision making both stagger back but then regain footing quickly as their Talent shattered windows, cracked cobbles.

Bruno heard his mother's cry – '*The plan, Bruno!*' – her voice like someone submerged. He left Nic, stood and sprang forwards and snatched his pocket watch out of the Clocktower as Temperate Thomas sounded his own call –

'Elders!'

Shrugging off their appearance (their pretence, Bruno realised) of dotage and weakness, the other nine Elders were on their feet immediately. They extended their arms and added their Talent to the Temperate's and Bruno saw his mother falter, almost fall and Bruno forgot himself, any plan, almost called to her –

The other Widows rushed to Sara Atlas's side. The Elders turned their Talent on the women.

Bruno felt Nic's hand at his ankle, a weak but determined force trying to pull him down, so he crouched, but with senses struggling to make sense of the battle: Talent formed hands of fire then fingers of ice, then white light, white noise, charging smoke and sea mist with figures forming like strangers seen through rain then unseen, the atmosphere of the square like quickening seasons, hectic with small storms, vying emotions, dying stars . . . And there was no telling who was closer to winning. Not until Bruno looked hard and deepest, and saw clearly – his mother was sinking, not under the press of the Temperate's Talent but with a hand clutched to her side. *Blood*. A gunshot, a wound spreading dark wings and he knew that only time – minutes maybe? – stood between the victory of the Elders and the failure of the Widows. Seeing his advantage, Temperate Thomas spared blows of Talent for the other Widows. They crumpled without a cry.

Not minutes then – moments. And all Talent dissipated.

Bruno's hearing sang with it, senses still fumbling, pocket watch cold in his hand. He couldn't know what to do.

349

Temperate Thomas stood over his mother.

'So where's yer son?' he asked her. 'Where's yer rightly-decent boy?'

His mother said nothing.

Temperate Thomas kneeled and whispered to her, 'I understand so much now, Widow. I rightly understand my mistake in not ensuring you and yer boy burned in that house ten turns ago. Ye see, there's nothing in this town – no secret, no whisper, no prayer uttered in the dark – that I'm not knowing of. I knew yer husband was a Rebel. And I knew it would've been the most horrific thing if a Rebel turned on his own wife and wee boy and burned them in their beds.'

Bruno didn't move but wanted to, felt Nic's fingers on his ankle tighten, heard him say, 'Wait.'

'And that could've been yer ending,' continued the Temperate. 'Martyrs, the two of ye, and then Forgotten. That's the fate I'd decided for ye, Widow Atlas. But now ye'll have a different ending. One not so rightly-noble.'

Temperate Thomas stood. Talent stiffened his fingers and like Pace, Bruno's mother was being commanded to leave – flesh plucked from bone, dust and ash joining the breeze as Nic told Bruno, 'Don't show yerself, it's what he wants.' But Bruno had already the cry in his mouth – '*Stop!*'

He abandoned his Talent. The Temperate did the same.

Bruno's mother had enough left of her to whisper, 'Bruno. No.'

'I'm not hiding,' said Bruno. 'Not being silent any more.'

Bruno felt Nic, unseeable, snatch again at his ankles, but he stepped away.

He and the Temperate faced one another.

'Well done,' said Temperate Thomas. 'So rightly-noble, and in front of all of Pitch End too.'

But although the Temperate's arm swept to include the townsfolk, draw them back into affairs, Bruno thought the Pitch Enders not there at all. They were only bland reaction; as in the Discussion Chamber, only what the Temperate wanted from them, what he needed them to be. Bruno wished he could tell them otherwise. Shake them into thinking, doubting, fighting.

'Ye can have my youth,' said Bruno. 'Just let the other children go.'

'Oh dear me no,' said Temperate Thomas. 'This isn't one of Dr Bloom's *Tall Tales*. No noble sacrifice here, no heroic exchange. This is no story. And if it were, there'd only be one ending – what *I* decide.'

The Temperate stared skywards, to the storm cloud squirming, separating, dark tentacles snaking up and out across the bowl of the sky, intent on the horizon.

'And this,' said the Temperate, his Talent entirely enclosing Bruno, his hand reaching to reclaim the pocket watch, 'is the most important pocket watch, ye know. The one Dr Bloom took most pride in. The one that matters most.'

'Ye don't know what's going to happen,' managed Bruno. 'When ye restart it. Dr Bloom never told ye.'

'I know enough!' the Temperate told him, and for the first time Bruno saw anger. 'I know that I need *The Book of Black & White.*'

An Elder approached, limping, grey-eyed, and from beneath worn robes he lifted *The Book of Black & White* and settled it on the Temperate's hands. It opened, spine snapping like small bones.

Bruno had enough will only to turn his eyes – to look down on Nic, who'd stopped, eyes shut. To his mother, who was just as still. No one to help him, no one to save or be saved by. Bruno could only witness. The Temperate returned Bruno's pocket watch to its place in the Clocktower and with one of his long, precise fingers turned the hands to midday, midnight, matching the Clocktower.

A single strike from the Clocktower: a hard, colourless note.

'Ye see how important yer watch is?' said Temperate Thomas. 'How I couldn't have done it without ye.'

Bruno stared.

Another blow then, no echo, and more again as –

'Elders!' called Temperate Thomas. 'Free the children from their cage and be bringing them before me! Now we'll be seeing what Dr Bloom's Clocktower can do.'

XXXIV

One-Footed Ravens

Bruno counted twelve dull strikes, then everything moved
– cobbles wriggled loose, cracks opening the town square
like something dormant beneath was waking; Pitch Enders
were forced into toppling, desperate hands snapping out
for support and then returning to useless prayer as their
children – released from their cage, near tears, no comfort
– began to separate, unanchored vessels on a tempestuous
sea.

'Don't be afeared!' Temperate Thomas cried to all. 'We
are favoured! We have knowledge and therefore power!'

But even Temperate Thomas couldn't remain grounded
as the Clocktower itself moved – rising, twisting like a
screw releasing itself, its tip intent on the storm, it struck
louder and deeper. Then stopped. A weight of silence.

Bruno wondered: will it work? After ten turns, what's
going to happen?

An answer came when the point of the structure split

and one-footed ravens inside were thrown upwards like tossed gravel. They were eaten by the storm.

'I see now,' Bruno heard the Temperate say to himself. 'Just like in yer precious *Tall Tales*, Jonathan. I see how you imagined it. Just like that accursed Cinder-Folk woman indicated to that old fool, all those turns ago.'

Clara? thought Bruno. The Cinder-Folk woman from the *Tall Tale*. He remembered the raven she'd kept, the one she'd looked to when the old man had demanded the secret to youth. And another man at the close who'd stood and watched the old man burn – Temperate Thomas.

'And now . . .' the Head of the Elders began, but didn't finish – no more was needed. Closing his eyes, one of his fingers went to the page of *The Book of Black & White*. Bruno heard the tear of skin as the Temperate began a journey across paper, through memory and imagination, paths opening that would allow his Talent to accomplish anything.

Then the ravens returned. Like shreds of ash they tore themselves from the storm, the same but different. Still one-footed, but Bruno saw one long claw, sharpened. A queasy crackling of grubby, grey wings brought the birds in an arrow downwards. Bruno glimpsed beaks clean and white as one raven detached from the flock and landed on the shoulder of one of the children. The boy's head eased back. Bruno noticed a look in the child's eyes – or a lack of a look, as though he'd vacated his body – of pure dreaming.

The boy's jaw jutted, and the raven with gleaming beak delved into his mouth.

Cries of protest from the cage of adults.

The raven shifted its claw, wrestling with something inside the boy's mouth.

'Entirely painless, I assure ye!' Temperate Thomas cried to the crowd.

But Bruno could see doubt, saw hands clench the bars of the cage, shake them, testing their strength.

Finally, from the boy's mouth the raven plucked a some-thing. Nothing so crude as flesh or blood but something deeper, harder to define – something small and glowing and twisting like a hooked worm, faint one moment and then rebellious and brilliant the next. Something that flick-ered between powerful and weak but all the while fighting to release itself.

'Childhood,' Bruno heard Temperate Thomas whisper. 'Youth itself.'

The Temperate raised an arm and the raven took off.

The boy returned, dazed, and then toppled to the ground.

A flash of grey and the one-footed, one-clawed raven landed on the arm of Temperate Thomas. And like the boy his jaw extended, but gratefully – the raven deposited the squirming shred of youth into his mouth.

In one moment Bruno saw two transformations –

Like Sabitha, age washed over the fallen boy, face sagging, skin loosening like damp cloth to gather in folds, eyes smaller, clouding, body gravitating inwards as though being

355

bullied into a smaller space. And in Temperate Thomas, the opposite effect – youth regained, he stood taller, face working to dispel wrinkles.

'Ye see!' he cried then. 'Ye see what we can achieve, my fellow Pitch Enders!'

But his audience was no longer captive. Something extraordinary to Bruno – the faith of Pitch End in their Elders was crumbling. All attention, all outrage, was focused on the boy the raven had stolen so much from – smaller, quieter, smaller again, he was soon a fossil of a child, an abhorrence. The worries of the townsfolk went to their own children –

'Cecil, get away from there! Run home!'

'Fight them off, son! Don't let those ravens come near ye!'

'Martha! Come to me!'

So many cries Bruno couldn't tell them apart as he saw Martha Tilly run to her mother whose arms snaked out between bars, reaching –

Temperate Thomas shouted, 'No!' his Talent springing across the space between mother and child. Martha fell backwards. The other children brought her back, clustered close to one another.

'Ungrateful!' the Temperate shouted. 'Rightly-disobedient behaviour towards yer Temperate! If ye'll not be decent enough to comply, then ye'll be decent enough to give whatever youth ye have to yer Elders, however many turns old ye are!'

356

Bruno struggled from his bones outwards, thinking that Temperate Thomas's Talent might have weakened with having to throw so much at Martha. But still it held him.

The one-footed ravens began a descent in a swirl tightening to a funnel –

And then a new presence in the town square.

Bruno saw and then looked away, then flicked attention back to see. He thought his own imagination had summoned something – behind the Marshall stood a tall, dark figure. Not stood – hovered. Wavered? Bruno found it easier to say what the figure wasn't than what it was – not smoke, not storm, not ash or fire . . . then a voice everyone heard, unable to be ignored – 'Ye've done too much, Ignatius Thomas.'

This voice silenced everything, even the storm. Ravens stalled, then scattered.

'Too much to be forgotten about.'

Bruno blinked. More figures, hovering, wavering. And then he realised what they were, though another voice named –

'It's a *Shadow*!'

Martha Tilly. She remembered, thought Bruno. And in his memory he heard words, a *Tall Tale* –

'*We linger on still. Shadows, our presence everywhere and nowhere, as long as we remain in the minds of the ones who loved us. And at times we can rise. Face any great evil, put a stop to what is not right—*'

Recognition arrived on the faces of the other children – they knew what a Shadow was, recalled that it held no threat. They knew – like Bruno – why the Shadows had come, and they had no fear of them.

The Temperate though –

'Back!' He slashed the air with Talent as the Shadows drifted towards him. But they felt nothing. Neither dead nor alive, only memory made visible, un-Forgotten, they couldn't be hurt. 'Back to the place ye sprang from!'

Bruno struggled again and was perhaps able to move, a little. He watched the other Elders retreat in their limp and stagger, to the town hall, Shadows accusing –

'Timothy Horrfrost – ye had me murdered after I saw ye drowning a bag of kittens in the harbour!'

'Marcus Pesters – ye had me arrested, starved to death when I refused to be giving ye half my land! Land that my family had been tending for sixty-six turns!'

'Basil Writtle – ye took my son, Herbert. Took him, stole his childhood.'

Enforcers too, blades still drawn for a battle that would never happen, were falling back to the steps of the town hall as the Temperate cried, 'Ye think ye can haunt me?'

The Shadows overlapped to one stretch of black, wrapped around the Clocktower. The world was visible to Bruno through their gathering, but darkly.

'Ye can't get to me!' shouted Temperate Thomas. 'Ye're only memories, nothing more! Ye can be banished,

Forgotten on my say-so like everything else in Pitch End! *Marshall* – drive them back!'

Bruno saw the Marshall fight to his feet. Where his pistol had exploded his whole hand was a wound – open and livid and deep. He did nothing.

The Shadows stopped, were silent, and Bruno's hope left him as the darkness began to part, disperse, leave them.

'Ye see!' the Temperate called. 'Nothing but memories, nothing but words! Now gather those children up, Marshall!'

But then more words, a voice low, strong –

'I wouldn't be hurrying to help him, Marshall McCormack – not after what he did to yer daughter.'

Bruno could turn then, to the source of the voice – Conn, beside him his father and the twin boys Dominic and Donal, all standing at the entrance to Old Town. In the keeping of Conn's father was a body, so shrunken Bruno thought it could've been supported by the breeze. And if Bruno hadn't known what he did, he wouldn't have recognised the person held there. But Marshall McCormack did –

'*Sabitha?*' he said. He staggered forwards.

'No!' shouted the Temperate. 'It's a trap, Marshall! They must've taken her. Don't trust them, they should've been destroyed in the fire, they—'

'The Cinder-Folk aren't so easily destroyed,' Conn interrupted. 'And I'm thinking, maybe not the Rebels either.'

Yet more sound, rising – something high, on the approach. A kind of splutter-grumble. A sound Bruno recognised from time spent in the skies with Nic, with Louise and David flying beside, with the world wide open.

XXXV
The Imagination of Bruno Atlas

The Clegg swooped over the town square, David flying, in his wake a small, bedraggled, but hardy flock of Bird-Sentries, their mechanical wings spitting arrows at one-footed ravens, exploding them in black flame and charred feather as more Sentries bounded from Old Town – hare, wolf, fox, stoat – and flowed across the square, chasing Enforcers into darkways.

An Owl-Sentry opened its claws and plunged towards Temperate Thomas, a Fox-Sentry leaping to the Clocktower, rusty-toothed and lithe, attempting to tear a pocket watch from the stone – both were snatched by Talent, crushed. Bruno went to Nic, to his mother, crouching in the place between.

The Marshall approached and Bruno held tight the hands of Nic and his mother, like he might protect them, or they him. But the Marshall continued – walked to meet Conn's father. In the pandemonium, a moment of quietness: the

Head of the Enforcers took his daughter from the arms of the Cinder-Folk man, and then descended, holding Sabitha close, closer. Perhaps not close enough to be consoled.

At the same time the Cinder-Folk twins ran forwards to lash amber flames at any Elders or Enforcers keeping them back. The Temperate faced their father, Conn. Talent from both men was flame then, knotting, rising and flailing as both tried to command and overpower the other. But too strong – Temperate Thomas drove Conn back –

A recorded roar, like the Elm Tree Mountains given voice, stopped them all.

Then the thing Bruno had been waiting for – the Tiger-Sentry – surged from Old Town, shocking in its reality, its size more than Bruno recalled, trailing mortar and glass, wound tight after ten turns of waiting, the thrash of metallic paws sending lamp posts into a lean, its spring and charge erratic but, on its back, almost guiding, was Louise.

Enforcers and Elders were no worry then – off into the town hall, double doors shut, bolted.

Temperate Thomas was deserted. He held *The Book of Black & White* like a shield as Louise turned the Tiger-Sentry to face him.

'I'm warning ye,' he said, but the threat was nothing to Louise Green –

'No,' she said, 'I'm warning *you*.'

She leaned low. The Tiger's eyes whirred, jaw opening, crammed with teeth. It charged, ground relenting into cracks, leaping, brass claws extending as Louise threw herself to the cobbles before the Temperate slammed the Tiger-Sentry into the ground on the force of his Talent –

Shortened shotgun in her hands, Louise rolled to a stop and fired two shots –

Temperate Thomas dismissed both with a flick but dropped *The Book of Black & White*. It landed beside Bruno, beside his mother, who discovered enough energy to fall upon it, embrace with eyes shut, infuse it with Talent – and *The Book of Black & White* imploded in her arms.

Temperate Thomas saw, appalled.

His anger went first to Louise as he threw the full force of his Talent. Her gun disintegrated but she discovered the depth of her own Talent and threw what she had back, all memory and emotion and imagination writhing in the place between –

'Conn!' shouted Bruno.

The Cinder-Folk family rushed to help as blood pricked Louise's hands, Talent gnawing at fingertips. But they were too far, too slow and Bruno was desperate in his looking, in his needing. He spied the Enforcer blade he'd used to free Nic and without thought or word and only instinct, a desperate flick of his own hand snatched the blade from the ground and his Talent drove it into the Temperate's shoulder.

All Talent died.

Louise rolled over, didn't move.

Bruno watched Temperate Thomas stagger, hands flailing, trying to reach for the blade, the attack he hadn't seen coming. But in the end he could only topple. He didn't move, but Bruno continued to watch him for life.

'Bruno,' his mother said then. Her voice was too faint, too desperate to be ignored and he looked to her, crept forwards and lifted her. 'Bruno – remember the last bit of the plan? Do ye remember what ye have to do now?'

'Not me,' said Bruno. 'That was for you to do.'

'No,' she said. 'Destroy it. I know ye can.'

Bruno shook his head.

His mother tried a smile. 'Always so disagreeable,' she said. 'Ye have imagination, ye could always see things others couldn't.'

Her hand was suddenly a firm pressure on his arm.

'*Go.*'

Hardest thing, returning to his feet, but Bruno stood. He looked up – the storm was failing, a dark coil at its heart; dry knothole surrounded by limbs of cloud dismembered, strewn across the sky like an unknown language.

Bruno laid his hands flat upon stone, upon the Clocktower, and shut his eyes.

He carved a route in his imagination to an idea, the thought of what Pitch End would be without the Clocktower. Couldn't see it. He thought again, differently: of the Clocktower as something lesser, not stone but sand; childish, a castle on Diamond Beach he'd turned out with his father, triumphant, then broken by the tide . . . He ground his forehead against stone, but didn't have enough emotion for it.

Bruno opened streaming eyes and saw Nic, unmoving, Louise the same. He saw Conn and the final Cinder-Folk family. Final, but still living, still together. Then his mother. Reality ignored, imagination his solace – he saw Nic and Louise and David and his mother all surviving. A Pitch End without Elders and Enforcers.

He breathed in, shut his eyes once more, and allowed images to harry him. Then emotion that held imagination fired his Talent; a dream, a happiness.

A crack like the breaking of the earth. He looked – stone was separating, springing apart between his hands, a fault line scaling the Clocktower. He concentrated – it isn't here, it's nothing at all, a mistake, gone –

A final crack, an explosion of glass, and he felt the Clocktower relent under his fingertips, coated with sand. With the last cries of the storm cloud Bruno kneeled to scoop his mother up, Conn and his boys there beside him to carry Nic and Louise to safety as the Clocktower sank, Bruno fleeing but needing to turn, watch, know –

A colossal, crunching *hiss* and the Clocktower vanished into the ground. This was all he saw before he fell, shielding his mother as dust overcame, such a ruthless tide that it ended all his watching.

XXXVI
The Wave

Bruno felt but didn't see – a single, gentle finger touched his cheek.

'Bruno,' he heard his mother say.

He leaned close, brought her closer. And as on a morning ten turns before, when time had been taken by the Elders, he felt her press something into his hand: metallic, warmed by her touch, thin and no wider than a whistle.

'It's something all Widows have,' she told him. 'Called an Esteem. We were allowed to be keeping one thing with us, always. Just one. Something rightly-special.'

Bruno didn't speak. He realised he was waiting, though not wanting to. Knowing, and waiting for so long that light began to peel away dust, to part it.

He saw Nic, and then Louise – their eyes were open, faces bland masks of blood and filth. They moved. The final Cinder-Folk family too – they'd all survived.

'Ye see,' said Bruno's mother, and he looked to her again.

'Ye'll be okay. Not as alone as ye thought.' Her finger twitched against his cheek, began to sink. Bruno said nothing. He watched her watching him. He watched her go.

'Look for me in the dark,' said his mother. 'In the night-time, in the whispers. In the Shadows. I'll be there, so long as ye remember.'

Bruno shut his eyes. He could take no more seeing. He felt the burden of last breath leave her, and waited for her to take another. Waited, and waited still. There were perhaps moments, minutes, before Louise's voice, hoarse – 'Bruno. He's escaping.'

Bruno looked up. As though commanded by his Talent, the rough, weightless curtain of dust rose completely to let him see: Widows were finding energy to rise, Pitch Enders still cowering in their cage, but beyond was a lone figure in plum robes, staggering towards the Sea of Apparitions. And further out, something darker: the edge of the world curling in on itself, sharp as singed paper.

'A wave,' said Bruno. 'He's going to destroy Pitch End.'

Bruno settled his mother's head on the ground, and then somehow stood, her Esteem in his fist. Conn came close, saying nothing, waiting for direction. Bruno looked to the Pitch Enders so collapsed, helpless.

'Get everyone out of Pitch End,' Bruno told Conn. 'No one is gonna survive if they stay.'

'Where to?' asked Conn, sounding as frightened as any in the cage.

'Out,' said Bruno, eyes on the harbour. He swallowed,

and then added: 'Up into the Elm Tree Mountains. It's the only chance we have now.'

Without hesitation Conn, his father and the twins rushed to the cage holding the townsfolk, and with their Talent in small flames broke open the locks. The Pitch Enders remained, even as Widows joined and reached for them, encouraging. Bruno wondered if old, entrenched fears could be conquered. Could they accept help, could they help themselves?

Nic and Louise came close, supporting each other, stepping over the carcass of the Tiger-Sentry.

'I know what ye're thinking,' said Nic. 'Bruno, don't go after him.'

'Aye,' said Louise. 'Let him run. He can't be hurting us now. Ye don't need to be afeared of him.'

Bruno swallowed, said, 'I'm not. That's why I have to go after him.'

And he ran – down South Street, bare feet slamming and everything leaping, emotion a maelstrom, so strong he felt he could've levelled Pitch End with Talent. He didn't stop until his soles touched shingle, the shore.

Temperate Thomas faced the sea, one shoulder sagging. He had removed the blade Bruno had thrown at him with his Talent, dropped it by his feet. He was lingering as though awaiting collection soon, or obliteration. So much unknowable time passed, and then the Temperate turned – his face could muster no expression. His age in turns was an irrelevance – he was simply old.

He didn't look at Bruno as he said in quiet tones, 'I'm wondering if I stood here, would ye let me die? I'm wondering if you would stand here too. If ye'd let that wave destroy ye, just so ye could make sure I'd be destroyed.'

Bruno didn't speak, didn't need to.

'Ye would end yerself?' said the Temperate, looking at him then. 'For what?'

'For them,' said Bruno. 'For my mother. For the Cinder-Folk, for Louise and David. For Nic.'

'And the other Pitch Enders? Ye'd die for those that bullied and condemned? Not one amongst them who was for standing up and saving ye in the town hall?'

Bruno said without hesitation: 'I would. I will.' He looked out, saw darkness rearing, and trembled. 'Ye can stop it,' said Bruno. 'It's yer Talent that made that wave.'

'Oh no,' said the Temperate. 'That wave is as much yers as it is mine, Bruno. Ye read *The Book of Black & White*. Ye know what can be done with wishes and hopes and Talent. Truth-told: ye'd like to see this town wiped away as much as I.'

Bruno opened his mouth to disagree, but couldn't.

'It won't be stopped,' said Temperate Thomas. 'Because neither of us truly wants to stop it. We are Pitch Enders, we don't have the emotion needed.'

'What emotion?' asked Bruno.

'The want to save others. The desire to save those that would watch us perish.'

The Temperate took a small step back, towards the water.

369

'I brought down the Clocktower because I wanted to save others,' said Bruno.

'That was easy,' said the Temperate. 'That was considering people ye actually think something of, not strangers ye despise.'

From shingle to water then – the Temperate stepped but didn't sink. In support, transformed by his Talent, the surface of the water froze around his feet. He continued his slow retreat, and like an invitation he left ice, faint as worn lace, for Bruno to follow on. Bruno went. His feet were stung cold but he didn't care. He kept his eyes on Temperate Thomas.

'I've seen more things pass from this place than ye can imagine,' said the Temperate, still moving, Bruno still following. 'All things arriving and leaving. All those little worries and woes like little storms, those things ye seem to think so much of – they're all dust as soon as tomorrow, Bruno. Nothing, not important. Written-down words, *Tall Tales*, dead fathers and mothers – they all go with the tide. And after that, forever Forgotten. There's nothing that keeps on going, Bruno. Nothing lasts.'

'Liar,' said Bruno. He slipped, then regained himself – he'd moved beyond the harbour, alone with the Temperate on their small platform of ice only feet wide. He glanced behind – a rapid thaw, no retreat. In his hand he still clutched his mother's Esteem.

'A lie is not a lie if someone believes it,' Temperate

Thomas said. 'Words are more powerful than any Talent, Bruno. A man who can master words is a man who decides what truth is. Let me tell ye what ye should be saying: *Forgive me, Temperate. Forgive me, for I should never have left my mother on her own, never have believed such silly stories. I, in fact, should never have been born. My father never even wanted me.*'

'*Liar!*' cried Bruno, again.

Temperate Thomas said nothing more, and Bruno knew what was next –

A swipe from the Temperate's hand tried to topple him but Bruno threw himself forwards. They locked hands, struggling against one another, feet shifting on a shrinking circle of ice.

'*Dust,*' said the Temperate between clenched teeth. 'All Forgotten. Just like yer father, just like yer mother.' Both their eyes went to the Widow's Esteem. And Bruno began to sink – Temperate Thomas's strength was too great. But he decided that he wouldn't go without words. Like Pace – not silent, not obedient, but fighting.

'Some things last,' said Bruno. 'I remember being five and seeing two boys killed when ye ordered it. I remember my mother covering my eyes to protect me from seeing. I remember my father telling me a *Tall Tale* that took me into the town hall, led me to winding keys, a key that brought that Tiger-Sentry back that ye thought would never return. I know that my father rode it into battle – I've been told these things, they didn't die. And I'll remember my mother and father. And as long as I'm cared about, others will remember me too.'

Ice so brief at their feet was all the space they had to stand. Any slip and either could fall. All was black to Bruno as he sank – the backdrop of the coming wave, eyes of the Temperate, ice beneath them. Bruno looked down – darkness threaded the water.

'*Shadows,*' he said, and Temperate Thomas looked too.

Not vague as in the town square, not unknowable, but faces flowed beneath their feet. Almost human – not just faces but soft shoulders, arms long, dripping like slim stalactites, they rose in host around Bruno and the Temperate, rippling, enclosing. Bruno heard whispered threats, promises, accusations, but not for him – these words widened the eyes of the Head Elder as old enemies returned to torment him. Faces. Bruno recognised Gumbly, Pace, the two boys shot on the beach ten turns earlier, the face of the man who had called Bruno and his mother to safety from their burning house. All recalled, all enduring. And then his mother –

'*No more, Ignatius Thomas. As ye sentenced me, so be sentenced yerself – death, and rightly-swift Forgetting.*'

Hands, almost human, on all sides grabbed Temperate Thomas, held him, stifled his screams as they wrenched him free of Bruno and brought him down, pulling him under the surface as they returned to the water, a mass of eyes, fingers, whispers, and then gone. Bruno watched their darkness like a fading wish. He had one breath, and then he fell.

The water was shallow but the current was against him, the Sea of Apparitions being pulled out to feed the wave. He didn't pause to look, only began a fight for the shore, but surely too far?

Then a grumble-stutter, a cry from above – '*Atlas!*'

He looked, saw David, then turned back to see the wave scrub out the sky, fathomless, rushing towards him –

The Clegg swooped out over the harbour, one wing tucked tight to its side, banking hard as it fell into a dive, outstripping the wave, David dropping a rope that skimmed the skin of the Sea of Apparitions and there was one chance, Bruno knew, or nothing. He shut his eyes, trusting himself to know when, to see without seeing –

'*Now, Bruno!*'

Bruno felt rope in his hands and clutched it –

He was lifted clear –

He opened his eyes and stared into the dark maw of the wave –

The Clegg's engine groaned and it struggled to surge higher as sea soared over the harbour, water clutching Bruno's legs, climbing quickly to chest, neck, over –

And then he was free of it, was flying up and over Pitch End. Bruno looked down to watch the town taken, wave invading every street, darkway and doorway, pouring into the chasm where the Clocktower had stood. Then he looked away, too pained with the worry: had they escaped, Nic,

Louise, Conn and the Cinder-Folk family? And the Widows, the children, the other Pitch Enders?

David flew them higher, to the wall and further.

Bruno began a climb of the rope, hand over hand, and when he reached the top David offered his own hand, heaving Bruno up onto the glider.

'Before ye bring it up,' said David, straightaway, 'I *had* to lead that Temperate to the chapel. Had to make him think I'd given up. Otherwise he'd have been for burning all Pitch End, killing everyone he could. And even then he'd still have been finding the chapel anyway. It was the best decision, in the circumstances.'

David didn't look at him.

Bruno said, 'Of course. Sure I knew all that.'

David looked at him.

'Alright, Atlas,' he said, with the barest smile. 'No one likes a know-it-all.'

David looked down, Bruno too – small scraps were heaped like unwanted wares on the mountainside. No home, no role, no cage to be assigned to, no place. And Bruno realised: no role for him, no place; no card under the door to tell LIGHTHOUSE-KEEPER, no shadow to say WORK or SHUT-EYE. No time.

'Take us down,' Bruno told David.

The wings of the Clegg tilted back and in moments the world came close – this tree, that face, clear and then clearer – and Bruno leapt before he should have done but landed without a stumble.

He looked for certain faces. Then came first sight, first people as though formed by his need to see them – Nic and Louise. They saw and ran for him, Conn close behind with his father and boys, faces black, eyes red-rimmed but relieved. All were smiling.

Louise leapt on him and he almost recoiled, so unused to a thing like affection; all he could do was struggle to stay upright. Nic gave him a thump on the back and said, 'There's no telling ye, is there? Ye just had to play the hero.'

'Bloody right he did!' said Louise, as David arrived and eased her away, letting Bruno breathe.

For many moments Bruno saw only who he wanted, but then a din rose that took his attention – the other Pitch Enders, children and adults who'd managed to escape. Whether farmer or fisherman, Enforcer or shopkeeper, man or Widow, all moving towards him, crawling. They wanted answers, guidance, as though he might tell them what to do, what to say. What to think and be like. Tell them how they could exist, like an Elder would've done. Bruno found himself seeking one – alone, far but not so far he couldn't be noticed, the Elder Horrfrost had found himself the only rock to sit on. He had his back to the mountain, face to the drowned Pitch End. Bruno heard his sombre mutterings on the air and knew that soon the Pitch Enders would turn to the Elder, would follow an instinct so many turns old to listen and be grateful for easy orders. They were in a place other than Pitch End, so Bruno wondered: were they Pitch Enders

375

still? And if not then who were they? If they asked, the Elder would tell them, and Bruno knew that he needed his own words, needed to speak or he'd lose the townsfolk forever.

He looked to Louise, David – they were waiting too. Looked to Nic who nodded, knowingly, to Bruno's hand.

His mother's Esteem had remained, and before anything else he opened it, unscrewing the top, fingers reaching in. Inside was coiled paper, corners bitten down by flame. Saved from a fire. It was a pictograph of Bruno and his mother and father on Diamond Beach. He looked, and didn't just see it but recalled it – a memory in shades of ash, but it struck Bruno as more alive than anything around him, containing more light. He examined his own face in the picture, his parents'. All eyes were narrowed to the sun. Bruno expected to see some doubt, some foreshadow of what was to come. But there was nothing to darken it. He was grateful.

'Bruno, look!'

Louise, pointing back towards Pitch End.

A sheet of troubled sea was tucked close to the mountainside, had stopped there but covered the town completely. Only one clue was offered to what was hidden below, and this was what Louise pointed to, what the townsfolk all looked to. Bright as blood, boughs like ancient kindling, leaves unfurling flames, flourishing behind George Pitch's nightmares, testament to his hope – the Faerie Fort, free of the town hall, was rising. Not just surviving but, Bruno thought, beginning to thrive.

Bruno cleared his throat and the waiting of the assembled deepened, pressing against him. He swayed where he stood. He realised that he would have to trust – start, and maybe more would follow without too much thinking. He kept his eyes on Pitch End, and imagined.

Bruno Atlas opened his mouth and began to speak.

Nigel McDowell

Nigel grew up in County Fermanagh, rural Northern Ireland, and as a child spent most of his time battling boredom, looking for adventure – crawling through ditches, climbing trees, devising games to play with his brother and sister, and reading. His favourite book as a child was *The Witches* by Roald Dahl.

After graduating with a degree in English (and having no clue what to do with it!), he decided to go off on another adventure, spending almost two years living and working in Australia and New Zealand. With him he took a small notebook containing notes about a boy called 'Bruno Atlas', and a seaside town called 'Pitch End'. When he returned to Ireland after his travels, one notebook had multiplied into many, and eventually his notes for *Tall Tales from Pitch End* filled a large cardboard box . . .

Nigel now lives in London. He has written articles on film and literature for a number of websites. He is always on the hunt for books about folklore and fairytale. He wishes he had more time to climb trees. *Tall Tales from Pitch End* is Nigel's debut novel.

Follow Nigel on Twitter: @NMcDowellAuthor